National bestselling author Kathleen Bridge presents a delightful new series set on a barrier island where waves meet sand—and mayhem meets murder . . .

The Indialantic by the Sea hotel has a hundred-year-old history on beautiful Melbourne Beach, Florida, and more than a few guests seem to have been there from the start. When Liz Holt returns home after an intense decade in New York, she's happy to be surrounded by the eccentric clientele and loving relatives that populate her family-run inn, and doubly pleased to see the business is staying afloat thanks to its vibrant shopping emporium and a few very wealthy patrons.

But that patronage decreases by one when a filthy rich guest is discovered dead in her oceanfront suite. Maybe this is simply a jewel theft gone wrong, but maybe someone—or many people—wanted the hotel's prosperous guest dead. Only one thing is sure: there's a killer at the Indialantic, and if Liz lets herself be distracted—by her troubled past or the tempting man who seems eager to dredge it back up—the next reservation she'll book could be at the cemetery . . .

Death by the Sea

A By the Sea Mystery

Kathleen Bridge

LYRICAL UNDERGROUND
Kensington Publishing Corp.
www.kensingtonbooks.com

LYRICAL UNDERGROUND BOOKS are published by

Kensington Publishing Corp.
119 West 40th Street
New York, NY 10018

All Kensington titles, imprints, and distributed lines are available at special quantity discounts for bulk purchases for sales promotion, premiums, fund-raising, educational, or institutional use.

Special book excerpts or customized printings can also be created to fit specific needs. For details, write or phone the office of the Kensington Sales Manager: Kensington Publishing Corp., 119 West 40th Street, New York, NY 10018. Attn. Sales Department. Phone: 1-800-221-2647.

Lyrical Underground and Lyrical Underground logo Reg. US Pat. & TM Off.

First Electronic Edition: April 2018
eISBN-13: 978-15161-0520-5
eISBN-10: 1-5161-0520-6

First Print Edition: April 2018
ISBN-13: 978-1-5161-0523-6
ISBN-10: 1-5161-0523-0

Printed in the United States of America

To my firstborn, Joshua Evan. Thanks for all the encouragement and LOVE.

XO, Mommy

And this was the reason that, long ago,
In this kingdom by the sea,
A wind blew out of a cloud, chilling
My beautiful Annabel Lee;
So that her highborn kinsmen came
And bore her away from me,
To shut her up in a sepulchre
In this kingdom by the sea.

—Edgar Allan Poe

Chapter 1

"I curse you, Barnabas! May your undeath haunt you through all eternity. I'd rather die a mortal than live year to year preying on innocent blood, watching those I love buried in hallowed ground. You will not take me with you!" She jerked the knife toward her chest and fell to the floor.

After a few beats, Aunt Amelia opened her eyes, cracked a smile, then pulled herself up with the help of a sturdy piano bench. For a minute, Liz feared her eighty-year-old great-aunt had fractured a hip.

"Bravo! Bravo!" Barnacle Bob called out.

Liz applauded. Her great-aunt performed a deep bow, the tip of her bright red *I Dream of Jeannie* ponytail grazing the threadbare Persian carpet. When she stood, her sea-green eyes gleamed under black liner that extended from the corners of her eyes in true sixties style. "Enough theatrics," Aunt Amelia said, adding a schoolgirl giggle. "I must talk to Pierre about dinner." She wrapped a neon-pink scarf around her neck, kissed Liz on the top of the head, and exited the music room.

Amelia Eden Holt, Liz's favorite—and only—great-aunt, had starred in three seasons of the 1960s vampire-themed television soap drama, *Dark Shadows*. "Starred" might be an exaggeration, because she'd only had a small part as a Collinwood maid. However, that was what Liz loved about her paternal great-aunt; she was bigger than life and more colorful than the tail feathers on Barnacle Bob, Aunt Amelia's thirty-year-old macaw.

"Drama queen... Showboater... Diva," Bob squawked.

Her great-aunt adored Barnacle Bob. Liz just hoped Aunt Amelia never heard the parrot's two-faced comments. "Hush, BB, that's not nice." Liz took a seat next to his cage, inhaling Aunt Amelia's signature scent, L'air du Temps.

When Liz was five, after her mother passed away, she and her father came to live with Aunt Amelia in the old family-run hotel. At one time, the Indialantic by the Sea Hotel was Melbourne Beach, Florida's premier ocean-front resort. Unfortunately, the monikers "premier" and "resort" no longer held true. The Indialantic sat on a barrier island sandwiched between the Indian River Lagoon to the west and the Atlantic Ocean to the east. Last fall, Liz's father invested a sizable percentage of his attorney fees from winning a class-action lawsuit into the coffers of the hotel. With Aunt Amelia's and the staff's hard work and dedication, along with the rent coming in from the new shops, the establishment was finally inching its way toward the black, affording them one more year to stave off the bank and real-estate predators.

Aunt Amelia insisted on adding to the old hotel's name by calling it the Indialantic by the Sea Hotel and Emporium. The name was a little long-winded for Liz's taste, but no one dared cross Aunt Amelia.

In 1945, a fire had destroyed the entire midsection of the Indialantic Hotel, and the north and south parts of the resort had been made into two separate buildings, with a large courtyard in between. The south building was the hotel, and the north building housed the emporium shops. The shops consisted of Home Arts by the Sea, a women's lifestyle collective; Deli-cacies by the Sea, a gourmet deli and coffee shop; Sirens by the Sea, a women's clothing boutique; and Gold Coast by the Sea, a rare coin and estate jewelry shop. It had been Liz's idea to have her best friend from childhood, Kate Fields, leave her booth at a local antique mall and rent out the remaining space at the emporium. Kate called her used book and vintage shop Books & Browsery by the Sea.

Before she'd left Melbourne Beach for Manhattan, Liz had considered the hotel too old-school and boringly quaint. Now, after six weeks of being home, she felt cocooned, cozy, and safe when she stepped inside. It was a far different feeling than she'd had in the city, turning the three dead bolts on her SoHo loft's door. Life was simple on the island, and Liz embraced the laid-back beach-town vibe, something she hadn't been able to do at eighteen when she was young and beyond restless.

The upper level of the Indialantic had large guest suites that had become a refuge for Aunt Amelia's occasional "strays," usually senior citizens with small Social Security checks and small pets, "no bigger than a bread basket." Although Liz knew Aunt Amelia made exceptions to her own rule, as evidenced by Killer, the Great Dane who looked longingly at Liz's lap.

"Sorry, pup, don't even think about it. I'll have to spend the next few weeks at the chiropractor." Her father called the upper floor of the hotel

Aunt Amelia's Animalia, and chose to live in an apartment next to his law office on the first floor. Liz lived in the Indialantic's former beach pavilion, now turned beach house. It was a nice distance away from the Indialantic and a quiet place to work on her writing career, or more accurately, her *non*-writing career.

Liz glanced around the music room and reminisced about past years with her father at the piano and Aunt Amelia singing, dancing, or replaying one of her scenes from *Dark Shadows* or a myriad of other midcentury television shows in which she'd had small roles. Aunt Amelia had been considered a character actress—and she was quite a character. While some children had Dr. Seuss and *Goodnight Moon* read to them before falling asleep, Aunt Amelia would tell Liz about the evil witch Angelique and the beautiful Josette who fought each other for the handsome vampire Barnabas's love. "Barnabas didn't want to be a vampire, Lizzy dear, but he had no choice. Sometimes you just have to face who you are and make the best of it..." Liz smiled at the memory and patted Killer's large noggin. She'd been loafing too long. She thought about all the things she had to do to get ready for the Indialantic Spring Fling by the Sea. It had been Liz's idea to have the event on Saturday in the hopes of drumming up more business for the emporium shops. Although Melbourne Beach was, as advertised, a casual, beachy surfer's paradise, Liz knew there were celebrities hiding in nearby ocean-front homes with tons of disposable income who might enjoy an off-the-grid dining and shopping experience.

If Liz was honest with herself, she'd been using her role as her father's and great-aunt's assistant as an excuse not to write. It was amazing that her agent hadn't given up on her, especially after the scandal that had rocked the literati and her life as she knew it.

She got up, walked to the window, and looked out at the Atlantic. The hotel was perched on a sandy cliff, east of State Road A1A. The hotel's property also encompassed the west side of the highway, with its own dock on the Indian River Lagoon. Lost in thoughts of the past, Liz startled when she heard Barnacle Bob squawk, "Places to go. People to see."

Liz moved over to the parrot's cage. "The only place you're going is dreamland. Catch ya later, BB. Time for my dinner. Try to behave yourself."

"Okay, Scarface! Keep it real."

She gave it back to him. "Whatever you say, bald-as-a-billiard-ball Barnacle Bob."

The parrot was missing all the feathers on the top of his head. What remained were little pinholes, like a child's connect-the-dots puzzle.

Liz traced the scar on her right cheek. She'd had two operations with a plastic surgeon in Manhattan, and a week ago, the third procedure with a surgeon in Vero Beach. Each skin graft was an improvement, but she was told that a scar would always remain and that a fourth operation would have to wait for at least another year. She now thought of her life in terms of before-the-scar and after-the-scar. Surprisingly enough, life after-the-scar was the better of the two. Her before-the-scar life had included a tempestuous relationship with Travis Osterman, the Pulitzer Prize–winning author of *The McAvoy Brothers*, a five-hundred-page novel following three generations of brothers and their triumphs and sorrows through countless women and wars.

She'd left Melbourne Beach when she was eighteen and spent six years at Columbia University and then two years writing her novel, *Let the Wind Roar*, while modeling and bartending. After her novel won the PEN/Faulkner award, it flew to the top of the *New York Times* best sellers list. Liz spent the following year living every author's dream. Then she met Travis and her dream turned into a nightmare, due to a scandal and a defamation-of-character lawsuit, not to mention a night of terror she would never forget. Liz had been acquitted of any wrongdoing in the lawsuit, but it was too late. She was branded a pariah and ostracized from every Manhattan literary salon. Liz had returned home to Melbourne Beach, her wings clipped by her father, and rightly so. It was a little embarrassing for a twenty-eight-year-old, but she'd welcomed his broad shoulders to cry on and she loved that her father never questioned her choices, saying instead, "If it wasn't for the contrast in your life, you'd never have known what you truly wanted."

Since Liz had returned to Florida, though, everyone at the Indialantic had been walking on eggshells around her, including Aunt Amelia. Of course, the whole sordid affair had been plastered all over the tabloids, but not even the tabloids knew what had really happened. Only her father, Betty, and her best friend, Kate, knew the entire story. Liz had given Aunt Amelia a kinder, gentler version of the events that had gone down.

Barnacle Bob spun around in his Mercedes of a birdcage and faced the wall, aiming his colorful tail-feathered rear end at Liz. Aunt Amelia had found him after a hurricane at a local pet rescue facility. She'd had her pick of other pets needing a good home, but she always went for the less fortunate, in this case Barnacle Bob. Owing to his colorful language, Barnacle Bob's former owner had probably been a crusty old sailor or a Florida fisherman, no doubt male. Barnacle Bob had a soft spot for Aunt

Amelia and he never said anything disparaging to her face, only behind her back. He was less kind to the rest of humanity.

Liz covered the parrot's cage. "Early to bed, early to rise, BB."

As she and Killer walked out of the music room, it was hard to ignore the muffled expletives spewing from Barnacle Bob's foul beak.

Chapter 2

Sunday dinner at the Indialantic was the only time the guests, help, and emporium shopkeepers all ate together in the huge hotel dining room. However, today was an exception because it was Thursday. Aunt Amelia had asked Pierre to whip up a special thank-you feast to kick off the first annual Indialantic Spring Fling by the Sea, scheduled for Saturday at the emporium.

The hotel's original dining room had been double the size that it was now, but it was still big enough to seat sixty people. There were fifteen square tables topped with white Irish linen tablecloths dating from the hotel's opening, personally ironed by Aunt Amelia. Liz's great-aunt found ironing a therapeutic distraction. Liz didn't even own an iron. She looked guiltily at her white cotton blouse that her great-aunt had insisted on pressing. In the past, all Liz had had to do was leave a bag of laundry outside her Soho loft door on Monday morning and it would be picked up by Mr. Kim, the owner of the dry cleaner at the end of her block, then delivered back by Monday evening.

Three of the Indialantic's hotel guests sat together at a table by a huge window overlooking the Olympic-sized pool—the same pool where old-time film star and synchronized swimmer Esther Williams had performed one of her water ballet scenes for an MGM movie. Captain Clyde B. Netherton, the septuagenarian owner of Killer, looked dapper as usual, his gold-handled walking cane leaning against his chair. The captain was retired from the Coast Guard and skippered the sightseeing and nature-watch cruiser *Queen of the Seas* from the Indialantic's river dock every Monday, Wednesday, and Friday. He'd been staying at the Indialantic for the past two months. Also at the table was eighty-three-year-old Betty

Lawson. Betty had lived at the Indialantic for over twenty years and was one of the reasons Liz had become a writer. In the sixties and seventies, Betty worked for the Stratemeyer Syndicate as a ghostwriter for five Nancy Drew mysteries under the pseudonym of Carolyn Keene. Even under duress, she never revealed exactly which books she'd written. Betty had also penned a slew of other teenage mysteries for girls and boys under different nom de plumes. Sitting next to Betty was a new guest whom Liz had never met, but she'd seen her face plastered all over the society pages or attending local A-list events in the Melbourne Beach and Vero Beach area. Regina Harrington-Worth came from of one of the area's most prestigious families. Her grandfather Percival Harrington I, built his oceanfront estate, Castlemara, a few miles south of the Indialantic. Later, Regina's father, Percival II, commissioned a salvaging company to look for sunken treasure in the remains of the Spanish ship *San Carlos*—and scored big-time. The rest was Treasure Coast history.

Regina Harrington-Worth wasn't one of Aunt Amelia's typical strays. In fact, she looked and dressed like she belonged in West Palm Beach, or on a yacht moored at Fisher Island, where the residents had the highest per-capita income in the United States. She appeared to be in her early fifties, perhaps a little older, in no small part due to Botox and fillers. Her bottom lip was three times the size of the top. Near the woman's feet was a rhinestone-studded pet carrier. Two ice-blue eyes looked out from behind the mesh window. Liz couldn't tell what species the animal was, but she knew one thing: bringing a pet into the hotel dining room was a definite no-no in Aunt Amelia's book.

Everyone had served themselves from the twenty-foot buffet against the stucco wall. Pierre Montague, the hotel's live-in chef, who had his own suite of rooms on the second floor, stood in the doorway to the kitchen surveying the scene. He looked so much older than he had ten years ago. When her father and Aunt Amelia made the trip to Manhattan to visit her, she'd invited Pierre, but he refused to fly, saying, "Who would make the meals, Lizzy Bear?" He was right: Her father and Aunt Amelia could barely boil an egg. Liz was the only other cook in the family. When Liz was small, she called Pierre "Grand-Pierre," a play on the French name *Grand-Pere*, which translates to "grandfather," because that was how she thought of him. Like Betty, Pierre was family.

Pierre winked at Liz, and she pointed to her full plate, giving him a thumbs-up. At least he hadn't lost the mischievous twinkle in his pale gray eyes. His furry white caterpillar eyebrows matched an unruly mustache whose tips were waxed and curled each morning in true Hercule Poirot style.

Liz filled her Baccarat crystal glass with water and a floating lemon slice from the pitcher in the center of the table. The lemons were plucked from the Indialantic's own trees. At her table were her father and best friend, Kate Fields. Barnacle Bob called her "Crazy for Cocoa Puffs Kate," and for once, the parrot wasn't too far off with his 1960s advertising jingle. Kate was the girl at school who did anything on a dare, a fantastic athlete, competing in Ironman competitions and skydiving events, she was also passionate about saving the environment. In her emporium shop she had a sign: Upcycled and Better Than New. You could see the "crazy" side of Kate in the way she repurposed and displayed her vintage and antique items, changing the shop around daily in one wacky way or another. Also, just this side of crazy, was the fact that Kate talked to her books like people talked to their plants.

Kate wore a fluorescent yellow tank top over bicycle shorts, her long, light brown hair was pulled up in a sleek ponytail.

"Elizabeth Holt, do you think you could pile any more food on your plate?" Kate was a quasi-vegetarian, occasionally eating fish and poultry, never red meat.

Liz was on her second course. Her first course had consisted of mini crab cakes with a mustard remoulade and creamy seafood chowder. She pushed her twice-baked Brie-and-chive potato up against a large slab of medium-rare prime rib smothered in Pierre's famous horseradish sauce. "Now I have room." She tucked a rogue strand of strawberry-blonde hair behind her ear and took a bite of the potato. "Oh boy, did I miss Pierre's cooking when I lived in New York."

"You're as good of a chef as Pierre," Kate said. "Isn't she, Uncle Fenton?"

Liz's father wasn't Kate's real uncle, but the ties were just as strong.

"Yes, she is, Katie." He looked at an open file on the table. Liz couldn't remember a time when he wasn't immersed in one of his cases. Even though her father was a retired Brevard County public defender, he was still an active member of the bar association and took on small cases for the locals in the Melbourne Beach area.

Liz wiped her mouth with a napkin. "I love cooking, but there's nothing better than someone cooking for you, especially if that someone is Pierre. I have to admit, with all the top restaurants in Manhattan and their molecular cooking hocus-pocus, using foams and freeze-dried techniques, not one came close to providing a meal that could match this." She took another bite of prime rib, noticing Kate staring at her fork. Liz waved it in front of her. "Sure you don't want a teensy bite?"

Kate looked around to see if anyone was watching, opened her mouth, and said, "Hurry!" She swallowed the bite in ecstasy, her eyes glazing over.

Did Kate think the vegetarian police would arrest her? Liz knew her friend's Kryptonite—Kate never turned down a dare. Liz's Kryptonite was the scar on her cheek. Kate had driven her to Vero Beach for the last procedure. Now that the healing on the outside had begun, she needed to focus on trying to heal the inside. Liz got up from the table, headed to the sideboard, and snatched a couple ramekins of crème brûlée.

When Liz got back to the table, Kate whispered, "What the heck is Regina Harrington-Worth doing here?"

"I have no clue. I'll have to ask Aunt Amelia." Liz turned to her father. "Dad, do you know?"

He said, "Apparently, they couldn't find an open hotel that would take pets. You know your great-aunt—you need refuge for a four-legged pet or even a two-legged bird, the Indialantic by the Sea Hotel and Emporium will accommodate you."

Kate laughed. "Boy, did you say a mouthful, Uncle Fenton. I think she'd even take in a no-legged snake—possibly drawing the line if it was poisonous." Kate reached over and grabbed one of Liz's brûlées.

"Hey, hands off. Get your own."

"Try and stop me. Too much sugar for you. You have to learn balance." Kate finished the brûlée in three spoonfuls.

Aunt Amelia was on the other side of the dining room, her arms gesturing wildly in their theatrical splendor as she talked to the hotel's housekeeper, Iris Kimball, or "Battle-axe Iris," as Barnacle Bob called her. Iris was the lucky one assigned to feeding him and cleaning his cage. BB was a creature of habit, bordering on obsessive-compulsive. He didn't like his routine upset. "Two p.m. Polly wants his freakin' cracker. Dammit!"

Liz glanced over at Brittany Poole, proprietress of the women's boutique Sirens by the Sea. Knowing Liz and Brittany's murky history, she was surprised her great-aunt would rent out a space in the emporium to Brittany. In the center of Brittany's plate were three spears of asparagus, which explained her waif-like appearance. Sitting at the table with Brittany were Edward Goren and his son, Nick. Edward rented Gold Coast by the Sea and was well-known in the area as a deep-sea treasure hunter. Per Aunt Amelia, he'd sold his business to another salvager based out of Miami. Edward's son, Nick, assisted him in appraising gold and coins and had recently started dating Brittany. Liz wished him good luck on that one.

Francie Jenkins and Minna Presley, who leased the emporium shop Home Arts by the Sea, sat at the table closest to the arched French doors that opened to a view of the ocean. Both women were in their forties and recently divorced. Like Liz and Kate, they'd been friends since childhood and lived together in a small cottage a mile south of the hotel.

"Pops" Stone, the elderly proprietor of Deli-cacies by the Sea, sat at a table near the open doors to the hotel's inner courtyard, the crowning glory of the Indialantic's early twentieth-century Spanish Revival architecture. When Pops's wife died a year ago, he'd sold his thriving deli in Melbourne and rented one of the emporium spaces. At Pops's table was someone Liz had never seen before. Almost on cue, the guy turned toward her, his gaze stalling for a moment on Liz's face. Was he looking at her scar? Doubtful, but something about him irritated her. She just couldn't put her finger on it. Liz turned her head toward Kate and whispered, "Don't look now, but who's that sitting with Pops?"

Of course, Kate twisted in her seat and looked straight at him. When she finally caught the guy's attention, Kate frenetically waved, like she was ushering in the winning car at the Daytona 500.

"Kate, stop!" Liz said, then slapped her friend on the wrist. "Could you be more obvious?" Oh no. Liz had just given Kate a dare.

Kate stood, grabbed Liz's shoulder, and pulled her back from the table, chair and all. "Stand up. Let's go meet that raven-haired, dark-eyed, scowling man of your dreams!"

"Say what? You mean man of *your* dreams, Kate Fields."

By the time they got to the table, both Pops and the man were gone.

Just as well. Who needs complications. The next chapter of Liz's life would be all about serenity.

Chapter 3

Liz helped Pierre in the kitchen with the cleanup. It was usually Iris's job, but she was MIA. Aunt Amelia had even checked the housekeeper's rooms. Iris had come to work at the hotel four months ago and had rooms on the second floor. The housekeeper was stiff and proper, almost emotionless, and she performed the mechanics of cleaning the hotel with military precision. She wore rubber-soled work shoes that always made it easy for her to appear silently in a room like a ballerina-toed cat burglar, causing Liz to startle on more than one occasion.

After they were finished, Liz sent Pierre off to bed, took off her apron, and hung it on the hook by the door. As she was ready to leave for home, the intercom buzzed and a light lit up next to the Oceana Suite. Liz pushed the button on the panel, and Aunt Amelia's acting voice boomed over the intercom. "Dar-r-rling Lizzy, could you please be a peach and gather the valises in the lobby? Mrs. Worth's husband has arrived and I still can't locate Iris."

She heard laughter in the background and a man's voice telling Aunt Amelia that he could get the luggage himself, and then his wife saying, "Don't be absurd, David! Let the girl grab them." Liz recognized the voice as Regina Harrington-Worth's, their new celebrity guest who'd been sitting at dinner with the caged blue-eyed pet.

Liz went to the lobby and grabbed David's valises, aka suitcases, and hauled them up the spiral staircase to the second floor. At the top of the landing, Liz paused for a breather. Captain Netherton must have heard her drop the heaviest of the two and opened the door to his suite. He held a pipe in his hand and looked like the actor from the late-sixties television show *The Ghost and Mrs. Muir*, with his VanDyke beard and mustache, tall, lean frame, and erect posture.

Through osmosis from her thespian great-aunt, Liz was a sixties television aficionado. After Liz's grandfather's death, Aunt Amelia moved from Burbank to take over the responsibility of the hotel. The first thing she'd done was to turn the old card room next to the library into her "viewing" room—a theater that also passed as a shrine to Amelia Eden Holt's early days of television glory. Liz had grown up watching a myriad of sixties shows with her great-aunt. From her earliest memory, Liz and Aunt Amelia would typecast hotel guests as characters from one of Aunt Amelia's shows. On Liz's first day home from New York, before Aunt Amelia had had the chance to christen Captain Netherton with his alias, Liz had yelled out, "Captain Daniel Gregg!" Then they'd both leapt in the air for a community high five. Liz knew from that day on, Aunt Amelia's jocularity would be the perfect balm to banish Liz's dark, *woe-is-me* thoughts.

Captain Netherton stepped out of his suite and laid his pipe on the hall table, then reached inside and grabbed his cane. He walked toward the suitcase Liz had dropped. "Elizabeth, dear. Let me help you with that."

"Please call me Liz. Where's your better half? As if I don't know."

He smiled. "You got it. Killer's with his lover, Caro, in Betty's suite. He spends more time with Caro than he does with me."

Carolyn Keene, nicknamed Caro, was Betty's black and white cat, who had an adorable white milk mustache. Aunt Amelia told Liz that the dog/cat love affair had started the day Captain Netherton came to the Indialantic. The Great Dane and Caro both had black fur with white tuxedo fronts. Caro could be found sleeping in Killer's humongous arms most afternoons on the second-floor veranda that overlooked the back garden.

Captain Netherton picked up the designer-emblemed suitcase.

Liz said, "Thank you, kind sir."

"My pleasure, Liz. What's in this thing? Gold bullion? Point the way, fair maiden."

"We don't have far, just next door to the Oceana Suite," Liz said, with a laugh. "But I still appreciate your help."

He had a limp, but seemed strong enough to carry the suitcase in one hand and use his cane in the other.

"Ahh, Mrs. Regina Harrington-Worth. You wouldn't happen to know if she's still married, would you? There's lots of buzz at the Eau Galle Yacht Club that she was seen dancing at some social event with a star polo player from the Vero Beach Polo Club."

Recalling what she'd overheard on the intercom, Liz said, "Yes, Captain Netherton, as a matter of fact, there still seems to be a Mr. Worth."

"'Captain' is sufficient, young lady. You can drop the 'Netherton'."

Liz might have only been home for a short while, but she'd seen the effect Captain Netherton had on octogenarians Betty Lawson and Aunt Amelia. Liz had even witnessed a shared intimate moment next to the dumbwaiter between Iris and the captain. He must be twenty years the housekeeper's senior, and now he was asking about the fifty-something Regina. It seemed the captain was an equal-opportunity lothario.

Captain Netherton placed the suitcase in front of the largest guest suite in the hotel and went in search of Killer. There couldn't be too many places a dog his size could hide. Perhaps Betty had shanghaied the Great Dane as an excuse to steal a private minute with the distinguished captain.

As Liz raised her hand to knock on the suite door, it flew open.

Aunt Amelia filled the doorway, wearing one of her flowing green-and-mauve peignoir sets, like something from a Doris Day–Rock Hudson movie. Her bright red hair was piled on top of her head, coiffed into large-sectioned banana curls. There was something strange about her face, and Liz realized what it was. One eye had her signature pearlescent baby-blue eyeshadow that went straight up to her pointy arched brow, along with black eyeliner, and false eyelashes. The other eye was wiped clean. Liz smelled Pond's cold cream from where she stood. David Worth's arrival must have caught Aunt Amelia at the beginning of her nighttime beauty regime.

Liz would never let on to Aunt Amelia that in her later years she reminded Liz of Endora from the sitcom *Bewitched*. When her great-aunt looked in the mirror, she probably saw the same young ingénue from her first television appearance. It was a commercial that had Aunt Amelia standing on a tree swing in a petticoated, floral dress with a lit cigarette dangling from her mouth as a young man pushed her from behind. In the background a song played, "Fresh as the breeze. Inhale the great outdoors with every puff..."

Aunt Amelia said, "Thank you, Liz. Just place the luggage on the stand next to the bed."

A man, whom Liz assumed was David Worth, hurried toward her. "Let me help you." He grabbed one of the suitcases, then reached in his pocket, took out a twenty-dollar bill, and stuffed it into Liz's now-empty hand. He had sharp features on a weatherworn face and eyes the color of Kalamata olives. His thinning, dark hair had patches of shiny scalp showing through. He wore casual but elegant clothing, and a gold- and diamond-encrusted Rolex watch.

"Not necessary," Liz said.

Aunt Amelia gave her the *zip-it* glare, the one she usually reserved for Barnacle Bob.

"'Not necessary' is right, David. We've been waiting for over an hour!" a nails-on-chalkboard voice said from the other room. Regina entered the sitting room, still dressed in what she'd worn at dinner, a low-cut jersey dress in a medallion print that hit well above her knees. Her hair was dark brunette, with a slight curl, and way too long for her age. Liz suspected she used hair extensions. She had the same dog-sticking-its-head-out-the-window expression she had at dinner on her lineless face.

"If that's all, Auntie, I'm going to turn in." Liz gave Aunt Amelia a kiss on her cheek and started toward the door.

"Wait!" Regina barked, snapping the fingers on her right hand, which was laden with a huge emerald and gold ring that must have come from one of her father's treasure hunts.

Liz turned, her expression hard as she searched her brain for a nice thought about the abrasive woman. What was Aunt Amelia thinking? "Yes?"

"Egads, what happened to your face?"

After months of living with the scar, Liz and her therapist had christened it her badge of courage. Liz walked up, nose to nose with the woman, and said, "It's really none of your business."

Regina looked at her husband and shrugged her shoulders. "I was only going to offer the name of a good concealer I special-order from Milan. It would camouflage that shiny raw skin beautifully, but that crevice might need a good plastic surgeon or collagen injections."

Liz's attorney had suggested that she leave off the bandage during the trial to play on the sympathy of the judge. Liz had refused. Besides, the *Daily Post* reissued a close-up photo of Liz's face on the night it happened, before the paramedics had arrived, followed by a blurb about golden boy Travis Osterman's defamation-of-character lawsuit. And, of course, the media wasn't allowed in the courtroom to hear her *truthful* side of the story.

Liz said, "Gosh. 'Concealer.' I never thought of that. Thanks for the beauty tip."

Regina snarled, "Well, I never!" She looked to Aunt Amelia. "Is that the way you have your staff talk to your guests?" She walked over to a tiger-maple credenza and tugged on a table runner from under a handblown aqua bottle filled with flowers from Aunt Amelia's cutting garden. The bottle teetered and water splashed onto the glossy wood. "Look at this ratty thing," Regina said, as she used her long nails to separate the runner's delicate silk threads. "David, in the morning, call around for another hotel. This one has seen better times."

Liz begged to differ. In the late 1940s Fred Astaire had stayed in the very same Oceana Suite while on hiatus from one of his films. A baccarat chandelier hung over a rattan love seat and mahogany coffee table. The table was topped with blue-and-white Chinese pots sprouting snowy white orchids. Granted, the carpets and some of the other furnishings were starting to show their age, but her great-aunt had a hard time parting with anything that came from the Indialantic's original glory days. Liz's favorite part of the suite was the balcony beyond the French doors that had a stunning view of the ocean, where guests could lounge on a pair of cushioned chaises, or have their morning coffee at a marble bistro table. In her opinion, the Oceana Suite was perfect, and she didn't want Regina Harrington-Worth to tell Aunt Amelia otherwise.

Before Liz could defend the beauty of the room, David Worth said, "I've tried to find a place that will take Venus, but every hotel on the island that takes pets is booked. April is apparently their busiest month." He took a half-dozen tissues from the box on the credenza and mopped at his perspiring brow. He was about six feet tall, but he seemed smaller than his wife, who was probably five-foot-two without her skyscraper footwear.

Regina turned toward him, eyes blazing, "Well, try to look a little harder. I don't know how you came up with this old dinosaur of a flophouse. I remember it from my childhood, and there's not one modern improvement that I can see."

David lowered his head in acquiescence, but his right hand was clenched in a fist. "You wanted to stay close to Castlemara while it's under construction. This was the most convenient."

Regina continued, "Daddy left me the old decrepit thing…" She looked around the sitting room, then continued. "As soon as they tear the damn thing down, I've been promised a five-month completion on my new *pied-à-terre.*"

Castlemara was a gorgeous, oceanfront Spanish Colonial mansion built in the early twentieth century, around the same time as the Indialantic, and was situated east of A1A, ten miles south of the hotel. Liz glanced at the bamboo dining table. On top were unrolled architect's plans, showing a three-story box of metal and glass. Liz admired modern architecture, but the renderings for Castlemara's replacement were more akin to a suburban office building than a beach house and it looked like the perimeter of the proposed structure would gobble up most of the property's natural terrain. Once, when Liz was on a book signing tour in California for *Let the Wind*

Roar, she'd stayed at a friend's Malibu beach house. When Liz opened the blinds in her guest room for a glimpse of the Pacific Ocean, she was stunned to see the couple in the glass box next door, sharing a shower. Talk about awkward.

Liz couldn't believe what she was hearing. "You're not thinking of razing that beautiful mansion, are you? Didn't Ponce de León land on the beach near Castlemara? I thought it was about to get historical status?"

Regina said, "Not anymore, thanks to a fabulous stable of New York City lawyers. Now, get on your way. I am having a private conversation with my husband." Regina looked at Aunt Amelia. "If we must stay here, I will make up a list of things I need. Also, do you have a girl you could loan me for our stay?" She glanced around the room, then stopped on Liz's face. "And I don't want her."

Liz turned and walked through the open door and into the hallway before saying, "Good. Because you couldn't afford me!"

Chapter 4

Liz waited for Aunt Amelia near the staircase going down to the lobby. When her great-aunt finally appeared, her cheeks were the same shade as her hair. "That woman! I'm so sorry I got you involved, my pet. Iris should have been there instead."

"Auntie, why are you letting them stay? Since you've been collecting rent on the emporium shops, I thought you were okay for the time being. It's too much work for you now that you're…"

"Now that I'm what?" Aunt Amelia put her hands on her wide hips, made famous by a Hula-Hoop commercial she'd starred in that had all the women in the sixties Hula-Hooping to create trim waistlines above their wide, baby-boomer-bearing hips. "Don't even go there. I feel as good as I did forty years ago. As Wayne Dyer once said, 'If you change the way you look at things, the things you look at change.'"

"How does that apply to your age?"

"I don't look at things as an eighty-year-old. I look at them as a forty-something."

"Well, you'll always be eternally young in my book. Can I make you a sandwich from the leftover prime rib?"

"No, no, dear. Think I'll turn in. I wish I knew what happened to Iris. Maybe you can ask your father if he's seen her before you head home?"

"Will do. Sweet dreams, Auntie." Liz kissed her soft, powdery cheek.

Aunt Amelia put a hand on either side of Liz's face. "Listen to me, young lady. Don't you ever let anyone make you feel less than the wonderful, giving, precious child I see by pointing out superficial flaws. When you are ready to talk, you know I'm here."

"Of course, I know that. We'll talk soon. I promise. Now, give me the list Regina gave you and I'll take care of things until we find Iris."

Aunt Amelia handed her the list. "It's a doozy. Maybe they'll find a place tomorrow. I thought having a Harrington stay here might bolster our popularity rating a bit. Regina's father, Percival, was the nicest man. He did so many wonderful things for our little barrier island. Also, I feel sorry for the poor wee thing."

Liz said, "I know Regina's father died recently. He died of natural causes. Right?"

"Elizabeth Holt, what are you implying?"

"Oh, nothing. But I wouldn't feel sorry for her. Regina's not 'wee.' She could trample us both in her six-inch heels and keep on walking."

"I was talking about Venus."

"What *is* Venus, anyway? Cat? Dog?"

"Not sure yet. But why should it suffer? Every creature needs shelter."

"Okay, what television character were you thinking for David Worth?"

Aunt Amelia fingered one of her curls and looked up at the ceiling, "That's a hard one. There's something familiar about him. I feel like I've met him before, just can't remember where. Maybe the actor Jack Webb, who played Sergeant Joe Friday on *Dragnet*? I'll have to sleep on it. You?"

"I'm not sure about him, but her, it's as clear as day—Joan Collins with long hair."

"Hmm...maybe. I was thinking Regina looks like Morticia from *The Addams Family*."

"She does resemble Carolyn Jones."

"Did I ever tell you about *The Addams Family*...?"

"Yes, you did. It was the episode called, 'Cupid Aims for Fester,' and you played Miss Carson, the Avon lady whom Uncle Fester mistook for his dating penpal. Now, get to bed, Auntie. It's getting late."

Aunt Amelia shuffled down the hallway toward her four-room suite in kitten heels affixed with lilac feathered pom-poms. Liz wouldn't have been surprised to hear a scream when her great-aunt looked in the mirror and realized she was wearing only half of her eye makeup.

As Liz walked down the curving, wrought-iron staircase, she worried about her great-aunt. No matter what "psychological age" she was, Liz couldn't help but think of her advancing chronological age and all the financial worries that seemed constant when running—yes—a run-down hotel. On top of that, Liz knew her aunt worried about her even more than the Indialantic. What would she and her father do if anything happened to Aunt Amelia? She pushed the thought aside, placing it next to all her other worries, and went into the kitchen.

The terra-cotta floor gleamed in the low light. It amazed Liz that this was the same kitchen where only hours before she had helped Pierre prepare dinner. She thought she heard a sigh, but it was just the wind. The kitchen seemed a lonely place without Pierre's bustling presence. Pierre had been working at the Indialantic since before Liz was born. He'd gone to the same French cooking school as Julia Child and he'd given Liz her first cooking lesson when she was only six years old. He'd even had a stool made for her with her name painted on it so she could reach the counter and be his "sous-chef." The stool still stood in the corner of the Indialantic's huge original Spanish-style kitchen, now updated with stainless steel appliances.

Another thing Pierre and Liz shared, besides a passion for cooking, was a love of mysteries. Her first Agatha Christie, *And Then There Were None*, had come from Pierre, its pages well-worn and dog-eared. The book still held a place of honor on Liz's bedroom bookshelf.

Pierre was the same age as Aunt Amelia, and since she'd come back to Melbourne Beach, Liz had noticed him forgetting to add key ingredients to the dishes he'd been making for decades. She tried to make it a point to go to the kitchen during the prep stage and taste everything before it was served, adding any missing items when Pierre's back was turned. When she had confided in her father and Aunt Amelia about her suspicions of Pierre's memory loss, they'd tried to get him to see a doctor, but he refused to go. Pierre was proud of the fact that, in eighty years, he'd never been to a doctor—not even when he cut off the tip of his pinkie finger while deboning a chicken. Luckily, one of the hotel's guests at the time was a retired nurse. She'd stitched it back on, as good as new.

Homeopathic remedies were Pierre's go-to cure for a myriad of ailments. He used herbs from his kitchen garden years before they came into vogue. Instead of Neosporin and a Band-Aid, Pierre had applied aloe and a mystery poultice to Liz's childhood boo-boos, then, as a distraction, they continued to bake gooey cinnamon buns or letter-shaped sugar cookies that spelled new words for Liz to learn. She wished she could return the favor and restore Pierre's memory, and she made it a point to look up what herbs might improve his memory loss.

Liz exited the kitchen via the door leading outside to the south garden. A heady scent of mint and rosemary rose from the ground as she passed Pierre's herb garden. In the distance, a light mist hovered over the ocean.

She took a path west toward the outside entrance of her father's apartment. Through the panes of glass in the arched Spanish Revival window was the welcoming glow of her father's desk lamp. He was at his desk in his usual, hunched-over position, pouring over an open law book. Since she'd been back, Liz had acted as his sounding board. Her father rehearsed closing arguments in front of Liz to see if she thought they needed tweaking from a stylistic writer's point of view. They never did. Many a time, Liz sat in the back of the courtroom, watching her father in action. His lean, six-foot-two frame, graying hair at the temples, and green eyes that matched Aunt Amelia's, made him an impressive figure, but it was when he opened his mouth to defend a client that he truly shined. Her father was on heart medication, which was the reason he'd retired as the county's leading public defender. She had tried to get him to lighten his caseload, but he was a sucker for a good sob story, occasionally getting hoodwinked by a bad guy or gal. In his estimation, if he could save one innocent person from jail, then he'd done a good job.

Aunt Amelia had encouraged her nephew to hang his shingle on the side entrance of the Indialantic—Fenton Holt, Esquire—reassuring Liz that the best thing for a strong heart was a passion for living.

Originally, she and her father had lived in the caretaker's cottage on the part of the Indialantic's property that faced the Indian River Lagoon. When Liz left for college, her father moved from the caretaker's cottage into the hotel to be closer to Aunt Amelia. The cottage was then rented to one of Aunt Amelia's fellow actresses from *Dark Shadows*, Millicent Morgan, who played the spunky, gap-toothed barmaid at Collinsport's Blue Whale Tavern. Sadly, Millicent had recently passed away and now the cottage remained vacant.

She knocked on her father's door, then walked in. He never locked it.

"Lizzy, you're a sight for sore eyes." Fenton rose and took five long-legged strides, then embraced Liz like he hadn't seen her in years, let alone a few hours. It reminded Liz of the panic her father must have felt when she'd called him from the hospital in Manhattan.

"What are you doing still working? Thought you'd have your feet up, watching reruns of *Law and Order*," she said, glancing at the tower of papers ready to spill off his desk.

"About to close up shop. I have a new case I might need your help with, but you'll have to go undercover."

Liz laughed. "I'm game."

"And why are you still hanging around the hotel? Shouldn't you be home with *your* feet up, or better yet, at your desk with your feet on the floor, writing your next blockbuster? You have a gift, Lizzy—you shouldn't squander it."

"Can't seem to get on track. I do have a title now, though. What do you think? *Read This and Do the Complete Opposite of What I Did for a Happy, Guilt-free Life.*"

"Catchy. I do like the last four words...'happy, guilt-free life.'"

"Auntie wanted me to ask if you've seen Iris. She's disappeared."

"No, sorry. I haven't seen her."

She and her father talked for a few minutes longer about her new covert assignment. After saying good night and shutting the door, Liz burst out laughing. She could only imagine what the tabloids would say if they ever got a photo of her doing what her father had just asked her to do. Liz took out her penlight and followed the cement sidewalk until she met the sandy path leading to the ocean. The moon peeked out from behind the clouds and helped to light her way. This stretch of the island was wild and untamed, backing up to the thirty-four-acre Barrier Island Sanctuary Center. On any given day, you might see huge blue crabs side-winding their way along the shoreline, endangered turtles laying eggs, snakes, owls, bobcats, and even the occasional panther on the prowl. Luckily, tonight the only creature she encountered was a screech owl with a pair of beaming yellow eyes. It whinnied and trilled as she passed.

Chapter 5

Before taking the crushed-shell path to her beach house, Liz stepped onto the sandy trail leading to the hotel's planked boardwalk that overlooked the ocean. At one time, the boardwalk followed the shore for the entire width of the original Indialantic by the Sea resort, but after decades of storms and hurricanes, the boardwalk had been reduced to a tenth of its original size. She stood at the railing and looked out across the dark ocean, the sound of the waves soothing and tranquil. She reveled in the sensation of the gentle wind caressing her face and felt a trickling of the desire to write. Maybe she'd write something less heavy than *Let the Wind Roar*, something with humor and a touch of romance—but *just* a touch.

April in Florida was Liz's favorite time of year, and she felt happy to be home and at peace with her surroundings. Through the mist, a ghostly lit cruise ship headed southeast toward the Bahamas. Liz had grown up with stories of sunken ships filled with treasure, none of which were fairy tales. In 1715, an entire fleet of Spanish ships carrying gold, silver, and decorative pottery sank in a storm off the Sebastian Inlet, ten miles south of where Liz stood, close to Regina's father's estate, Castlemara. A hurricane hit the shoreline in the mid-1950s, exposing a survivors' camp from the ship *El Capitana*. Soon after, a large cache of treasure was discovered. To this day, usually after a hurricane or storm, salvagers could be seen excavating odd pieces from *El Capitana* and other lost-at-sea vessels.

On Liz's tenth birthday, Aunt Amelia had given her a metal detector. The morning after a tropical storm slammed the island, Liz and her great-aunt hurried to the beach where the *El Capitana* survivor camp had been discovered, pretending they were shipwrecked from the S.S. *Minnow*. While they sat on the beach drinking Pierre's lemon-limeade and eating peanut butter and mango sandwiches, Aunt Amelia reminisced about her days on the set of the television show *Gilligan's Island*, where she'd met Mel Blanc, the man of a thousand voices. Mr. Blanc had been doing the voice-over for Gilligan's parrot and had given Aunt Amelia an unprompted montage of his most famous cartoon voices, including Daffy Duck, Porky Pig, Tweety, Sylvester, and Liz's favorite, Yosemite Sam. He'd ended his performance with a Bugs Bunny, "Eh, what's up, Doc?"

Aunt Amelia had also confided in Liz that the actress Tina Louise, aka Ginger, wasn't anything like the ditzy character she played on the show. Soon after her guest appearance, her great-aunt dyed her hair what she now called Tina Louise Red. It was no wonder Liz had become a writer. There was so much rich material to draw from, living with Aunt Amelia.

Liz did find treasure that day on the beach, not a gold coin from a shipwrecked Spanish galleon, but a 1926 Morgan silver dollar—from the same year the Indialantic by the Sea Hotel had been built. Liz still had the coin in a small trunk at the foot of her bed, where she kept her childhood keepsakes, including things that had belonged to her mother.

Regina Harrington-Worth's father had also found treasure near where the *El Capitana* was shipwrecked, reminding Liz about their irritating new guest. Regina's mother had died decades ago, and now, with her father's recent death, Liz wondered why Regina wasn't staying on her daddy's yacht while waiting for Castlemara to be torn down. Anywhere but the Indialantic.

The fog off the ocean was getting thicker, but Liz could still see the light of the moon reflected off the rolling waves. It was low tide. Soon that would change and the water would reach the bottom step, sometimes going farther inland, right up to the cyclone barrier fence that protected the twenty-foot dune. Down the shoreline, she observed two figures; one short, one tall.

Liz crept down the steps, then shined her tiny light on the damp sand. It was unusual for someone to be out on this stretch of the beach so late at night. She continued toward the couple, who seemed to be arguing about something, their voices carried on the wind in angry, broken syllables. She couldn't see their faces in the mist. The smaller female pushed against the man; he pushed back. As Liz reached in her pocket to dial 911, the man pulled the woman into an embrace and they fell to the sand. Liz turned, embarrassed by the passionate scene. She headed back up the steps, then hurried to her beach house. She retrieved the key from under an orchid pot, opened the French doors, and stepped inside her cozy haven.

Six weeks ago, when Liz had come home to Melbourne Beach from Manhattan, her father and great-aunt had surprised her with the beach house—they'd even taped a huge, pale aqua bow on the front door. Not only had her father invested money into the Indialantic, but he'd also paid to have the falling-into-ruin beach pavilion restored into a home for Liz— the perfect place to refocus on what was important and hopefully a serene environment to get her "writing mojo" back on track. Bestie Kate and the ladies from Home Arts by the Sea had helped with the interior design of the cottage, adding one-of-a-kind vintage items, hand-blown glass bowls, paintings by local artists, and fluffy, lightweight throws made from raw silk yarns in shades of aqua, coral, and cream.

The beach house had an open floor plan. The great room and kitchen were separated by a long counter with six bar stools and an open pass-through, making it easy for Liz to chat with guests while cooking in her dream kitchen, which Chef Pierre had designed as part of her homecoming surprise. She went to the fridge, grabbed a bottle of water, and headed to the bedroom. As she passed her office, she glanced inside. Her desk mocked her from its lack of use; her open laptop, a mere prop in case someone dropped by unexpectedly. Her favorite good-luck writing mug sat on the table next to the printer. Since her move back, it hadn't rekindled her desire to write, but she liked that it waited patiently for her, like an old friend. She felt a familiar tingle in her fingers.

Perhaps it was time?

Then she shook her head and continued to the bedroom, then into the bathroom, where she quickly performed her bedtime routine. It only took her about ten minutes, compared to her great-aunt's sixty. She looked in the mirror at her fair skin and blue eyes the color of bleached denim. A pale face that wasn't allowed to tan because of the scar. She wanted to surf, feel the elements, feel alive. She wasn't a great surfer; she was actually pretty mediocre compared to Kate and Kate's older brother, Skylar. When Liz went down to the beach, she looked like Norma Desmond from *Sunset Boulevard*, wearing a humongous floppy hat, hiding from the sun under a huge umbrella, while staring out to sea or reading an Agatha Christie novel.

Thank heaven for Christie.

Last week, Liz walked into the Indialantic's kitchen and found Pierre with his feet up, reading *The Murder of Roger Ackroyd*, reminding her of her teenage days when she and Pierre would lounge on the terrace overlooking the ocean, reading Christies while sipping Pierre's famous lemon-limeade. Now, as a distraction from her past, and with the approval of her therapist, Liz was on a mission to read everything Christie had written. She kept a notebook of her progress—six books down—seventy-four to go, not counting the short story collections. Liz didn't want to read heavy literary best sellers, and she completely avoided the *New York Times Book Review*. The competition and pressure of trying to remain on top of the list had been one of the reasons leading to her and Travis's demise.

Liz went into the bedroom and changed into an oversized Columbia University T-shirt. Francie Jenkins had made an amazing hand-sewn quilt that she'd framed and hung on the wall behind the bed. It was made from vintage fabrics in sea colors, some of which had been donated by Aunt Amelia and came from old trunks stored in the hotel's luggage room. The king-sized bed faced a floor-to-ceiling glass window with a no-holds-barred view of the Atlantic. Every morning when she woke, she felt like she was on the deck of a ship, only there weren't any rolling waves to make her seasick.

She turned back the duvet, got in bed, and nestled down into cool, high-thread-count Egyptian cotton sheets, then switched on the bedside lamp and reached for *Evil Under the Sun.*

Chapter 6

Friday morning, Liz woke to a jewel of a sunrise. She took a shower, pulled her hair up into a clip, added some mascara and lip gloss, put on a simple pale aqua sundress, and went in search of her father. When Liz got to the outside door of her father's office, she didn't knock; instead she burst in. "What a morning! I'm ready to hear more about my new assignment, and I want to know what you think about a raffle for the Spring Fling by the Sea to raise money for the Barrier Island Sanctuary." She stopped short when she noticed the stranger from yesterday's dinner sitting in a chair across from her father.

"Uhh, sorry, Dad. Didn't know you weren't alone."

"Obviously not," the man said, twisting slowly in his chair to face her. He gave her the same annoying once-over he had at last night's dinner, and Liz's face heated in anger. His dark, almost black hair was on the longish side. His deep brown eyes assessed her from under hooded lids with thick lashes. She met his piercing gaze with what she hoped was cool disdain. He seemed the type that enjoyed making a woman squirm. But not this woman. Liz had to admit he was attractive, but he wasn't her type—actually the opposite. Kate would go for him in a heartbeat. Then she thought about Travis. He'd been her type, a bookish academician, and look how that'd turned out.

"I'll come back later," Liz said.

The guy snorted and turned back to her father.

Her father closed the file in front of him, oblivious to the negative vibes in the room. "We're almost finished here. Just give me five minutes." As an afterthought, he said, "Ryan Stone, this is my daughter, Liz. Ryan is on leave from the New York City Fire Department to help his grandfather in Deli-casies by the Sea, until Pops's new knee heals."

So much for typecasting him as a villain. Pops was kind and sweet, always smiling. Ryan must take after someone else in his family, not his grandfather.

Ryan turned and gave Liz a dismissive gaze her father couldn't see. His lip curled up on one side. "A pleasure, I'm sure." Then he turned and said, "Mr. Holt, I really should be getting back to my grandfather."

Liz could take a hint. "I'll be at Books & Browsery by the Sea. Come by, I'd love to show you what Kate has done."

Fenton said, "As soon as we're finished, Elizabeth."

Uh-oh. Liz knew that when her father called her "Elizabeth," she was in trouble. She regretted interrupting his meeting with Pops's ungracious, and yes, irritating grandson. What exactly was he doing, talking to her father in such a lawyerly fashion? Liz knew her father would never tell her anything confidential about an open case, but when she helped him with his paperwork, maybe she could find out. Liz was privy to where he hid the keys to his files and she knew the password to his laptop—her mother's maiden name and birthday.

If Ryan Stone had come from Manhattan, or one of the boroughs, then he probably knew all about the infamous Elizabeth Holt scandal, likely explaining his bristly posture.

Or he could just be a jerk.

Liz walked to the back of the office and opened a door that led into her father's apartment, then stepped inside his main living space. All four walls of the room had built-in bookcases packed with books—and not just law books, but fiction, biographies, psychology texts, and his favorite, courtroom thrillers—both fiction and true life. On the other side of the hotel was a library ten times the size of her father's. If her father wasn't to be found in his office, pouring over law books or with a client, he would be reading in one library or the other.

She walked through the room, loving the way her father had arranged things to be both masculine and cozy at the same time. Liz stopped next to a teak end table displaying a photograph of her father, mother, and herself at age four, standing in front of their apartment in Manhattan. It was impossible to believe that the vibrant, smiling woman with Liz's blue eyes would die of breast cancer the next year. She had only a few memories of her mother, but at least they were all good. And she had the video that was full of love and bright smiles that her mother had left her "just in case."

Opening a door next to her father's kitchen that led to the interior of the hotel, she followed a narrow-tiled hallway, passing the hotel's dumbwaiter that hadn't been used in decades. At the end of the hallway was an ornate wrought-iron staircase leading up to a Juliet balcony facing the Indian River Lagoon. When Liz was in middle school, she and Aunt Amelia would practice lines from Shakespeare, dressed in cone-shaped hats topped with a half dozen of her great-aunt's chiffon scarves, giving their productions, per Aunt Amelia, a Renaissance feel.

Romeo, O Romeo, leave me the hell alone, Romeo. As Liz knew firsthand, there was a thin line between passion and obsession, and once you crossed it, there was no going back.

She continued on through a curved archway that opened into the kitchen. Betty Lawson sat at the wooden farm table with Caro on her lap. Pierre stood at the stove, filling Betty's bowl with steel-cut oatmeal. Every morning but Sunday, Betty added two tablespoons of molasses to her oatmeal to "unclog the pipes" and keep her "regular."

Pierre wore his white chef's toque from morning to evening, making Liz wonder as a child if he slept with it on. "Liz, darling. Can I make you some breakfast?" Pierre asked, as he handed Betty the bowl with shaky hands. "I just made Betty some eggs."

Liz caught Betty's usually mischievous gaze, which now looked concerned and directed at Pierre's hands holding the bowl of oatmeal, not eggs. Liz had thought only her father and Aunt Amelia knew about Pierre's memory loss, but Betty didn't miss a thing. Maybe it had something to do with decades of writing teenage mystery novels.

"I wish I had time, Grand-Pierre, but I'm meeting with Aunt Amelia about the Spring Fling. I'll try to talk her into coming back to the kitchen afterward."

Betty motioned for Pierre to sit across from her, where his soft-boiled egg on a slice of homemade multigrain toast waited. He took a seat and smashed the egg into his toast with his fork. Yolk oozed onto the plate. Then he picked up a bottle of Tabasco sauce and shook it liberally over his egg. Liz was happy because she'd researched cayenne pepper and found it was beneficial when used in the diets of patients with memory loss.

The day's lunch and dinner menu wasn't on the center island cutting board like it usually was. She usually checked to make sure Pierre had everything he needed. Lately, she'd been prepping the ingredients and placing them in small bowls with numbers on top of the cellophane so all he had to do was lay them in order on the counter. "Chef, do you have today's menu? I have a feeling our new guests, the Worths, will be expecting one of your masterpieces."

"Of course I do, my dear." He reached up and took off his toque. Inside was a rolled-up piece of paper tied with string. "Voilà."

Laughing, she took it from his hand and unrolled it. Pierre's calligraphy was beautiful, full of flourishes and curlicues he'd learned as a young boy in primary school in France. Every morning at 6 a.m., Pierre would be at his desk in the butler's pantry writing out the day's menu with a pen he dipped in India ink that Aunt Amelia had special-ordered for him.

Today's menu seemed simple and elegant, but Liz doubted the poached salmon entrée he had planned for dinner would satisfy Her Haughtiness, Regina Harrington-Worth. She also knew how important it was for Aunt Amelia to impress the Worths.

In the butler's pantry, she found the cookbook she and Aunt Amelia had printed and bound with all of Pierre's signature dishes and had presented to him on his eightieth birthday. Liz had her own copy in the beach house that she referred to time and time again. To her, thumbing through *The Chef Pierre Montague Cookbook* was like walking down memory lane.

She decided on salmon wrapped in crêpes with a lemon dill sauce. They would add a little pizzazz to the meal, and Pierre's crêpes were the best she'd ever tasted. Pierre wasn't like the chefs seen on television—he had no ego. So when she explained about the change in the menu, he was on board with her selection.

After checking the pantry and huge refrigerator to make sure Pierre had all the supplies he needed for the upgraded entrée, Liz walked over to Betty, leaned down, and scratched behind Caro's ears, winning a few affectionate head butts. She asked, "Did Iris show up this morning?"

"She was up before me and left a note that she was going to the supermarket," Pierre said, pointing to the kitchen counter. "But she forgot to take the list." He stuffed the last bite of his toast into his mouth, got up, and put his dishes in the dishwasher. Then he said, *"Au revoir,"* and went outside to tend to his kitchen garden.

Liz sat next to Betty and Caro. The cat transferred laps, and Liz and Caro commenced a short discussion—Liz rolling her tongue in imitation of Caro's distinctive gravelly meows, while Betty laughed and joined in the conversation. She realized, after years of living with Aunt Amelia and her Animalia, that if she talked to an animal, it would no doubt talk back to her.

"I see that Percival Harrington II's daughter is staying in the Oceana Suite," Betty said, interrupting Liz's discussion with Caro. "You do know there are rumors she killed her father so she could inherit Castlemara and the treasure from the *San Carlos*?"

"That's not like you to believe rumors. Are you just bored and need a good mystery to solve? Although, I must admit, after meeting her, I wouldn't be surprised."

"He officially died of a heart attack. Captain Netherton told me the Coast Guard had him airlifted from his yacht, but he died before reaching the hospital. His daughter was the only one on board besides the crew."

"Well, if anyone can bring on a heart attack, that woman can. I'd better go. Auntie's probably wondering where I am." Caro jumped off Liz's lap, probably to find her buddy, Killer. Liz got up, kissed Betty on top of the head, and moved toward the door leading into the dining room, passing the cappuccino/espresso machine. She was jonesin' for a cup of French roast topped with a layer of frothy milk and one of Pierre's better-than-donuts beignets that called to her from under a glass-domed cake plate, but she resisted and went on into the dining room.

Only one table had been used for breakfast, and it was piled with a stack of dirty dishes. Liz guessed the Worths had breakfasted there, because she knew Captain Netherton and Betty usually ate in the hotel's kitchen for breakfast and lunch. She cleared the table, knowing Iris was out. As she folded up the tablecloth, she glanced at Regina's lipstick-stained napkin. The woman had actually used her white linen napkin as a makeup blotter. *What a piece of work*, Liz thought as she headed back to the kitchen. She balanced the stack of dishes, then used her shoulder to push open the swinging doors and walked inside.

Betty was gone, and the kitchen was now neat and spotless. Liz rinsed the dishes, put them into one of three industrial-sized dishwashers, and left the room. On her way back through the dining room, she spied a business card on the floor under the chair where she'd found Regina's lipstick-stained napkin. The card belonged to Captain Clyde B. Netherton; all that was printed on it was his name and a cell phone number. She put it in her pocket. Liz had to give him credit, the captain was a player and not afraid of going after the happily married—if, indeed, Regina Harrington-Worth *was* happily married.

Chapter 7

The dining room had three exits: one leading to the kitchen, another to the interior courtyard with the Indialantic's famous sixty-foot coconut palm in the center, and the third, which Liz took, had her entering a short hallway. She passed the closed door to the library, and continued through a twenty-foot archway that opened into the lobby. Everything in the lobby seemed copacetic—almost too quiet without Aunt Amelia's presence. She felt like she'd time-traveled and was back in 1926, the year the Indialantic by the Sea Hotel had opened to much fanfare and had been booked from September to June for almost fifty years.

Next to the antique elevator, she saw that the brass stand to Barnacle Bob's cage stood cageless. The Indialantic had a working service elevator off the kitchen, which Aunt Amelia kept up to code for any guests who couldn't use the stairs in the lobby. The old lobby elevator hadn't worked for as long as Liz remembered. Aunt Amelia held out hope that one day they would have enough money to repair the charming 1920s Otis elevator cab with its brass accordion gate and ornate art deco floor indicator. Family folklore had it that on its last voyage, the cab had stopped between floors with gangster Al Capone inside—angry as a bull in a zoot suit. And there were rumors that the elevator operator went missing and was never seen again.

The décor in the lobby was the same as when Liz had left ten years ago, when she'd moved to Manhattan. And it had changed little from when she and her father had arrived twenty-three years before. Aunt Amelia always said, "If it ain't broken, why fix it?" Liz glanced down at the Persian carpet that covered the lobby's terra cotta–tiled floor. She was sure Regina would notice the carpet's worn spots and frayed edges.

The lobby had a vaulted ceiling and stucco walls, and it was filled with six-foot potted palms, bamboo tables, and bamboo chairs with comfy upholstered cushions in tropical prints. Aunt Amelia hadn't needed a porter or a reception desk clerk for years, because even though the Indialantic had the word "Hotel" in its title, it was more of a boardinghouse—that was until Aunt Amelia let the Worths stay. Her favorite part of the lobby was its long, highly polished wood registration counter. On top of the counter was the hotel's original guest register, filled with famous and infamous names dating from the 1920s.

A wooden cabinet behind the counter had mail and telegram cubbies corresponding to the hotel's original guest rooms. Now only the top two rows were used for sorting mail and messages for Liz, Aunt Amelia, Betty, Captain Netherton, and Iris.

She thought about the constantly disappearing housekeeper. Iris was hard to warm up to. Aunt Amelia must have felt sorry for her for some reason or another to have hired her. Liz often heard the housekeeper tell whomever would listen that she "ran" the hotel, not "Old Lady Holt." It wasn't any of Liz's business how much the housekeeper earned at the Indialantic, but she knew room and board came with the job and she didn't want Aunt Amelia to be taken advantage of.

Then she remembered that those in glass beach houses shouldn't throw seashells. Wasn't she doing the same thing as Iris? Freeloading off of her father and great-aunt? Liz had some money saved up from the proceeds of her book and the sale of her loft, but her father had refused to let her sink it into the Indialantic. Not that Liz had spent much time in the past cleaning the guest rooms, but how hard could it be to vacuum, dust, fluff pillows, and leave a couple of mints on each bed? Then Liz stopped dead in her tracks, when she remembered Regina and the list. She suddenly wished Iris the best. It would be interesting to see the unflusterable Iris tackle Regina's list of demands. She had glanced at the list last night, stopping after she read the first item: Fresh Parboiled Tuna Three Times a Day. It looked like the mystery of the species of Regina's pet, Venus, had been solved—she must be a feline.

Liz left the lobby and continued down the hallway to the screening room. When she opened the door, it was dark inside. Only a faint light spilled onto the back row of seats from the projection booth. She felt her way down the aisle. As she got closer to the screen, she saw the outline of Aunt Amelia's head, front row and center. Liz slid into the seat next to her and took her soft, ring-bejeweled hand in hers. "What are you doing sitting here in the dark?"

"I was getting inspiration for the Spring Fling by watching the episode of *My Three Sons*, where Ernie tries to raise money for a charity event at school, spends some of the proceeds on a candy bar, then is called into the principal's office."

"Let me guess, you played the principal?"

"Nope. The secretary. Complete with cat-framed glasses on a pearl chain and an angora twinset that had me sneezing from all the little rabbit hairs I inhaled. It took eight takes for a one-line speaking part."

Liz jumped. A voice from the other side of Aunt Amelia said, "Ernie Douglas, does your father know you're here?"

"Barnacle Bob, you scared the crap out me!" Liz scolded.

He seemed to enjoy Liz's reaction and kept repeating, "Does your father know you're here? Does your father know you're here?" The parrot did a perfect imitation of a young Aunt Amelia.

Aunt Amelia said, "Behave, BB. You have to be nice to Lizzy."

"Nice to Lizzy. Nice to Lizzy. Scared the crap out of me!"

"Silence, rude boy," Aunt Amelia scolded, then turned to Liz. "Our weekend event is such a great idea. Thank you, my lovely. All the emporium shopkeepers are on board, except for grouchy Edward. He's worried someone might steal one of his gold coins. I told him, this is a sleepy barrier island where crime is nonexistent and everyone knows each other. You must agree that Edward's the spitting image of Cesar Romero in *The Computer Who Wore Tennis Shoes*. That Kurt Russell was such a charming young man, and those adorable dimples..."

"Hmmm, love Kurt Russell, but I beg to differ. I think Edward looks more like Vincent Price than Cesar Romero."

"Romero."

"Price."

Aunt Amelia laughed. "I guess it's a draw. What's funny is that both Price and Romero were characters in TV's *Batman*—Romero as the Joker and Price as Egghead." She stopped and said, "Here I go again. Rambling on about the past. How do you put up with such a crazy auntie?"

"Oh, that's pretty easy," Liz said. "I'm your biggest fan."

"I only met Vincent Price once on the set of *Alfred Hitchcock Presents*. Well, I didn't meet him *per se*, but I'm sure he winked at me. My favorite episode of his was 'The Perfect Crime.' Price's character is an egomaniac detective who is proud he's never committed a crime..."

"I remember when we watched that one! A lawyer tells a detective that he sent an innocent man to his death, the detective kills the lawyer in a very original way—thus creating the perfect crime."

"Whomever Edward reminds us of, he sure is a cranky-puss."

"He and Regina would make a good couple," Liz said. "I feel sorry for David Worth."

"I'm sure no one put a gun to his head to marry her. Her family has owned Castlemara for generations. It's such a shame they are going to tear it down."

"Maybe the Barrier Island Historical Society will stop them. We might look bad to the locals, harboring the Worths. Betty said there are rumors that Regina killed her father." Liz purposely put the bug in Aunt Amelia's ear in case she felt any future regrets about kicking the woman out, especially if Regina continued with her unrelenting demands.

"Percival II was an old man with a bad heart. I've heard the rumors, but I don't believe them for a second. I've invited Mrs. Harrington-Worth to share high tea with me in the courtyard this afternoon. Try to get her to see the charm of our hotel from a different perspective."

"If I were you, I'd take a shot of bourbon first."

"Elizabeth!" Aunt Amelia got up and reached for Barnacle Bob's cage. "Vincent Price and his wife were gourmet cooks, just like you. I think I have his cookbook somewhere, *A Treasury of Great Recipes.*"

Liz stood and wordlessly took the heavy cage from Aunt Amelia's hand. "I'd love to see it. Speaking of food, let's finish our discussion about the Spring Fling in the kitchen. Maybe we can get Dad to join us?"

"That would be splendid."

"I burst in on Dad this morning. He had Pops's grandson with him. Any idea why the guy needs an attorney?"

As they continued up the aisle, Aunt Amelia said, "No. Not a clue. But that Ryan is such a nice, polite boy and hot as a Carolina Reaper."

The Carolina Reaper was the winner of the hot pepper contest Pops had a few weeks ago at Deli-cacies by the Sea.

"If you say so. Auntie." She wanted to change the subject before her great-aunt came up with a name for Ryan Stone from the midcentury TV vault in her head. Liz thought the guy resembled the actor who played Ross Poldark on the PBS television series *Poldark.* Darn. Now Liz was playing the twenty-first-century naming game.

"I let Ryan rent out the caretaker's cottage until he goes back to New York," Aunt Amelia said.

"You what!"

"It makes sense. On the days when Pops isn't feeling good enough to put in a full day, Ryan will be nearby to open and close Deli-cacies. Pops lives in a one-bedroom condo. It can't be that comfortable for Ryan."

Liz would protest more, but she'd grown fond of Pops. He was always so jolly, and he sure knew how to prepare all the home-style deli foods she missed from New York, while still offering local seafood, produce, and an amazing cheese and wine selection. Ryan would never be considered jolly like his grandfather. The thought of Ryan living in the caretaker's cottage, which she and her father had called home for thirteen years, also rubbed Liz the wrong way, but she let it go. Aunt Amelia could do whatever she wanted when it came to the hotel, but that didn't mean Liz would let her guard down when it came to people who could take advantage of her great-aunt. Iris Kimball also came to mind; something wasn't right with the woman. Later she would ask Aunt Amelia if she could take a look at Iris's references. "Come on, Auntie, let's go to the kitchen for some rocket fuel and beignets. You really need to bring a flashlight with you the next time you come into the theater alone. I don't want you falling and breaking your hip or something."

"Ha. My bones are as strong as an ox's. Had a bone-density test last week. I have the skeleton of a forty-year-old. So there."

"Okay. Okay. No more 'old' comments. Got it."

Chapter 8

Liz returned to the lobby after her discussion with her father and Aunt Amelia about tomorrow's festivities. She found Captain Netherton and David Worth seated by the door to the inner courtyard, chatting amicably. Regina's loud presence was notably missing, and Liz exhaled with relief. When the captain noticed Liz, he excused himself, stood up, and grabbed his cane, which had been leaning against his chair.

She said, "It's Friday. Are you taking the day off skippering *Queen of the Seas*?"

The captain nodded his head in David's direction. "The Worths have chartered the entire ship. They want to check out their building site from the water."

Once again, she wondered why Regina wasn't living the high life on her recently departed father's yacht, usually moored at the ritzy Eau Galle Yacht Club. Liz looked toward David Worth, who was intently reading his newspaper. Seconds earlier, Liz had seen him leaning forward in his chair, trying to overhear their conversation. Maybe if she used the word "bedbugs," he would pass it on to his wife and they would vacate the hotel.

Captain Netherton and Liz talked a little while about the upcoming weather pattern, then she excused herself. She planned to meet Kate to talk about tomorrow's Spring Fling. She walked toward the lobby's massive revolving door and stepped inside. It took all her strength to get the heavy thing moving. A little WD-40 might be in order. Finally, Liz was spit out the other side, onto the green carpet under the hotel's main portico.

She inhaled the salty air and surveyed the seascape in front of her. The temperature was in the upper seventies, and the ocean wind was calm, but you never knew what storm might blow in this time of year in coastal

Florida. Liz looked toward a huge fountain encircled in coral hibiscus, whose backdrop was the glittering Atlantic. In the center of the fountain was a statue of Hercules holding a bow and arrow. Water trickled from the bottom of his quiver and into the fountain. From a distance, it looked like the Roman god with six-pack abs had a prostate problem. The statue's left foot was missing and the tip of his aquiline nose was gone, adding, per Kate, rescuer of all things old, a "rustic charm and air of antiquity."

When Liz was small, the hotel had a live-in groundskeeper. Now, every Tuesday, a six-person crew came to cut the grass. They did a little trimming, then were gone in under an hour. Pierre tended to his kitchen garden, and Aunt Amelia took care of the cutting garden and flowering shrubs. The responsibility for the upkeep of the flowers and foliage in the interior courtyard was shared between Pierre and Aunt Amelia.

Once upon a time, the hotel had its very own mascot in the form of a magnificent peacock. When Liz was a child, she saw a snapshot in an old photo album of Preston the Peacock in full plumage, strutting across the Indialantic's expansive lawn. She re-created the peacock's jewel-toned colors with Crayolas supplied by her father and drew a picture of Aunt Amelia's head on top of Preston's body, because that's what her showbiz great-aunt reminded her of—a beautiful peacock. She remembered how disappointed she'd been after a trip to the Brevard County Zoo, when she'd learned that all the pretty peacocks were male, compared to the female peahens, which were a dull mud-brown. Her father had wisely pointed out that it was far better to be a female peahen, because they could camouflage themselves better in the wild and avoid predators.

She stepped under the canopy and onto the circular white flagstone drive and headed north. When the sun peeked out from a chubby marshmallow cloud, she suddenly realized she wasn't wearing a hat to protect her scar. She released the clip that held her long, wavy hair in a loose chignon and let it cascade onto her face. Instant sunscreen.

Minna Presley drove by in one of the hotel's golf carts and Liz waved hello. Minna waved back, her short spiky hair and brightly colored geometric print spandex dress clinging snugly to her lean body. Six months ago, Minna had been talked into going in fifty-fifty with her buddy Francie on the rental of the emporium shop Home Arts by the Sea. Forty-something Minna certainly didn't need the money. She had a large following for her one-of-a-kind mixed media art and was featured in numerous galleries in the area. Minna was considered a VIP in nearby Vero Beach, known for its art community, galleries, and multimillionaire residents.

Thinking about Minna's celebrity status, Liz remembered that tomorrow there would be a juried showcase at Home Arts by the Sea of Minna and Francie's clients' works. Kate planned on having a buy-one-get-one-free used book sale at Books & Browsery by the Sea, and Aunt Amelia had talked Brittany into hiring a few models to meander around the emporium dressed in Sirens by the Sea clothing and jewelry.

Pops would be supplying a wine-and-cheese tasting at Deli-casies by the Sea. In his youth, he'd been a sommelier at Brooklyn's Peter Luger Steak House, and his selection of cheeses was becoming legendary in the Melbourne Beach area. Because of his recent knee surgery, she'd promised Pops that she would help with the wine tasting. Now that his grandson was in town, she doubted her services would be needed.

Liz turned left at the end of the driveway. There were five cars in the emporium's parking lot. Under a sign that read Indialantic by the Sea Emporium, were mammoth double-arched doors. She opened the door on the left and stepped into the foyer. She corralled her unruly mop of hair and clipped it up into a messy bun. A lock of hair fell onto her right cheek, covering her scar. Instead of leaving it there, she poked it back up inside her hair clip. Her therapist had warned her that she needed to be fearless, and that every time she looked at her reflection, she should thank her lucky stars she had a face to look at. Things could have turned out so much worse.

Liz marveled at the way the emporium had come together. The first-floor space had once housed the Indialantic's grand ballroom, men's smoking lounge, and billiards room. The second floor had been demolished and a two-story wall was erected on the south side of the building. The shops now had an open-air setting. Four-foot walls separated each shop from another, encouraging customers to meander and interact. Stucco walls extended up to a buttressed ceiling that came to a peak, like those in an old Spanish mission, and suspended from the pierced-tin tiled ceiling in the foyer was a huge Baccarat glass chandelier that had formerly hung in the hotel's ballroom.

Across from the windows that looked out at the old clay tennis courts was Brittany Poole's shop, Sirens by the Sea. A chain was up across the entrance, and the accessory showcases were dark. Liz didn't see Brittany, just four mannequins waiting to be clothed.

When she'd returned home from New York, she was surprised to find out that Brittany had rented a space for her women's clothing shop. On her first time in, Liz asked Brittany the price of an unticketed turquoise and silver ankle bracelet. Brittany had made it clear that their feud was still ongoing. She'd replied, "One hundred forty-five dollars for everyone else, one hundred eighty for you." Then Brittany picked up her phone and ordered a two-thousand-dollar pastel gossamer cocktail dress. Liz doubted anyone else was on the other end of the line.

She'd known Brittany since elementary school. Once, she'd invited Brittany over for a playdate. After Brittany left, Liz realized a few things were missing from her room. She waited until she was invited to Brittany's house, then, when Brittany left the room, she searched under Brittany's bed. Liz found two Nancy Drews, her *To Kill a Mockingbird* book that had belonged to her mother, a box filled with her favorite seashells collected along the barrier island's shoreline, and a framed photo of Liz's father from law school. When her father came to pick her up, Liz went on a rampage of indignation, filling him in on every last detail of Brittany's act of high thievery. He'd been empathetic—only not to her, but to Brittany. He explained that Brittany was jealous of Liz's close relationship with him because she'd never known her own father. Mrs. Poole was a single mother who worked twelve-hour shifts at a Melbourne Beach grocery store. And if there was one thing defense attorney Fenton Holt was known for, it was his compassion for the less fortunate.

On top of Brittany's childhood exploits, there was a very brief time in high school when Brittany had dated Kate's older brother, Skylar. Skylar had been like a brother to Liz, and Brittany had tried to thwart their friendship at every turn. Was she still supposed to have compassion for Brittany? Time would tell. But she had a feeling they would never be "besties."

She continued on to Home Arts by the Sea. Francie Jenkins sat at a long, burnished aluminum table and was giving knitting lessons to a young woman sitting next to her. The shop had been set up as an open workshop with three twenty-foot worktables and chairs. There were towering wood cubbies spaced around the shop filled with yarn, embroidery thread, bolts of fabric, batting, and artists' supplies. Across from the worktables were three tall easels holding works in progress. The two-story wall at the back of Home Arts by the Sea was adorned with art, including framed oil and watercolor paintings and three of Minna's mixed-media collages on six-foot canvases. There were also natural wood bookcases that held items for sale made by members of the Home Arts by the Sea Collective, including knitwear, blankets, pottery, primitive-style hooked rugs, blown glass, and handmade jewelry.

Liz's life in Manhattan left little time for leisure crafts. She'd learned to crochet as a teen from Betty, but she hadn't picked up a hook in ten years. Maybe she would get back into it. She knew from watching Francie and

Betty that there were many cathartic benefits to learning the needlecraft arts and that she should make it a point to take a few lessons in her downtime. Her nagging muse whispered in her ear, *Another excuse, to not write, Elizabeth Amelia Holt.* Darn muse.

When she passed by Home Arts, Liz called out, "Hey, Francie."

Francie looked nervously at the young woman next to her, put her finger to her lips, and pointed at a stroller that apparently held a sleeping baby. Francie handed the knitting over to her pupil. Then Liz heard Francie whisper, "Go on, you've got it, Beth. I'll be right back."

Liz met her at the entrance to the shop. Francie grabbed her arm and pulled her toward the bench under the windows and they both sat. Francie focused her large, chocolate-brown eyes on Liz. Aunt Amelia and Liz had mutually christened Francie with the name Gidget from the television series starring Sally Field. Her dark brown hair was styled in a sixties flip with short, razor-straight bangs. Francie wore clothing that she handmade, using her own trademarked sewing patterns. She sold the patterns at Home Arts by the Sea, online, and at sewing centers across the country. She would take a vintage pattern and update the measurements for a modern woman's silhouette, then add a flourish or two from her own imagination.

Liz looked at her apron. "Love the poodle."

The apron was affixed with pink poodle appliques trimmed in gold sequins. The cotton print polka-dot dress under her apron had a buttoned-up bodice and a Peter Pan collar. The dress flared at the waist and was cinched with a patent-leather belt.

"Thanks. I copied the poodle from a skirt I bought from Books & Browsery by the Sea. Kate's always on the lookout for vintage clothing I can duplicate."

"You all set for the Spring Fling?"

"Yes. Minna and I are anticipating a big turnout." She glanced toward Sirens by the Sea. "Do you believe that deadbeat, Brittany? This is the third time this week she hasn't come in on time. She makes the rest of us look bad."

"I'll talk to Aunt Amelia. I don't want to get involved. Brittany and I aren't exactly on good terms."

Francie stood, looked over the wall at her pupil, and gave her a thumbs-up. When she sat back down she said, "I've been giving the poor thing lessons since we opened the shop, and she still tends to make a mess of things. I must not be a very good teacher."

"You are a great teacher, Francie. Every class you give is packed and usually has a year-long waiting list."

"I'm determined to help her. That's why I had her come in before opening."

Liz stood. "Any more grumbling from Edward?"

"Edward wouldn't be Edward without a little grumbling. You should hear the way he talks to his son. Speaking of grumbling, I heard Regina Harrington-Worth is a guest of the hotel. What hole did she crawl out of? I'm the vice president of the Barrier Island Historical Society, and there's no way we're letting her tear down Castlemara."

"As far as I know, Regina sounds pretty confident she'll be moving into her new mansion in five months' time."

"Oh my gosh. She'll be staying here for that long?"

"I hope not."

"Her father and mine were the cofounders of the historical society. They say she bumped off her father, Percival Harrington II."

It was the second time today Liz had heard the rumors, and now that the Worths were staying at the Indialantic, she knew it wouldn't be the last.

Francie leaned in closer to Liz. "I know her father must have had a clause somewhere in his will that would keep Regina from demolishing Castlemara. When I was in the office a couple of weeks ago, Regina burst in furious after finding out that after her own death, Castlemara would go to the Barrier Island Historical Society. I won't let her tear down Castlemara. It's a travesty. You should have Fenton look into it." Francie had a pleading tone, tears pooling in her huge brown eyes.

"Another thing I'd better not get involved in. Why don't you stop by my dad's office later, though, and talk to him?"

"Maybe I will."

As they talked, the young woman called Beth came toward them, holding what Liz, who wasn't a knitter, could only describe by using Aunt Amelia's term, a "rat's nest" of tangled, variegated yarn. "Oops," the woman said to Francie.

Francie stepped toward her and took the hot mess out of her hands, patting her student on the back. "No worries, there's more yarn where that came from." Prodding the woman back to the table, she turned back to face Liz and mouthed, *"We'll talk later."*

She thought about what Francie had said. If Regina's father had put Castlemara in a trust for the Barrier Island Historical Society, how was Regina going to be able to tear it down? It wasn't Liz's problem, but she could tell by meeting Regina only once that the woman would move heaven and earth to get what she wanted. She took a right at the end of the aisle and passed Deli-casies by the Sea. When she saw the back of Ryan's head, she started to scurry toward Books & Browsery by the Sea, but not before Pops spotted her and called out, "No French roast today, Liz?"

She called back, "Not today, Pops. But thanks." She was dying for another coffee, but having to interact with his annoying grandson was too high a price to pay.

Chapter 9

Nailed to the four-foot wall at the entrance to Books & Browsery by the Sea was a worn, rustic sign that read Beware—Pickpockets & Loose Women. Kitschy, but no doubt original. Kate's shop was set up a bit differently than the rest of the emporium. It had the same short perimeter walls, but inside, Kate had created a mazelike obstacle course from a slew of seven-foot-tall barrister bookcases she'd bought at a retired judge's estate sale. The backs of the bookcases were used to hang vintage shelves, pictures, and mirrors. Scattered randomly around the shop were chairs, a couple of overstuffed sofas, tables, dressers, and crates, along with some items that Liz had no clue as to what they were.

"Yo, Kate. You in there?"

From somewhere in the back, she heard, "Right with you. I'm up here. See?"

Liz craned her neck and looked at the top of a bookcase near the middle of the shop. Kate was sitting on top, her legs dangling over the side.

"What are doing up there? Barnacle Bob is right about you."

Kate called out, "Pshaw, I'll eat that bird for dinner."

Liz knew Kate loved the crusty old parrot as much as she did. Kate placed a lamp on top of a teetering stack of books.

"Aren't you scared that the lamp might fall on a customer?" Liz asked. "Unless you're planning on busing in an NBA basketball team, how the hell can anyone read the book titles if they're up in the nosebleed section?"

"It's not about selling books," Kate replied. "It's about thinking outside the box and giving customers ideas on how to display their own vintage items." Kate leaned into the stack of books and mumbled something into their pages. Then she said, "Do you mind spotting me on the ladder? I'll be right down."

Liz made her way toward Kate, stubbing her big toe on a wooden pineapple crate filled with broken violins. She glanced at the price tag—you couldn't buy just one, you had to buy the whole kit and caboodle. When she reached Kate, she said, "What would you have done if I hadn't shown up to spot you on the ladder?"

"Oh, I'd be fine. I'm doing it for your peace of mind, not mine." Then she climbed down with the agility of Spider-Man. Kate wiped her hands on the back of her jeans, then gave Liz an air-kiss. "Did you check out Pop's grandson on your way in?"

"No, I met him in my dad's office earlier. Rude. Insolent. Need I go on?"

"Whoa Nelly. I think thou doth protest too much, my dear. He helped me bring in some of my recent finds this morning. It's time to dip your pinkie toe in the man pool again."

Liz's hand went to the right side of her face.

"I'm so sorry, darlin'. That was insensitive. But really, he seems to be such a nice guy."

"To you, maybe. You wouldn't happen to know what his business with my father might be, would you?"

"Not a clue," Kate said. "Come. Follow me, or you might get lost."

Kate wasn't kidding. Liz side-winded past piles of crates overflowing with stacks of books. Every shelf within the towering barrister bookcases they passed was packed with books and vintage/antique knickknacks that coordinated with the subject matter on each shelf. Nineteen-sixties tin globe banks were bookending nonfiction geography books. Victorian Gothic romances were next to Queen Victoria memorabilia, Staffordshire figurines, and floral-chintz English tea sets. Kate didn't "buy" used books from estate and garage sales; she adopted them. She also wouldn't let anyone buy a book unless she knew it was going to a good home.

When they reached the back of the shop, they both sank into an overstuffed, down-cushioned sofa. The sofa had huge magnolia blossoms printed on soft fabric. It wasn't for sale, because if it was, Liz would have already put it in her beach house.

Liz reached over and swiped a paper cup with a lid that sat next to the antique cash register. She almost swooned when she felt the cup was still warm. *Please be coffee, please be coffee*, she chanted in her head. She put the cup to her lips and took a long swallow. "Blech! Kate Fields! What is this stuff?" She gagged, wanting to spew the grainy, bitter liquid onto the floor or into the nearest brass spittoon, but she forced herself to swallow.

Kate said, "Chicory. Better than coffee. Who needs caffeine when you have a beach to walk each morning and sea air to clear your lungs? Haven't you ever heard of drinking chicory? They still mix it with coffee in New Orleans."

"I've heard of it. But the key words are 'mixed with coffee.'"

"Chicory is made from the roots of a rather beautiful flower. In France, during Napoleon's time, there was an embargo on coffee. The French mixed what little coffee they had with chicory to make the coffee last longer. The same was true in New Orleans during the Civil War when the Union Navy blocked coffee shipments from coming into the ports. Skylar got me into it."

Liz hadn't seen Kate's brother, Skylar, since returning to Melbourne Beach. The three of them had practically grown up together. Skylar was a big-time environmentalist and was currently in Washington, DC, trying to raise funding for the Barrier Island Sanctuary Education Center, a few miles down the road.

"Well, you can give me all the history lessons you want. I still think it tastes like crap."

Kate laughed. "All you have to do is walk next door and get a cup of java from Pops. What's the matter, scaredy-cat?"

As if on cue, Liz heard a rustling coming from a basket with double handles that butted up to the arm of the sofa. She scooched closer to Kate and saw two small ears surface from the basket.

"Wow," Kate said. "Bronte doesn't come out for strangers. Ever. She must know you're an animal person."

A gray-and-white striped tiger kitten hopped out of the basket and landed on Liz's bare leg, digging all eighteen claws into her flesh. Liz said, "Oww." Then she kissed Bronte on her pink nose. "She's adorable. Whom does she belong to? Not you, I'm sure."

Kate sneezed.

"Bless you."

"Thanks. She's everyone's—well, actually, she lives in the emporium. Someone left a box of kittens by the front door. We were able to find homes for them all, including Bronte, but she keeps hiding when it's time to hand her over to her new owner. Everyone but Brittany agreed she would be the emporium's mascot. Even though I'm allergic, I figure this might be the only way I can ever have a cat. She's worth a sneeze or two, don't you think?"

"Definitely. How'd she get her name? Let me guess. Your favorite author?"

"Not exactly, but the Brontë sisters are at the top of my list. For some reason, the section of classic books with *Jane Eyre*, *Wuthering Heights*, and *The Tenant of Wildfell Hall* is where Bronte loves to hang out."

"She doesn't seem unsociable to me," Liz said. The kitten was already sound asleep on her lap.

"Aww. She likes you. Hey, did you catch this in *Florida Today*?" Kate handed Liz a folded newspaper topped with a photo of Regina wearing the Queen Maria Louisa of Spain's gold-and-emerald necklace and matching pendant earrings. Liz realized it was the first time she'd ever seen the woman smile. Underneath the photo, it read:

Mrs. Regina Harrington-Worth will be the guest of honor tomorrow evening at the Carlisle Beach Ballroom for the Treasure Coast Spring Ball in Vero Beach, benefiting the American Heart Association. Mrs. Harrington-Worth will be giving a short presentation about her famous father, Percival Harrington II, and his contribution to the Melbourne Beach and Orchid Island area. Tickets will be $250.00 a plate. Please contact Gayle Kramer at carlislebeach.com/reservations.

"Ick. Her necklace and earrings are too gaudy," Kate said. "Aunt Amelia must be happy she has a celebrity guest, although I don't think Francie is too thrilled, especially with the proposed demolition of Castlemara. You didn't hear it from me, but I think they might even have protesters tomorrow at the Spring Fling by the Sea."

"I don't think there's any need to worry," Liz said. "Regina wouldn't dare show up at the Spring Fling, too lowbrow for her taste."

"Well, don't say I didn't warn you."

The door to the emporium slammed shut, the sound reverberating off the thirty-foot ceiling. Then they heard a female voice screech, "Who parked their damn golf cart in my parking spot?"

Hurricane Brittany had just blown into town.

"I have to go talk to Edward," Liz said. "He had quite the Grinch-face last night at dinner."

"When doesn't he?"

Liz stood and put a snoozing Bronte on the cushion behind her.

"Wow, she's staying on the sofa. You must have a magic touch," Kate said.

Liz smiled. Words she hadn't heard in a long time.

She left Kate to mind the shop and went over to Gold Coast by the Sea. Edward hadn't spent a lot of time trying to fix up his shop. It was bare boned, with locked display cases and a small desk with a lighted magnifying glass, desk lamp, and a laptop to look up current coin and estate jewelry values. He not only appraised gold items, he also sold some items that he would stack on velvet trays inside the two lighted show cases on either side of the shop. There was a scale for weighing the gold, and behind him, a vintage bank safe that Kate had sold him, in which he put his valuables at night after he closed the shop, ever complaining about the four-foot walls and the lack of security. Aunt Amelia had told him he could set up his own security camera for the interior of the shop. There was already one camera facing the parking lot that went to a feed on Liz's father's laptop, as well as to their security company in Melbourne. Another camera was stationed outside the front entrance to the hotel.

"You still going on with this Spring Fling idea?" Edward whined. "It sounds like a sophomoric high school dance. Who came up with the name?" With his peaked eyebrows and thin mustache, he looked the spitting image of Vincent Price.

The title, Spring Fling by the Sea, had been Aunt Amelia's, but Liz defended it to bristly Edward. "I like the name. It's fresh and perky."

"Have you seen Nick? I don't like him hanging around with that Brittany woman. He didn't come home last night."

Liz would love to chat with Edward, but not about his son and Brittany. They were both adults. She just wanted Saturday's festivities to go off as planned. "I know Brittany just came in. I'm sure you heard her. Why don't you ask her? I hope we can still count on you to do some free coin appraisals tomorrow."

"Yeah, yeah. If anyone had told me six months ago I'd be sitting behind a desk all day on my rear end, instead of out on the open sea, at the bow of *Mermaids Bounty*, I would have told them to kiss my keister."

"Why did you give up the business?" Liz asked.

"Too damn expensive, and I couldn't find a competent salvaging team, case in point, my deadbeat son. Plus, I needed the money from the sale."

Liz wanted to ask why, but figured it wasn't any of her business. She assumed *Mermaids Bounty* was the treasure salvager ship he'd sold before renting the space for Gold Coast by the Sea. "Well, if you need anything, let me or Aunt Amelia know."

He didn't answer, just put a jeweler's loupe on his right eye and began looking at a small gold coin.

The less contact she had with Edward and his son, the better, she thought as she exited the shop. Her next job was to seek out Brittany and make sure she'd chosen what clothing her models would wear tomorrow.

Liz sought but didn't find. The lights were on in Sirens by the Sea, and the mannequins were clothed, but Brittany was nowhere to be seen.

Chapter 10

Liz had borrowed a straw hat from Kate's shop and decided to take a stroll around the grounds to see if everything looked in order for tomorrow. She was a little concerned about the weather. What had started out as a perfect day was now beginning to cloud up, and she hoped that the forecasted mega-storm for Monday didn't arrive a few days early.

She followed a path along the south side of the hotel. Up ahead, she spied Minna's golf cart parked next to the gazebo steps. Most everyone on the barrier island, especially on this deserted stretch of land, got around on golf carts.

Minna looked toward her and waved. Liz waved back.

When she reached the gazebo, Minna said, "Love your hat."

"Thanks. I borrowed it from Kate."

"Come. Have a seat. I'm taking a creative early lunch before I have to relieve Francie."

The white wrought-iron gazebo had been built in the 1970s and fashioned after the one in *The Sound of Music*. After the first hurricane season, most of the small panes of glass had been blown out by the hundred-mile-an-hour wind gusts. Now only the frame remained, making it much cooler inside—after all, this was Florida, not Austria. As Liz knew, it still made for a fun stage to re-create the scene from the movie with the song "Sixteen Going on Seventeen." As a teenager, Liz would dance in the gazebo with an imaginary partner under a star-filled sky, the sea air smelling of gardenias and the promise of future love.

Minna sat on a stool that faced an easel with a large stretched canvas. In front of her was a panoramic view of the ocean. A large toolbox rested on top of a small folding table. Next to the toolbox was a coffee can filled with brushes and other strange-looking utensils, reminding Liz of dentists' tools.

Liz sat on the bench that followed the perimeter of the gazebo. "What are you creating today? I bet you're low on stock because your pieces sold so quickly at your last gallery showing."

"Thanks to all the support everyone at the Indialantic gave me."

"I loved that showing. I wanted to buy a piece for my beach house, but as soon as I turned my back, someone else bought it."

"It was probably Brittany. She still owes the gallery for one of my pieces. On the first day of my show, she bought *Tempest in a Teapot* with a check. Sonja, the gallery manager, usually requires a credit card or money order. Brittany told Sonja she was the proprietress of the Indialantic by the Sea Emporium and Sonja took her check. It bounced the next day, but I still had to pay Sonja her commission. Then, when I presented Brittany with the bounced check, she said she'd pay the balance and bank fee."

"I'm not surprised. I hope you got your money."

Minna ran her fingers through her short, spiky brown hair, highlighted on the edges in auburn. Last week, the highlights had been green, and the week before pink. "It's been two weeks. So far all I've received is a lot of heartache. I even offered her a discount. I wouldn't mind if she was grateful at all. But every time I ask her about it, she has this snotty attitude, like I should feel lucky anyone bought one of my works."

Liz said, "You are one of the most popular artists in Florida. Why didn't you just go take it back from her?"

Minna opened the toolbox and took out a large jar marked Thick White Gesso and placed it on the folding table. "I'm not that desperate. I'll wait awhile and then send one of my Italian nephews." She laughed. "That will get her motivated." Minna commenced with ripping white tissue paper into small pieces, then placed them in a bucket at her feet.

Liz hadn't ever seen one of Minna's works in progress, only her amazing finished pieces on the walls of Home Arts by the Sea or at Sun Gallery in nearby Vero Beach. "Will this piece be completed in time for tomorrow's Spring Fling?"

"No, it takes me a couple of months, at least. I like to take my time. Introduce new materials and think about the composition. A lot of people have the misconception that all you do is glue a bunch of unrelated items onto a canvas. I like to do layers. The viewer might not even see what lies underneath, but I know it's there, and that resonates with me. It's like the secret to the *Mona Lisa*'s smile—you never know what lies beneath da Vinci's masterpiece, only what he wants you to see on the surface. Using reflective light technology, a French scientist has found another woman's portrait behind the iconic painting. Not that I'm comparing my work with The Master's."

"It's like writing a novel, too. There's so much background, research, and character analysis you need to do before you even write a single word, and most of it doesn't ever find its way onto the page—it just remains in the author's head."

"Great analogy."

"Hey, I just saw Francie. Home Arts looks fabulous for the Spring Fling."

"It was a great idea," Minna said, as she started to pack up. "I hope your new hotel guest, Regina Harrington-Worth, doesn't show her face here tomorrow."

Liz was intrigued. "Why?"

"She almost sabotaged a showing of my art at the Vero Beach Women's Club. I had a line of women interested in my pieces, until she came up and told everyone to save their money because Sotheby's was going to have an auction of some of her father's recovered jewelry and other items found on the shipwrecked *San Carlos.*"

"Wasn't her father still alive at the time?"

"Well, that's the kicker. There never was an auction because her father wouldn't allow her to sell anything he'd given her. It was all to go to local museums after her death."

"How'd you find that out?"

"After I came home from the luncheon, I got ahold of one of my contacts at Sotheby's. She told me there was going to be an auction and sent me the link to look at the pieces online. Later, I got an e-mail saying the auction had been canceled, so I called her back and she told me that Percival Harrington II *himself* had called to cancel—and the reason why. It seems his daughter, Regina, had tried to do the same thing at Bonhams in London."

Liz stood. "Why am I not surprised." She looked at her watch. "Oh boy, I better run. I still have a list of things to do. Thanks for donating one of your pieces to the Barrier Island Sanctuary, Kate told me her brother called to say he was over the moon about it."

* * * *

When Liz returned to the Indialantic, she checked to see if her father was in his office or his apartment, but he wasn't. She wanted to warn him about the possibility of people picketing the hotel because of their new celebrity guest, Regina Harrington-Worth. As she turned the corner on her way to the exterior kitchen door, she found Pierre in his garden.

"Lizzy, why don't you join me and Betty for a late lunch?" he offered.

Her stomach growled, and she responded with an emphatic "Yes!"

Twenty minutes later, Liz's plate was so clean, it looked like it had just come out of the dishwasher. The goat cheese quiche and microgreen salad hit the spot. Which wasn't hard to do lately. Her "spot" seemed to be growing larger and larger since being back around Pierre's meals and all the gourmet goodies from Deli-casies that she kept stocked in her fridge.

While waiting for Pierre to bring out the dessert, Betty told Liz that Pierre and Aunt Amelia had been burdened that morning with packing an elaborate picnic luncheon for the Worths to take on their *Queen of the Seas* boat ride with Captain Netherton.

"And that loud, bossy Mrs. Harrington-Worth insisted your aunt Amelia go with them to serve it," Pierre added.

Liz was sorry her great-aunt had to go through what she imagined was such a trying experience. Especially since Aunt Amelia got seasick easily. "I should have gone instead, but perhaps it's all for the better. I might have been tempted to push Regina overboard."

Pierre scuffled to the sideboard, retrieved a folded piece of paper, and handed it to Liz. "Amelia said I should give this to you." He handed her the paper.

The note read: *Iris had a small family emergency and will be back before the dinner hour. Lizzy dear, can you do your auntie a favor and clean the Worths' suite? It can't be that bad, they've only been here for a night.*

Famous last words, Liz thought.

"Polly wants his damn kiwi, already," a voice called from the butler's pantry. Barnacle Bob wasn't allowed in the kitchen in case the health inspector made a surprise visit, but with his booming voice, he might as well have been shouting directly into Liz's ear.

"Ignore that brat," said Betty. "He already ate."

"Kiwi. Kiwi. Kiwi," BB chanted.

Betty stuck her tongue out in Barnacle Bob's direction. "We were out of kiwi, as you might have gathered," she said to Liz. "It's at the top of Iris's shopping list over there on the counter."

Barnacle Bob ate the same thing every day: half of a plum, half of a banana, half of an apple, and half of a kiwi. The first time Liz had fed the parrot, she'd made the mistake of peeling off the skin on the fruit. Barnacle Bob pouted and went on a hunger strike that lasted for about an hour.

Iris was shirking her duties. Aunt Amelia wouldn't be too happy if she found out her precious parrot had gone without his favorite food.

Chapter 11

Following a dessert of key lime pie squares, of which Liz had three, she left Pierre and Betty in the kitchen and proceeded to the housekeeper's closet to get the supplies needed to do the thing she dreaded the most—clean the Worths' suite. Liz filled a bucket on wheels with a mop, cleansers, and rags. She snatched Iris's ring of keys from a hook on the wall and took the service elevator to the second floor. After grabbing the hotel's prehistoric Kirby vacuum from the maid's closet, she hurried to the Oceana Suite. She knocked before she put the key in the door. *Phew! No Worths.*

The outer room and bedroom to the suite were a breeze to clean. As she dusted, polished, and vacuumed, she mulled over all the things on her checklist for the Spring Fling. One thing she'd been avoiding was asking whether Pops still needed her to help with the wine-and-cheese tasting at Deli-casies. The thought of working next to Ryan made her stomach flutter—she wasn't sure if she felt butterflies or the vampire bats from one of Aunt Amelia's episodes of *Dark Shadows*.

Liz placed a bar of imported dark chocolate on each king-sized pillow on the plantation-style four-poster bed. Feeling pleased at how easy it had been to clean the suite, she took her bucket of supplies and mop into the bathroom.

There was only one thing to say: Regina Harrington-Worth was a pig.

It took her a good hour and a half to get the bathroom cleaned. On top of the cleaning, she also had to collect Regina's dirty unmentionables, which were actually worth mentioning, because there were so many. Makeup paraphernalia was scattered on every available flat surface, including the ledge of the Jacuzzi bathtub. The inside of the tub had a lavender ring around it. When Liz proceeded to fill the tub with water to clear the jets, bubbles shot out and popped against the window she'd just cleaned, leaving more lavender circles on the glass.

After finishing the bathroom, she didn't venture into the walk-in closet and hoped that when the Worths came back from their boating trip they had picked up "a girl" to cater to Regina's every whim.

Liz sprayed sea breeze air freshener and left the suite. Then she thought of something. The cat! Where was Regina's cat? She stepped back inside the suite and searched under the bed, sofa, and dressers. No feline. Liz thought she heard a scratching from the walk-in closet.

"Here, kitty, kitty. Here, Venus."

She opened the closet door, and sure enough two pale blue eyes looked out from a crate, a larger bejeweled version of the one Liz had seen at dinner last night. She stepped closer. "What are you doing locked in the closet, Kitty?" She knelt next to the carrier and opened it. "Come on, pretty baby, let me get a good look at you. I know Pierre gave you parboiled tuna as instructed."

At the word "tuna," the cat torpedoed out of the carrier and latched itself onto Liz's chest. The cat's front claws stuck to her sundress like Velcro. Venus resembled the cat on the infamous poster with the tagline Hang in There, Baby. The only difference between Venus and the cat in the poster was that Venus was bald from head to tail. When Liz had lived in SoHo, she'd passed an exotic Manhattan pet shop that had a sphynx kitten in the window with a price tag of two thousand dollars. Venus was off-white and wore a pink collar around her tiny hairless neck that Liz guessed, by the amazing sparkle of the stones, was likely studded with real diamonds. When Venus finally relaxed her claws, Liz picked her up, her hand grazing the cat's collar. Something pricked her finger, drawing blood. As she placed Venus back inside the crate, she noticed sharp prongs where a stone used to be. Venus snuggled onto the leopard-print velour cushion and closed her eyes. Liz latched the crate and left the closet.

After wrapping a tissue around her bleeding finger, she left the Worths' suite and went down the hall to the linen pantry. Armed with fresh sheets and towels, she entered Captain Netherton's suite. His was neat and tidy, perhaps having something to do with the captain's military background. He got free room and board in exchange for skippering *Queen of the Seas*. Aunt Amelia didn't give him a salary, but he did get to keep all of his tips, and he also collected a pension from the United States Coast Guard.

In the sitting room, there was a mahogany bookcase filled with antique maritime books, and on a desk, a map showing the different water depths and currents off of Melbourne Beach, including the famous Sebastian

Inlet. The ocean side of the inlet was a surfer's paradise; on the western side, a snorkeler's paradise. Countless times growing up, Liz swam in the inlet's calm bay alongside friendly manatees.

She left the clean linens on the captain's bed, then exited the suite. After returning the Kirby to the maid's closet, she went down to the first floor, put away the cleaning supplies, and dropped the used sheets and towels in the laundry room. Her stomach growled. It was time for a snack.

When she entered the butler's pantry, she caught Barnacle Bob napping. He was a beautiful bird when sleeping, even with his bald head. The parrot must have sensed Liz's kind thoughts and decided to set her straight. He awoke and stood at attention. "Push Regina overboard. Push Regina overboard," the parrot shouted, mimicking Liz's earlier conversation with Betty. Then he added, "Liz is a bad girl. Liz is a bad girl."

She marched up to Barnacle Bob's cage and pointed her finger at him. "Keep quiet or else."

BB repeated, "Liz is a bad girl. Liz is a bad girl." Then he bit the tip of her finger, and she bled for the second time in an hour. She opened the pantry cupboards and found a rubber finger cot, something every good chef kept handy in case of accidents, and put it on her finger.

"Lizzy darling, where are you?" Aunt Amelia bellowed.

She grabbed an orange scone from the cookie jar, left the pantry, and closed the door, only to hear a muffled, "Who's got their hand in the cookie jar? Liz is a bad girl. Push Regina overboard."

Liz entered the kitchen to find a pale and disheveled Aunt Amelia. There were black trails on her cheeks left by her mascara and black eyeliner.

"We must get rid of that woman!" Aunt Amelia said as she plopped down on a chair at the farm table. "I don't know what I was thinking. Regina complained the whole time on the boat, and she actually spit out her Brie, prosciutto, and apricot chutney sandwich because Pierre didn't cut the rind off the Brie! What a prima donna. Then the water started getting rough and dark clouds rolled in. Clyde wanted to turn back, but "The Boss" wouldn't let him until we pulled up to the Harrington property. She took photos and made a million calls to her contractor, asking him why Castlemara hadn't been bulldozed yet, and then she went bonkers when she found out there was a holdup on getting permits from the town."

"That's good news for the historical society," Liz said.

"Not if it means the Worths will be staying here until it gets sorted out."

"True."

"Her poor husband, David, was at her beck and call the whole time, and he also made numerous phone calls. That guy's a saint, and he knows his way around a boat. I'm sure I've met him before somewhere. You know I never forget a face, but he's assured me that isn't the case. He said this is the first time he's ever been to the Indialantic. Lizzy, maybe you can make a few calls of your own to see if any rooms opened up elsewhere. I think I've made a big mistake letting the Worths stay here. Hell, I'll even keep her pet, whatever it is, for free, if you can't find pet-friendly lodging for them."

"Oh, Auntie, please don't get riled up. We'll figure something out. By the way, Regina's pet is a cat—a hairless sphynx, to be exact."

"Lovely creatures."

A clap of thunder made them both jump. Liz looked out the kitchen window and saw black clouds rolling in from the ocean. "Looks like a storm. I just got a lightning strike warning on my phone. You look like you need some chai tea, an orange scone, and a hot bath."

Her great-aunt stood. "That sounds wonderful."

She walked to the pantry and set Aunt Amelia's favorite teacup and saucer onto a sterling tray. The cup was trimmed in gold and had butterflies and cherry blossoms on the outside. The cup and saucer were one of a set of forty that had been Liz's great-grandmother's. The other thirty-nine and matching dinner service had been destroyed in the hotel fire, years ago. Liz opened the tea canister, took out a packet of tea, opened it, and poured it into the cup. She reached into the cookie jar, took out another orange scone, and set it on a cake plate.

On her way out of the pantry, Liz said to Barnacle Bob, "Hush, BB. Don't upset Aunt Amelia or I'll tell her what you did to my finger, you brute."

The parrot must really have had a soft spot for her great-aunt, because for once, he kept his big beak closed.

Liz went into the kitchen, placed the tray in front of the electric kettle on the sideboard, and filled the cup with hot water, while Aunt Amelia got out a napkin, spoon, and tea bag strainer.

Aunt Amelia picked up the tray. "I'll be in my suite for a little R-and-R. Is everything all set for tomorrow?"

"Yes, everything's taken care of. No worries. Go take a nice restorative bath."

"I'll let Calgon take me away… from the memory of my recent boat ride with Mrs. Harrington-Worth. Wish Calgon still made those bath oil beads today. I got a year's worth after I did that commercial."

"Ha, in this day and age, they would probably have something carcinogenic in the ingredients."

"Things were better before sell-by dates and ingredient lists," Aunt Amelia said. "GMOs, HMOs, and all the other stuff they make you worry about now. We never had expiration dates when I was growing up. My mother even left the butter out on the counter."

Craack!

Aunt Amelia's teacup shook, and tea filled the saucer. "That one sounded close. Hope we don't lose power. The generator is only good for the first floor of the hotel. Thanks for cleaning the Worths' suite. Iris should be here any minute."

"You hired her with references, I hope? She doesn't seem too dedicated. Always disappearing."

"She told me she has an ailing mother. And you have to admit, she does a great job cleaning."

"Yes, she does." Liz put her hand on her great-aunt's shoulder and gave it a squeeze, then held open one of the swinging doors to the dining room for her to pass through.

Halfway across the room, Aunt Amelia turned and said, "I don't want anything you're doing here at the Indialantic to take away from your writing, and I do appreciate all the time you've taken to plan the Spring Fling. I'll only ask one more time. Are you sure you don't want to do a book signing of *Let the Wind Roar* tomorrow?"

"No, that ship has sailed. But thanks. Sales are still brisk, anyway. Nothing like a good scandal to revive sales figures."

"It was a beautiful book. And your next one will be, too."

Aunt Amelia was under the impression that Liz was writing in the evenings. Liz did have a contract with the publisher of *Let the Wind Roar*. She had to produce a 90,000-word manuscript by February, only eleven months away, and all she had was an outline that she hated. She was on her third extension from her publisher, and her agent had told her there wouldn't be another. Apparently, three strikes and she'd be out. "I can put my writing on hold, if need be. I don't want you to worry about anything. Oh, I left clean sheets and towels for Captain Netherton."

"That poor captain. What he had to endure on our trip from hell. Thank you for all your help, my love."

"You're welcome. I think *you're* the saint for going on a boat ride with that woman."

Aunt Amelia turned and walked out of the dining room toward the lobby. She never used the service elevator, saying that climbing the spiral staircase helped to keep her young and spry.

It was only four thirty, but it was as dark as night. Liz ran out through the kitchen door with a basket on her arm to harvest some of Pierre's herbs. A raindrop hit Liz on the nose. She hurried and snipped some dill, parsley, and arugula, then sprinted to one of the four lemon trees, plucked two lemons, and made it inside before the sky let loose its fury.

She finished laying out the last ingredient on the marble counter just as Pierre walked in.

"*Mon cherie*," he said, kissing Liz on the cheek. "You are too good to me, my little sous-chef."

"My pleasure, Grand-Pierre."

He laughed, then took off his chef's hat, pulled out a paperback, and handed it to her.

Liz looked at the cover. It was the next Christie on her reading list. If he could remember what her next book was, then that said something for his memory.

She left the kitchen, confident that Pierre was his old self again.

Chapter 12

Liz took the back hallway to her father's apartment. When she opened the door and walked in, she found her father and a stunning blonde sitting at the small bistro table next to the galley kitchen, each with a glass of wine in front of them. The woman was somewhere in her mid-forties, dressed in a tailored, navy-and-white-striped blouse under a navy suit jacket. Her skirt came to just above her knees, and she had shapely legs atop two-inch navy pumps. Her large brown eyes were framed by perfectly arched brows.

Oops. Had Liz interrupted a date? Over the years, plenty of women had been attracted to her father. He'd dated sporadically, but no one else could measure up to Liz's mother, Chloe TreMellyn, whom her father had met at a party in Manhattan while attending Columbia Law School.

Her father said, "Liz, I'd like to introduce you to Charlotte. She and I work together at the courthouse."

Charlotte stood and extended her hand. Liz considered herself tall at five-foot-eight, but the woman was at least five-ten.

Liz gave her a firm handshake. "Nice to meet you. I hope my father invited you to the Spring Fling festivities at the emporium tomorrow?" She could tell by the way Charlotte dressed, she might love to purchase something from Sirens by the Sea.

Before Charlotte could answer, they heard a banging coming from the direction of her father's office in the adjoining room.

"I'll get it," Liz said. She went into her father's office and opened the door. Lightning illuminated the Wicked Witch of the West. A drenched Regina pushed against the door and charged into the office. She shoved Liz out of the way and stood in the middle of the room, then pointed at Liz, making a snarling motion with her top lip, exposing perfect teeth.

"My recently purchased Mikimoto seventy-thousand-dollar Hyacinthia necklace is missing. Your 'auntie' said you were the last one in my room!"

Fenton and Charlotte rushed in from the apartment. "My daughter is not a thief," Fenton said. "Remain calm. Tell us where you last saw the necklace."

Regina's wet hair was separated into snakelike clumps, and she glanced wildly around the room like an unhinged Medusa. She wore a red and white geometric print wrap dress with a plunging neckline that appeared Saran-Wrapped to her body from the rain.

"Why don't you have a seat?" Charlotte offered.

One of Regina's hair extensions fell to the floor with a *splat*. As she reached to pick it up, she exclaimed, "Who the hell are you! I don't want to sit. I want my necklace!"

"I'm Agent Pearson from the Brevard County Sheriff's Department." Liz was stunned.

"Well, then, arrest that girl," Regina said, pointing to Liz. "She probably wanted to get even with me because I made a helpful suggestion about her unsightly scar."

Unsightly! "How dare you!" Liz shouted. "I didn't touch your necklace!"

Aunt Amelia burst in from her nephew's apartment. "Am I too late? I didn't mean to imply that Liz took your item."

"Item!" Regina screeched. "It's not just *an item*!"

Aunt Amelia sat in the chair offered by her nephew. "I just meant that Liz might have seen it when she was cleaning. Maybe you misplaced it?"

"I didn't misplace anything," Regina spat out.

David Worth materialized in the doorway, holding a half-open umbrella, panting and out of breath. "Regina, I found it. It was under the bed." He closed the umbrella, hurried inside, then held up a pearl-and-diamond necklace.

Regina pointed again at Liz. "She probably put it there so she could come back later and steal it!"

David mumbled something Liz didn't hear, and Regina turned on him with venom in her eyes. David tightened his grip on the handle of the umbrella, like he might need to use it to fend off his wife's ire.

As Regina spun back toward Aunt Amelia on her gold sandals with four-inch heels, she lost her footing on the wet floor and nose-dived onto the tile.

Everyone held their breath as they watched her push herself up on all fours. She screamed, "My knee! My nose!"

David, Liz, and Aunt Amelia all ran to her side.

"Get that girl away from me!" Regina said, as blood gushed from her right nostril. "Call my lawyer!" Regina got into a sitting position, then leaned back against the sturdy partner's desk.

"Mr. Holt, please call an ambulance for my wife," David said.

"No ambulance," Regina screeched. "I'm not going to some subpar hospital. I need my plastic surgeon, and he's in Cannes."

Liz took a few steps back, then stood next to the safety net she called her father. She observed Regina's shrunken form: her plaited hair, bloodstained face, and left knee that was already three times the size of the right, and almost felt sorry for her. Almost.

Agent Pearson, aka Charlotte, grabbed a box of tissues from the top of a filing cabinet and handed it to Regina. "You should be checked out."

"Mind your own business," Regina growled, as she stuffed a tissue up her right nostril.

Aunt Amelia took out her cell phone from the pocket of her fuchsia and turquoise caftan and punched in some numbers. "Ryan. This is Amelia Holt. Can you please come to Fenton's office? One of our guests has taken a nasty spill and we might need your help." After she hung up, she said to Regina, "Don't worry, someone from the New York City Fire Department is on his way."

"'Don't worry...don't worry,'" Regina mimicked. "I'm plenty worried, and you will be, too, when I sue your ass!"

Aunt Amelia looked like she'd been slapped.

A few minutes later, all six-foot-three of Ryan Stone came into the office. Liz felt a weird sensation in her chest. Just because Ryan aroused a feeling of disquiet in her—that didn't mean she was attracted to him. Perhaps it had something to do with her insecurity after being everyone's "darling" in the publishing world one minute, then finding herself wearing cement shoes at the bottom of the East River, the next. Coming home had been the right step in her healing process, but for some reason Ryan brought her insecurities to the surface. She'd taken a bullet for Travis that day in court by agreeing that the trial transcripts wouldn't be made public. Now she wished she hadn't. There was nothing worse than being misunderstood and vilified for something you hadn't done.

Ryan locked eyes with hers, then turned away and began to administer aid to a surprisingly quieted Regina. After a few minutes of prodding and poking, he said, "Nothing's broken, but she needs ice and a pillow for under her knee. Her nose will be fine, but she'll have a bump and a black eye or two."

Regina was speechless for the first time since she'd entered the room. She looked up at Ryan like he was not just her knight in armor, but also the Holy Grail.

"She needs to be in bed," he said.

Aunt Amelia got up and walked to the doorway of Fenton's apartment. "Follow me."

Ryan scooped up Regina. She gazed up at him with a goofy grin on her face as he carried her through the doorway that led to the interior of the hotel.

Liz thought Regina should have gone to the hospital. How were they supposed to take care of her here at the hotel? Regina didn't want Liz around, which left only Aunt Amelia to deal with her. Poor Aunt Amelia. Perhaps the housekeeper might grace them with her presence. Now, there was an idea.

"I need to be on my way," Agent Pearson said, as she kissed Fenton on the cheek. "Nice meeting you, Liz." Then she headed to the door leading outside.

"I'll go with you," said David. He picked up his umbrella. "We can share my umbrella."

He opened the door and the two stepped through the doorway and out into the storm. Liz didn't understand why David hadn't followed Ryan and his wife. Well, maybe she did understand—the fury of the storm outside was a better alternative than Regina's wrath.

"I suppose I'd better go check on Mrs. Worth, from a lawyer's point of view," her father said. "Her talk of suing the hotel will give Aunt Amelia a sleepless night or two, I'm sure."

"That woman will be the death of us all."

Chapter 13

Pierre had made his salmon wrapped in crêpes and brought the meal up to the Worths' suite on a sterling silver tray. A tray that Liz had had to polish because Iris had been sent to the drugstore to buy gauze, Ace bandages, ice packs, and other sundries from one of Regina's extensive lists. Apparently, Liz wasn't allowed to go anywhere near Regina, which wasn't a hardship in her mind.

Aunt Amelia had been in a tizzy about the possibility of Regina suing the hotel for her injuries, recalling a *Perry Mason* episode in which she'd had a bit part that didn't turn out well for the main character, who was an innkeeper. Liz had tried to calm her by saying that Regina didn't have a leg to stand on, a fitting cliché, because Regina hadn't even gone to the hospital. Ryan seemed to be all she needed.

Betty and Captain Netherton ate dinner in the kitchen. Liz thought of joining them, but she knew Betty had the hots for the distinguished captain, so instead she packed up a healthy portion of Pierre's crêpes to take back to the beach house.

She stepped out the kitchen door and started on the path toward home. The storm had passed, but the winds remained. When she got to the south end of the Indialantic's drive, she saw Brittany, accompanied by Ryan, walking in her direction.

Brittany wore too much foundation, in a shade that didn't match her neck. In the time Liz had been away, Brittany had changed her hair color from brown to overprocessed blond and she'd begun to wear heavy, gold-toned jewelry that made her look forty instead of twenty-eight.

Liz stopped and waited until they reached her.

Ryan still looked like Ryan: dark, frowning, and slightly irritated when he glanced Liz's way. The difference in height between him and Brittany reminded Liz of Killer and Caro. Liz also remembered the couple of lovers she'd seen in the fog earlier—and their obvious height difference.

Liz marched up to Brittany. "Good. Just the woman I wanted to see. Have you confirmed that both of your models will be on time tomorrow and what they'll be wearing? We open at ten in the morning."

Brittany grabbed onto Ryan's arm. "I told you she was a bossy pants. I have everything under control as usual. I hope my advertising dollars have been put to good use."

Ryan remained mute, except for an irritated eye roll that said more than words.

Liz said, "I'll be on my way then."

Brittany took a step closer, and the heavy gold-toned chain around her neck almost looked like the real thing. "Yes. Do that."

As Liz walked away, a pebble got stuck between her sandal and the ball of her foot. She had to hobble along, feeling Ryan's gaze branding a big Loser sign across her back.

When she reached the end of the drive and the path to her house, she heard Ryan shout, "Stop!"

Liz ignored him. She wasn't at his command. Then she felt his large hand on her shoulder. She whipped around to face him. "What?"

Ryan looked behind him and held up his hand to Brittany, gesturing that he'd be right back to her. When he turned back to Liz, he tried a different tactic. He gave Liz an ear-to-ear smile that reached his deep brown eyes, just as a gust of wind blew a glossy lank of dark hair onto his forehead. With the stubble on his face, he reminded Liz of a pirate.

Liz had a thing about pirates.

"We need to talk about our assignment," Ryan said.

"Assignment! What assignment?"

Brittany started toward them.

"Your father didn't tell you?" He looked in Brittany's direction. "We should talk in private."

Liz hesitated, but her curiosity won out. "Okay, come to my beach house in an hour."

"How do I get there?"

Liz took off her sandal and got rid of the stone. "Ask around." Then she turned and walked away, head held high.

When Liz got to the beach house, she left her foil-wrapped dinner on the deck's railing, then went down to the shore. It was close to sundown, and the beach was shaded by the dunes. She got more than one mouthful of sand when she reached the bottom of the steps, and she had to keep her hand on her right cheek to protect the healing skin. She loved the ocean as much in foul weather as in fair. Even if the weather was rough for the Spring Fling, it shouldn't matter, because everything would be inside the emporium, except for the tables for the Barrier Island Historical Society and the Barrier Island Sanctuary. But if there was rain, the tables could easily be moved indoors to the large foyer on the other side of the double doors.

The surf was rough. It reminded Liz of Ryan's personality. She wasn't comfortable knowing he was living so close to her in the caretaker's cottage. And what "assignment" could he possibly be talking about? Well, she would soon find out. She reached for a conch shell, which lay perilously close to a royal-blue pearlized water balloon, which Liz knew wasn't a balloon at all. It was a lethal man-of-war, still wriggling with life. She pulled back her hand. Her thoughts strayed to Ryan again—was he the handsome conch shell or the stinging man-of-war?

Of course, Ryan didn't show up on time. It was two hours later when she saw his hulking form under the spotlight on the deck.

Liz opened the door. "You're late."

She didn't offer him a seat, but he sat anyway on the sofa, putting his feet up on the flat-topped trunk topped with beach-related coffee table books. He leaned back with his hands entwined behind his head, as if he was ready to settle in for a long snooze. She glared at him until he finally shifted his feet to the floor. Had he been raised in a barn? She pictured him and his fellow firefighters sitting around a pot of chili, talking sports, belching, and objectifying women.

He said, "I couldn't get away. Mrs. Holt noticed me walking with Brittany and asked me to check on Regina's injuries."

She felt a slight twinge of admiration for him helping Aunt Amelia, but it was short-lived. As he sat forward, his intense eyes focused on her, he said, "Before I agree to partner with you…"

"What? Partner with me!"

"You seem a little high-strung. Your reputation precedes you."

So. He *did* know all about Manhattan and Travis. Or at least he thought he did. "I'm not your partner. Are you delusional?"

He gave her a sly smile, acting like he knew he was in the driver's seat.

"Can you get on with it?" Liz continued. "I still need to eat my dinner."

"Is that what I smell? Have enough for two? We can discuss the case over dinner."

"No, there's not enough for two. Spit it out. What's all this business about an assignment or some kind of 'partnership'?"

"How about a drink, then?" he said, leaning back into lounging position again.

"This isn't a social call. And I don't drink."

He stood and walked toward the center of the great room. "That's not what I heard, princess." His smirk morphed into a sneer.

Liz walked up to him and poked her finger into his chest. "You mean, that's not what you read in the tabloids. You can leave now. We're finished here." Her face was warm and her knees unsteady.

He looked down at her and gave her one of those grins he most likely used on weak females when he wanted to get his way. Liz wasn't weak. He said, "Don't you even want to know why I came here?"

"Not really." She pushed against his rock-hard chest, forcing him to walk backward toward the door.

"Your father hired me to look into a case he's working on. He said you were already on board."

"What? You're a firefighter—why would he hire you?"

"I don't just work on the FDNY. I'm Kings County's lead arson investigator. And I'm very good at my job."

She walked toward the French doors and opened them. "Whatever. I'm not really in the mood to partner with you. I prefer to work alone. Time to go."

"We'll talk tomorrow. Granddad said you were helping with the wine-and-cheese tasting. See you at noon." Before going through the doorway, he gently touched her bottom lip with his index finger. "Take care. Lock up behind me."

As he sauntered out of sight, she locked the doors and set the alarm for the first time since she'd moved in. "Oh, Dad," she said to the empty house. "What have you gotten me into?"

Chapter 14

Liz sat on the sofa in Betty's suite. "Then the jerk said that Dad had hired him for a case he's working on. The same case Dad wanted me to help him with." She knew she sounded like a whining teenager. How many pouting sessions had Betty heard from her over the years? Too many. So Liz zipped it.

Betty poured tea into Liz's cup, then sat on the sofa, sinking into the crater left by Killer's one-hundred-sixty-pound physique. Caro hopped onto Liz's lap and head-butted her chin. Jealous Killer tried to do the same, then gave up and lay on top of Liz's feet.

"It can't be that bad," Betty said, picking up her crochet hook to fashion another granny square—a pile of about fifty towered next to her on a side table. "If Mr. Stone is an arson investigator, then I assume the case involves arson."

"It does."

Betty cut a piece of yarn, made a knot in the corner of the square, and added it to the pile. She noticed Liz looking at the stack. "We're making blankets for teens in local hospitals. Francie taught a class last week: 'Not Your Granny's Granny Squares'."

The colors of yarn Betty used weren't the avocado greens, golds, and burnt oranges from the granny-square heydays of the 1970s. These squares were made in neon colors that would keep you awake all night.

"There were ten of us in the class," Betty continued. "We're supposed to meet in a week and bring in our squares. Francie will take everyone's squares, mix them up, and make crazy mismatched blankets for the kids. Luckily, she'll be doing the final step of sewing the squares together. I just like making them."

"Obviously," Liz said with a laugh. She looked around at the Sea Breeze Suite. It was hard to believe Betty had been staying at the hotel for over twenty years. She'd moved in after her husband, a professor at Florida Tech, passed away.

By the far wall was a bookcase filled with photos of her grandchildren and two different sets of Nancy Drew mysteries. The first set was from the thirties; all had their pristine dust jackets and were covered in clear plastic sleeves. The second set was from the mid-sixties to the early seventies, the time period when Betty had worked as a ghostwriter for the Nancy Drew line and a few other mystery series, including the Dana Girls and the Connie Blair mysteries. Having voraciously read all of Betty's yellow-spined hardcover Nancy Drews as an adolescent, Liz thought she caught subtle differences in a few of the writing styles. No matter how hard she'd pleaded over the years, Betty stuck to her binding nondisclosure contract and was taking *The Secret of the Ghostwriter Mysteries* to her grave.

Next to the Nancy Drew books was a set of twelve pale-lavender hardcovers that Betty had authored using her real name, Beatrice Lawson. The Island Girl Mysteries took place on a fictitious island off of Florida's east coast, and featured a surfboard-wielding sleuth named Kit Sullivan and her plucky dolphin sidekick, Misty. The books were published in the mid-sixties and had a great following. Betty could have continued the series, but she'd run out of ideas for mysterious adventures involving a fifteen-year-old girl and her pet porpoise.

Liz finished her tea and roused Killer, waiting a few minutes until the pins and needles in her feet subsided from the Great Dane's weight. She stood and said, "I got up so early, it was too soon to go to the emporium to make sure everything was going according to plan."

Her alarm had gone off at seven. Liz had popped out of bed, taken a shower, dressed, chugged a cup of coffee, and was out of her beach house by seven thirty. The sun had still been low in the sky, and the water was glistening with lines of silver atop each gently rolling wave. She couldn't have asked for a better day for the Spring Fling. The emporium doors opened at ten, and Liz wanted to make sure everything was ready. Instead of stopping by the Indialantic's kitchen, like she usually did each morning, she'd gone directly to Aunt Amelia's rooms to coordinate the day's activities, and then to Betty's.

"You've always been a planner," Betty said, starting a new square. "I remember you plotting out all your stories with meticulously detailed outlines. I am so happy it paid off with *Let the Wind Roar*."

"Thanks to your proofreading and editing. If it wasn't for you, I probably wouldn't have even found an agent."

"Oh, I'm sure you would have, you're that good. How's the next one coming?"

Liz was saved by someone knocking on the suite door. Betty was tangled up in fuchsia yarn, so Liz answered.

A dapper Captain Netherton stood in the hallway. Instead of a cane, he held a walking stick. "Liz, my dear. No need to answer the question I was about to ask. I see the big galoot lounging beyond you with his paramour, Caro."

"'Big galoot' is right," Liz said. "Although he carries on like he's a quarter of his size. A few minutes ago, Caro chased a ball of yarn under the coffee table and Killer followed her. When he tried to stand up, he looked like a giant tortoise with a coffee table shell."

Captain Netherton laughed.

Killer glanced their way, his unclipped black ears rising to half-mast. *"You talking about me?"* they said.

Liz turned to the captain. "I hope you got your fresh linens yesterday?"

"I did, and thank you. You didn't happen to see the nautical chart I had of the waters off the island, did you? I'd just ordered it, thought I'd left it on my desk. Now it's missing."

"Yes. It was on your desk. I saw it there yesterday, around three o'clock."

He said, "That's strange. A mystery is a-brewin'. I might need the assistance of a mystery writer to help me go on *The Quest of the Missing Map*. Liz, do you know anyone?" He looked at Betty and winked.

"Can't think of a one," Liz said, then winked back.

Betty pretended to be crocheting, but Liz saw the corners of her mouth turn up.

"I really appreciate that you're working the raffle table," Liz said to the captain. "I hope you got the box of brochures I left outside your door yesterday for *Queen of the Seas*?" Pictured on the front of the brochure was a photo of *Queen of the Seas* and a distinguished Captain Netherton, with his dark gray eyes and white-toothed smile. He wore a navy blazer and white pants with a sharp crease. His cap sat at a jaunty angle, and he had one hand on the wheel in a relaxed fashion, instilling confidence and an air of experience. In bold-faced letters below his photo was printed: Indialantic by the Sea Hotel and Emporium Invites You to Join Captain Clyde B. Netherton for a River Cruise on *Queen of the Seas* to Tour the Barrier Island's Riches. You Will See Dolphins, Bald Eagles, Manatees, Birds from the Nearby Bird Sanctuary, and Even the Occasional Alligator, While the Captain Fills Your Head with Natural History Lessons and Tales from the Old Days of Pirating and Sunken Treasure Ships.

"No problem, my dear." He gave Liz a small salute. "Anything to help out your darling Aunt Amelia."

If Liz wasn't mistaken, he added the "darling" to make Betty jealous.

"Although the Worths have asked me to leave all of next week open in case they want to use *Queen of the Seas* to check out Castlemara again," he said, as he reached into his left pocket and withdrew a treat for Killer, then reached into his other pocket and took one out for Caro. "Apparently, there's no access from the highway, because it's cordoned off with a chain-link fence topped with razor wire. Someone's been breaking in, even though Regina said there's nothing left inside."

Regina? Liz and Betty exchanged glances. Regina Harrington-Worth and Captain Netherton were on a first-name basis?

Liz left Betty and the captain and went in search of Iris. She and Aunt Amelia needed Iris's help while they played hostess at the Spring Fling. And Iris needed to make sure the Worths remained in their suite. No one needed Regina hobbling out into the emporium, shouting and making a scene.

Earlier, Aunt Amelia had told Liz that when she'd brought up the Worths' breakfast, Regina had told her she still planned to go to the Treasure Coast Spring Ball—even if she had to be pushed in a wheelchair. She wouldn't let her minions down, and she planned to wear a floor-length dress that would hide her swollen knee. The same knee that had been expertly wrapped by Ryan. Aunt Amelia said the dress had been special-ordered by Brittany from one of her designer contacts. Liz hoped Brittany paid the vendor and didn't write a bounced check like she'd done for Minna's mixed-media piece. Aunt Amelia had also been tasked with finding a hairstylist and makeup artist who was up to Regina's rigorous standards. She'd finally located a duo from West Palm Beach who had a few celebrities as clients. They'd assured Aunt Amelia over the phone that they could camouflage Regina's swollen nose and black eye. Revenge-minded, Liz thought about going to the Oceana Suite and asking if Regina wanted to borrow Liz's concealer.

Liz followed the second-floor hallway until she reached the Indian River Lagoon Suite. She knocked on the door, and Iris answered, looking like she'd had a sleepless night.

"What time is it?" Iris asked, rubbing her eyes as she tried to focus on Liz.

"Eight thirty. Can I come in?" She didn't say yes, and she didn't say no, so Liz walked inside. The room looked the same as it had before Iris moved in. There were barely any personal touches, unless you counted a bottle of champagne and two glasses on the table in the sitting room. Liz wondered what celebration could warrant champagne, then she thought of Captain Netherton, who was now courting Betty. Could he be sneaking down the hallway for a secret assignation with the housekeeper? She didn't see a framed photo of Iris's ailing mother or any children. The woman was becoming an enigma, and Liz was determined to find out more about her.

"Did Amelia send you?" she asked. Even for being so short, Iris stood with military posture. Her plain face, hazel eyes, and hair, the color of wet sand, didn't meld with her wide, expressive mouth, which was now turned down in a frown.

"Yes. We need to make sure that you cater to the Worths today while Auntie and I oversee everything at the emporium. I hope she can count on you?"

"Of course she can depend on me. Why would there be any question of that?"

Liz wanted to say, *Because we haven't seen you in the last two days and Aunt Amelia is eighty years old.* Instead she said, "There is no question. I just wanted to touch base."

They stood looking at each other for a moment, like gunslingers at the O.K. Corral. Liz blinked and lost. She turned and walked away.

Later, after Liz said good-bye to Pierre, she left the hotel through the revolving door in the lobby. The possibility of thundershowers had been forecasted for the afternoon, but for now, Liz couldn't have asked for a more glorious day. She took a golf cart to the emporium's parking lot. She tried to use the Indialantic's golf carts as little as possible, preferring to walk, especially during the spring when Florida's weather was an eleven out of ten. No need for a gym membership when you lived in the tropics. But today Liz needed to zip around as quickly as possible. She didn't own a car, as she hadn't needed one in Manhattan. But Betty had given Liz the keys to her 1970 baby-blue two-door Cadillac DeVille convertible. It was the same color as Aunt Amelia's trademark eyeshadow. Liz kept it parked at her beach house because Betty rarely drove it. She'd told Liz that living at the Indialantic was like living in your own ecosystem; everything you needed was right within reach. Every fall, when Betty taught her writing classes at the Melbourne Beach Community Center, Betty preferred taking one of the hotel's golf carts, only driving the Caddy in foul weather. Liz doubted she even had a driver's license and made a mental note to offer her chauffeur services come September.

Although she'd lived in New York City for a long time, Liz realized she had no burning desire to go back. Sure, there were things she missed, but for now she was content with her life in the bosom of a loving family, which included her father, Betty, and Pierre—together they were the Four Musketeers. And if she was, indeed, a writer, there was no better place to write than by the sea.

Chapter 15

When Liz reached the emporium's parking lot, she was happy to see a white van with a black logo of a huge violin, followed by the words Strings on Wheels. Check.

A flamingo-pink camper was parked near the entrance to the emporium. Painted on the side of the camper, airbrushed in turquoise daisy-chain letters, was Josie's Traveling Flower Shop. Check.

One six-foot folding table was stationed on each side of the huge double doors. Check.

Relieved that everything seemed on point, she parked the golf cart and got out.

Kate pulled up next to her on her bike—not a motorcycle bike, but a *bike*-bike. She took off her helmet and hung it on the handlebars. "You sure picked an awesome day. I wanted to walk here, but I stepped on a shard of glass from a broken beer bottle on my morning beach run. It went clean through the sole of my Nikes."

Liz winced at the mention of a broken beer bottle and her hand went to her scar. "Are you okay?"

"I'm fine, just a small wound. It won't stop me from enjoying the day."

"You sure?" Liz asked.

"Of course I'm sure. Let me know what you need. Francie and Minna will take turns at the Barrier Island Historical Society table."

As they walked, Liz said, "Captain Netherton will be at the other table handling the raffles for the Barrier Island Sanctuary and handing out brochures for *Queen of the Seas.*"

"Sounds like you have everything under control. Let's get some java."

Liz wanted to avoid Ryan. But if she was going to help Pops at twelve with the wine-and-cheese table, then what would it matter if she stopped in now for a coffee? Maybe Ryan would be more cordial in front of his grandfather.

Kate opened the emporium door and ushered Liz through it. "Age before beauty."

Before the scar, Liz had taken her looks for granted. This morning, she'd thought of concealing the scar with makeup for the Spring Fling, then decided against it. Her surgeon had told her she should wait before applying anything topical that wasn't from a prescription until after her next appointment, because the last graft needed time to heal.

Liz said, "I'm only older than you by one month, young'un."

When they stepped inside, the foyer looked fun and festive. Josie had filled the space with flowering tropical plants and potted palms. The plants were for sale, along with the ones in her traveling flower shop camper, now stationed in the emporium's parking lot. Pops, or Ryan, had relocated six iron bistro tables and twelve chairs from Deli-casies by the Sea into the foyer, to make room for the wine-and-cheese tasting table. They gave Liz the great idea to have Aunt Amelia buy similar tables and chairs for the entrance, where people could relax while their significant others shopped till they dropped. In the corner, against the back wall, were four musicians practicing on their stringed instruments—Liz had thought it would be nice to have live music instead of canned. At two o'clock, they would be replaced with calypso/reggae musicians.

Everyone was busy getting ready for the opening, including Brittany. Before Liz could ask if Brittany's models had arrived, she saw two long-legged twin amazons seated at the counter of Deli-casies by the Sea, being catered to by an attentive Ryan Stone.

Six weeks ago, when she'd first walked into Deli-casies, Liz thought she was back in SoHo at her favorite Parisian brasserie, Balthazar. The shop floor had small white tiles interspersed with an occasional black tile, forming a honeycomb effect. The iron bistro tables and cushioned iron chairs were set inside three rough-hewn wood partitions, making the space appear like a separate café. Across from the café section was the barista counter, also constructed of wood and topped with an old-fashioned glass confectioners' case. It was filled with sweets, some of which Pierre had contributed. Pops was a great cook, but he wasn't much of a baker.

She looked toward Ryan. He wore a black form-fitting T-shirt and jeans, very New York, not at all Melbourne Beach. Of course, the black suited him and gave him that bad-boy vibe many women seemed attracted to.

Kate noticed her looking Ryan's way. "You have to admit, he is one tall, cool drink of water."

"And so are those two models who should be dressed in Sirens by the Sea clothing with price tags dangling from their armpits."

Kate gave Liz her coffee order, then left Liz in order to get her shop in shape and feed Bronte. Liz strode toward Ryan and the models. "Sorry to interrupt, but I think it's time you ladies went and changed into your first outfits. We open soon."

Ryan said, "You'd better listen to Bossy Pants, girls. Let me transfer your macchiatos into to-go cups. And don't forget to text your friends about the wine-and-cheese tasting from noon to five."

"That's if they're twenty-one?" Liz added.

"Yes, Debbie Downer." Then Ryan handed the "girls" their cups, and they strode away on their giraffe legs toward Sirens by the Sea.

After an awkward pause, Liz said, "Where's Pops?"

"He'll be here at eleven. He had a rough night's sleep."

"It must be a relief having you here."

Ryan turned his dark-eyed gaze on Liz's face. He looked puzzled by her compliment. "Well, if you have nothing else to do, princess, why don't you help me cut up some of the cheese."

"Don't call me 'princess'—and cut the cheese yourself!" Suddenly realizing how that sounded, she turned and stomped away. "And I have plenty to do," she called back over her shoulder.

At the thought of the word "princess," Liz felt her temperature rise. The 911 tape from that night long ago had become public. Liz could still hear it playing in her head, with Travis's voice, "Princess. My princess. How could you do this to me?" followed by some indistinct garbling, then Liz's voice, "Help! Please help! He's out of control!" Followed by crying—Travis Osterman's—the macho Pulitzer Prize–winning author of the best war novel in the last hundred years, sobbing like an infant. The nightly news had played the tape repeatedly. She'd first heard it in her hospital room, before her father had had a chance to jump up and turn off the TV. But it was too late. Until she'd heard her voice on the recording, Liz barely had any memory of what had gone down. But once she heard it, it had all come rushing back in vivid 3-D IMAX detail.

Ryan wasn't playing fair. Liz would make it her mission to pay him back one way or another.

As she walked out of Deli-casies, she realized she'd forgotten to get coffee for her and Kate. She did an about face and stomped toward the barista counter. "Two dark roasts. One milk and sugar. One black."

"Yes, ma'am, Bossy Pants. Let me guess, Kate is cream and sugar and you're…"

"Wrong again," she said.

"You wake up on the wrong side of the bed?" he asked.

"None of your business what I do in bed." She realized how ridiculous that sounded and took the tray with the coffees from his outstretched hand.

"See you soon for the wine and cheese. I don't think we need you, but my grandfather insists."

Liz didn't answer, just turned and clopped off toward the exit.

After she delivered Kate's coffee, she headed to Home Arts by the Sea. Both Minna and Francie were inside. Minna wore one of her geometric form-fitting spandex dresses that hugged every curve. Francie looked like a character from the movie *Grease* in a cotton candy–pink circle skirt with an applique of a young teen lying on her stomach, holding a turquoise slimline phone, the receiver coiled to her ear.

"Love your skirt," Liz said to Francie.

Francie twirled. Her vintage style suited her. Even though Francie was in her forties, she didn't care how everyone else dressed. Liz needed to take a page from Francie's playbook when it came to her scar.

Minna and Francie were doing their own raffle. A few lucky winners would receive two free lessons from Francie for the needlework project of their choice in any of the categories offered: quilting, knitting, crocheting, needlepoint, cross-stitch, primitive rug hooking, or sewing. Minna was giving away free painting or mixed-media art lessons. Liz was tempted to fill out slips of paper with her own name and phone number and drop them into each box.

Liz's next stop was Edward's shop, Gold Coast by the Sea. Edward wasn't there, but his son, Nick, was.

"Edward's in the back storage room." Liz always found it interesting that Nick called his father "Edward," not "Dad." Nick was tall and thick-necked, with massive shoulders. His tousled hair looked professionally highlighted. He wore an aqua polo shirt and plaid shorts that didn't mesh with the huge snake tattoo that traveled from below his elbow and then disappeared under his shirtsleeve to the top of his bulging, weight-lifter biceps. Offsetting his attractive facial features were yellowed teeth, no doubt stained from cigarettes. He reeked of them. Brittany was close to Liz's age, and Nick looked like he was in his early twenties. An odd pair.

Liz walked over to the front show case on her right. The top was smudged with fingerprints. She might be overstepping her bounds, but she said, "Maybe you get some Windex and clean off the show case? We open in a few minutes."

She heard from behind her, "Don't worry about my shop. I pay my rent on time and pay you for advertising. Though I doubt that tiny ad you placed will do any good. I don't need decorating advice from you. I've been in the business for forty-eight years." Then Edward turned to his son and said, "I thought I told you to clean the cases last night? Another night not at home. Maybe you don't need free room and board, not to mention a job anymore?"

Nick said, "Okay, old man. Settle down. It takes two minutes to clean a case. You're always bitchin'. How about all my help and the time I spent salvaging on *Mermaids Bounty*? I suppose that counts for nothin'."

"Your 'help'? You never took time out of your social schedule even to learn to dive."

"I'm claustrophobic. Mom would have understood. Clean your own damn case. I'm outta here." Nick whipped past Liz and went in the direction of the storeroom.

Liz was embarrassed to have witnessed the emotional exchange between father and son, and she quickly turned toward the shop's entrance, bumping into something solid. David Worth.

"So sorry. My apologies," he said.

Liz laughed. "My fault completely."

David looked nervous. Sweat beaded on his upper lip. He was probably on a timed errand for his demanding wife.

Edward came from behind his desk. "Can I help you with something? Ms. Holt was just leaving."

David looked into the show case on the left. "Um, I'm looking for something for my wife. Apparently, I'm in the doghouse and I saw you listed in the brochure in our suite."

Edward gave Liz the stink eye. She left the shop, worried that if she didn't, he might physically push her out. She wondered who'd let David Worth into the emporium before the opening. No doubt, it was Aunt Amelia.

As she headed toward the emporium's main doors, she heard David say to Edward, "It's not gold enough. It has to be eighteen-karat gold-plated or above, no cutting corners." His tone was forceful, and he sounded angry. Perhaps Regina was rubbing off on him. Gold Coast by the Sea had some nice pieces, but nothing compared to Regina's father's eighteenth-century jewelry from the *San Carlos*.

Upbeat music floated toward her from the string quartet. It was almost ten, time to open the doors. She heard Aunt Amelia accompanying the musicians with a few lines from the song "Send in the Clowns," using her exaggerated Broadway voice, even though she'd never been on Broadway, only performing at the Pasadena Playhouse when she'd lived in California, and the Melbourne Beach Theatre. As she sang, Aunt Amelia added an extra dragged-out sound at the end of each line she belted out: "Isn't it riiiich... Aren't we a paaaiiir..."

Liz rushed up and steered Aunt Amelia away from the quartet. "Time to send in the crowds, not the clowns."

"I originally wanted to sing Babs's 'Don't Rain on My Parade,' from *Funny Girl*, to ward off any bad weather, but they didn't know how to play it." She wore one of her colorful Hawaiian muumuus from the set of *Hawaii Five-O*. The wardrobe and set departments on many of her great-aunt's "shows" had allowed her to take home a memento from each of her roles. What wasn't plastered on the wall in Aunt Amelia's screening room, could usually be found in the room-sized closet in her suite. Each item was catalogued and promised to Liz in her will. A girl couldn't have too many plastic shrunken heads.

Liz looked out the emporium's window and saw a few clouds rolling in from the ocean. She crossed her fingers. "Maybe the calypso band scheduled for the afternoon will know the song?"

"You're right!"

Liz and Aunt Amelia opened the doors. Everyone was at their stations. A buoyant, upbeat crowd filled the emporium, exceeding their expectations. Liz and her great-aunt gave each other a fist bump. They'd done it.

* * * *

An hour later, Liz spied her father coming out of Kate's shop, Books & Browsery by the Sea, with a vintage golf club bag in one hand and a book in the other. He held up the book, *Go for Broke!* by Arnold Palmer. "Your best friend wouldn't let me leave without a book. She even gave the book a stern talking-to, saying, 'You'd better teach him all your tricks. He needs a little help with his swing.'"

Kate and Fenton played together at Spessard Holland Golf Course in Melbourne Beach. Of course, there was no contest. Kate always whipped his butt, big-time.

"So, what do you think?" Liz opened her arms to encompass the emporium.

"You and Aunt Amelia should feel very proud of yourselves."

"Thanks, Pops."

"Speaking of Pops, I just ran into Ryan. He was asking about you, said you'd promised to help him cut the cheese. Then he laughed for about five minutes."

"He's too much. Why is he helping with your case? We've never needed anyone to help us before."

"This one is out of my expertise, and Ryan has an excellent reputation as an arson investigator."

"Okay, okay. I'll play nice if Ryan will. I know he knows about Travis. I can tell."

Minna touched Liz on the shoulder. "Sorry to interrupt, but Francie is at the table outside, and I need to use the restroom. Do you mind manning the cash register? It's been crazy busy."

"Of course." Minna scurried away, and Liz said to her father, "You'd better go find Aunt Amelia. She might need to be told to sit down and rest."

They walked together toward Home Arts by the Sea.

She asked, "Have you seen any protesters against the demolition of Castlemara?"

"Not protestors holding signs or boycotting the Indialantic, but a lot of them handing out petitions from Francie and the rest of the historical society. I promised to look into it next week to see if I can help them."

Liz gave his arm a squeeze. "Did I ever tell you that you're my hero?"

He smiled down at her. "I think I've heard that a few times. Don't build a person up too much, you might not like what happens when they fall."

"Ha. That applies to anyone but you, Dad."

Chapter 16

Liz showed up at Deli-casies by the Sea at eleven thirty. Thankfully, Pops was standing next to Ryan in front of the wine-and-cheese tasting table. Behind the barista counter was a huge stainless-steel coffee and espresso machine where one of Pops's part-timers, Ashley, a senior at Melbourne Beach High School, worked the levers and nozzles like a pro, the top of her auburn hair lost in the fog of steamed milk and coffee vapor.

On the east side of the shop was a long, double-sided refrigerated case displaying a plethora of sliced meats, cold salads, cheeses, and a dozen types of olives. With each purchase of Pops's legendary homemade hummus, customers had a choice of a container of fresh minced garlic, olive tapenade, or roasted red-and-yellow peppers to mix into their hummus. On TGIF Fridays, Pops stayed open until seven and offered a raw bar of fresh local clams and oysters, cooked lobster, and in-season crab, along with discount prices on craft beer and wine. Exotic vinegars, oils, jars of roasted peppers, and artichoke hearts filled a shelf against the wall. Scattered around the shop were wooden fruit crates turned on their sides, stacked with boxes of crackers, cheese straws, and imported cookies. Liz sniffed the intoxicating air. Betty was right. Living at the Indialantic was like living in your own ecosystem, everything at your fingertips.

Pops called out, "Liz! What do you think?"

She looked at Ryan and grudgingly gave him credit for putting out an amazing display on the marble-topped table that usually stood against the back wall as a condiment bar. She was tempted to taste each small square of cheese. The wine did nothing for her, except remind her of Travis; it was as if she now had an allergy to alcohol. "It looks amazing, Pops. Do you need me to taste anything to make sure it's up to snuff?"

Ryan put his hands on his hips. "Thought you didn't drink?"

"I don't. I'm talking about the cheese."

He gave her a questioning look, and she could tell that he'd softened his stance with her. What had changed?

Ryan handed her an apron printed with Deli-casies by the Sea, next to a drawing of a lobster, a wheel of cheese, and a bottle of wine. She put the apron on and said, "Okay, what do you need me to do?"

"Just look beautiful," Ryan said.

Huh? What was his deal? Was that a compliment or a dis? A ploy to get her to collaborate with him on her father's case, or did it have something to do with Pops being nearby? She didn't have time to dissect the situation, though, because a line had formed in front of the table, snaking its way out the entrance to the shop.

Sometime around three, when Liz, Pops, and Ryan were still serving the crowds, they heard calypso music and the distinctive voice of Amelia Eden Holt, doing a hackneyed version of "Don't Rain on My Parade." The upbeat tempo from the band stayed with Aunt Amelia's enthusiastic rendition, then would morph into the music from the classic "Yellow Bird." Remarkably, it seemed to work. Liz knew that when her great-aunt made up her mind, there was no dissuading her. Liz also knew that when you suggested something to her that was a little on the crazy side without thinking it through first, you were in big trouble. Nothing was impossible unto Amelia Holt, the little girl from Melbourne Beach, Florida, who made it big in Burbank.

When six thirty came, Liz was exhausted. Pops was in the back, resting. He'd been quite the trouper, but Liz was happy she could be there to help. Liz and Ryan had worked nonstop, with little time for chitchat.

Ryan asked Liz to help him return the marble table to the back wall. She went opposite him, and as she was about to lift her side, Fenton walked in.

"Lizzy, stop. Let me get that."

Thinking about his heart, Liz said, "It looks pretty heavy, Dad. I can do it."

"Nonsense."

Kate passed in front of Deli-casies, carrying one of the collapsed folding tables from outside. "Kate! Can you help?" Liz shouted.

Kate leaned the folding table against the outside half wall, came inside, and helped them put the table back against the wall.

"Thanks. Now I'm going to bring back the bistro tables and chairs from the entranceway," Ryan said.

"You guys go find Aunt Amelia, I'll help Ryan," Kate said to Liz and Fenton.

On Ryan's way out, Liz saw him give her father a knowing nod. Suddenly it all came together: Her father must have talked to Ryan about what really went down the night of the scar. She doubted he'd revealed too much. Fenton Holt was known for his ability to keep a confidence; he'd staked his reputation on it. No doubt, he'd pointed Ryan in the right direction, and would let Ryan do his own research into Liz's guilt or innocence.

The emporium lights dimmed, and Liz and her father went in search of the colorful butterfly called Aunt Amelia. Liz hoped she was resting her wings.

They found her with Betty and Pierre sitting at a table in Home Arts by the Sea. Liz and Fenton went inside and sat across from them. The consensus was that the Spring Fling by the Sea had been a rousing success.

A short time later, Kate and Ryan walked by, each carrying a chair in their hands. Ryan stopped at the half wall to the shop and said, "Everyone's invited to Deli-casies to finish the cheese samples and open bottles of wine." Liz noted the effect that this new-and-improved Ryan had on everyone, including herself.

Aunt Amelia spoke for the group. "Be right there, Ryan. I think you're right, our hard work warrants a well-deserved respite."

"Hear, hear," Kate said, in a celebratory tone.

Aunt Amelia stood and they filed out of the shop, following Ryan and Kate to Deli-casies.

Ryan instructed everyone to have a seat in the café section. Pops was at the cash register closing out the day's receipts. Aunt Amelia called out, "Good day, Pops?"

"A very good day. Thank you, Amelia, and thank you, Liz. We couldn't have done it without you. Right, Ryan?"

"Yes, Grampa. It was a good day. Hang up your apron and come join us. We need to celebrate."

Everyone chose a seat. Ryan turned the sound system up, then passed out small, clear-plastic plates and cups. Five minutes later, he came toward them with a huge tray of assorted cheese squares spiked with toothpicks, his biceps bulging in all their glory.

Liz grabbed the last wedge of Parmesan reggiano infused with flecks of black truffles that she'd been eyeing all day. She put it in her mouth and moaned in ecstasy.

Ryan returned to the kitchen and came back with an open bottle in each hand: rosé in his right, pinot noir in his left. He skipped Liz, but then returned with sparkling water, even adding a slice of lime to her glass before he poured. Then he pulled a chair up next to Pierre and his grandfather and introduced himself to Pierre, praising him for the fabulous baked goods he'd contributed to Deli-casies.

Pierre's eyes were bright, and Liz wondered if maybe he should also forgo the wine and stick to the cheese. "You're welcome, and this wine is a perfect pairing with the smoked Gouda," he said, lifting his cup in the air. Pierre had once told Liz that he'd been raised on wine. His mother had even added it to his bottle as a baby to help him sleep—or more likely she'd added it so *she* could sleep. Liz doubted that story was true, but you never knew with the French.

Liz asked Pierre, "How is everything next door? All quiet on the Harrington-Worth front?"

"There was a little problem."

"I bet Regina was involved," Liz retorted.

Pierre swirled the wine in his cup, then took a sip, smiling approvingly at Pops. "Indirectly, Mrs. Worth was involved. Sometime in the afternoon, when Mr. Worth was going out on an errand, he found the windshield of his Bentley shattered from a rock that was tied with a note."

Kate chimed in. "Let me guess, the note said something to the effect of 'Leave Castlemara alone'?"

"I didn't see the note," Pierre said. "Iris was in the lobby when Mr. Worth stormed in. He told Iris that his wife wouldn't be too happy when she heard about it. Then he instructed Iris to order a limo to take them to the ball. Later, when I brought up their dinner of seared sea scallops, truffle risotto, and haricots verts, Mrs. Worth screeched that they would be eating dinner at a two-hundred-and-fifty-dollar-a-plate affair catered by one of those young *Top Chef* TV stars. I wanted to throw the whole meal at her."

Liz had been with Aunt Amelia when she'd told Pierre that the Worths would be eating at the ball. "Yum," she said, looking toward her great-aunt, who nodded and looked toward Pierre with concern in her eyes. "All the more for *moi*, Grand-Pierre."

Betty said, "Save some for me, too, chef."

Liz guessed the stone throwing was by someone from the historical society. She didn't agree with the method they'd used. Picketing in a calm and peaceful manner would be Liz's choice. She knew violence begot violence,

The conversation changed course to the subject of the returning sea turtles, something every true islander felt resonance with. Ninety percent of sea turtles that have laid their eggs on America's beaches have laid them in Florida.

Aunt Amelia shouted over the music, "We need a toast. Here goes. May those who love us, love us. And for those who don't love us, may God turn their hearts. And if He doesn't turn their hearts, may He turn their ankles so we'll know them by their limping!"

Liz said, "Auntie!"

Aunt Amelia grinned. "It seemed to fit—an old drinking toast from my Irish mother's side of the family."

After Aunt Amelia's toast, the discussion veered back to Regina and the fate of Castlemara. Soon, all the samples of cheese were eaten and the last drop of wine was poured. A few minutes after, Aunt Amelia cupped her hands around her mouth and shouted to Ryan, "Do you mind turning down the music a tad? I'm afraid my hearing's not as good as it used to be, and I'm missing all the juicy conversation."

Ryan said, "Of course, Amelia."

"I told you to call me 'Aunt Amelia,' young man."

Liz looked over at her great-aunt in surprise.

"Okay, Aunt Amelia." Ryan got up and turned down the volume. When he sat back down, he said, "I don't think Regina Harrington-Worth is that bad. Seemed amicable to me. And she did incur a bad twisting of the knee." He paused, then said, "Do you hear that?"

They all then heard the wail of a fire truck.

Aunt Amelia said, "Ryan, being a firefighter, you probably hear that sound in your sleep. The Brevard County Fire and Rescue is only a mile away."

Fenton lifted his glass. As he rose to speak, the emporium doors slammed open.

A woman's voice called out in a calm manner, "Fenton, are you in here?"

"I'm in Deli-casies by the Sea, come join us." He glanced at Liz and said, "Charlotte. I told her to stop by, was hoping it would have been earlier, during the festivities."

Liz's palms itched. "What kind of agent is Charlotte?"

"Homicide," he replied.

A minute later Agent Charlotte Pearson stood in front of the group. Her detective's shield hung from one of three gold chains around her neck. "Fenton, can I have a word with you?"

"Of course," he said, worry lining his forehead.

They walked out of earshot, and everyone left at the tables looked at each other in stunned silence.

Chapter 17

Liz pulled her chair up next to Aunt Amelia's and took her soft, freckled hand in her own. "I'm sure everything's okay, Auntie. Don't worry." Liz wished she could convince herself of the same thing. She felt oddly comforted by the fact that those she held near and dear were all gathered around her and unhurt. Ryan didn't exactly fall into that category, but with his sudden change of behavior, she'd almost added him into the mix.

No one said a thing. It was like they were all holding their collective breath, waiting for her father and Charlotte to return.

Within two minutes, Fenton was back. They heard Agent Pearson's shoes clicking across the wood floors, then out the door. He said, "Apparently there has been a robbery. Regina Harrington-Worth is dead, and her husband has been taken to the hospital."

Aunt Amelia asked, "Oh my God! Where did this happen?"

"In the Oceana Suite," Fenton answered.

Aunt Amelia gasped and stood up. "How was Regina killed, and what happened to David?"

When Aunt Amelia sat back down, Liz pulled her close, selfishly not to comfort her great-aunt, but to be comforted.

"Mrs. Worth was strangled, and her husband stabbed. That's all I know. It happened just a short time ago."

"The sirens—we missed them because of the music," Kate said.

Liz turned to her father. "What was stolen?"

Fenton sat, rubbing the area between his eyebrows like he was trying to erase what he'd just heard. "The necklace and earrings Regina had planned on wearing to the Treasure Coast Ball. We'll know more soon. The ME and forensics team are up there now. Char—Agent Pearson said the body will be moved shortly. She wants everyone to wait to reenter until they can secure the suite."

The body... the body... kept repeating in Liz's head.

Pierre stood and pulled up a chair next to Aunt Amelia. "Amelia, *mon cher*. We are together. Everything will look better in the morning. If the Worth woman was killed for her jewelry, no one else is in danger."

Impressed by Pierre's words and the clarity with which he spoke them, Liz left Aunt Amelia's side and went over to Betty. "I'm stunned. Murder at the Indialantic? Even with its long history and list of gangster and rumrunner guests, we've never had a murder!"

"You forget about Cissy Bollinger," Betty said.

The fire that took out almost half of the Indialantic had happened on the same day as V-E day, at the end of WWII. There had been one casualty, Cissy, the Indialantic's chambermaid. She hadn't died in the fire; she was discovered floating in the swimming pool. Everyone assumed Cissy had purposely set the fire, then killed herself. Ever since the age of ten, when Liz uncovered Cissy's things in a small suitcase in the back of the hotel's luggage room, Liz and Betty had been sleuthing the possibility that someone had framed the young eighteen-year-old, then murdered her.

"No one is allowed on the second floor at this time," Fenton said, "but on my suggestion, Charlotte said we can use the rear entrance to my office and stay in my part of the Indialantic until she comes down and tells us the coast is clear. Ryan, of course, you are free to go to the caretaker's cottage."

Liz had watched Ryan's face since Agent Pearson had first walked in. He'd focused first on the detective's words, then on her father's without moving a muscle.

"If you don't mind, Fenton," said Ryan, "I'll try to get more info on what went down from one of the first responders, then meet back at your apartment as soon as I can." Liz felt the confidence in his words. He was used to highly-charged situations. He added, "Granddad, will you be okay until I can drive you home?"

Pops was on the frail side, but he had a fire in his eyes that reminded Liz of his grandson. "I'll be fine. Go see what you can find out."

Liz said, "I'll make sure he's okay. We'll take a golf cart to my father's. He won't have to walk at all."

"Thank you, Liz." It was the first time Ryan had said her name. She wasn't going to go all soft on the guy until he atoned for his past behavior, but she was happy they seemed to have passed the sparring portion of their relationship. If you could call it a relationship...

"The cat. The poor baby," Aunt Amelia said, her voice cracking. "Ryan, please ask Agent Pearson if you can bring Mrs. Worth's cat to my nephew's apartment?" A single tear coursed down her cheek, making a line in her rosy blush. Aunt Amelia stood and stuck her chin out. "Let's do as my nephew suggests. We will reconvene in his apartment. Katie, do you mind making sure the emporium is locked up? Set the alarm on your way out, then meet us at Fenton's."

"Will do, Aunt Amelia," Kate said.

Chapter 18

Liz and Pops got in the golf cart parked outside the emporium. Before heading to the rear outside entrance to her father's apartment, Liz's curiosity won out, and she drove the cart to the front entrance of the hotel, stopping far enough away from the emergency vehicles not to get caught by Agent Pearson. The pulsing strobe lights in the near distance seemed out of place under the moonlit sky. She heard the sound of the waves hitting the shore and wished she could just go home, crawl under the covers, and wake up knowing she'd just had a bad dream.

Pops pointed out Ryan at the back of a rescue truck, talking to a first responder. "I'm so proud of my grandson. He not only got commendations from his hook-and-ladder company, but he was recently promoted after he solved an arson case. A single mother and four children barely survived a fire set by an ex-boyfriend. Ryan found proof that the fire had been deliberately set, leading to an arrest and conviction. That investigation took a lot out of him. I don't really need him down here, but I could tell he needed a break from New York."

Liz told Pops that she knew all about the pressures of big city life. Barrier Island living was the perfect balm—that was, until Regina's murder.

A half hour later, everyone was settled in her father's apartment. Liz and Pierre snuck off to the Indialantic's kitchen to make coffee. They tiptoed around the kitchen, not knowing whether they were legally allowed inside. Liz made coffee in the stainless steel urn, then filled two silver carafes, both with regular. At this point, decaf was not an option. They had a long night ahead of them. There was again no sign of Iris. Had the housekeeper been down the hall in her suite during the time Regina was murdered? And what about Captain Netherton? Liz had seen him in the emporium in the late morning, stopping here and there, charming the women. He hadn't said good-bye after manning the raffle table. His room was right next to the Worths'.

She hurried Pierre along the back hallway, hoping that when they got to her father's apartment, Ryan would be there with more information. Liz held the two carafes of coffee and Pierre brought the mugs; her father had the milk, sugar, and spoons. They passed the service elevator, ice machine, and dumbwaiter, not seeing any law enforcement personnel. Pierre pointed out the water pooling on the floor next to the ice machine and warned Liz to be careful. Ever-caring Grand-Pierre.

When they entered the apartment, not only were Ryan and Agent Pearson there, but also Venus, Regina's sphynx cat, sitting on Aunt Amelia's lap like the goddess she was named after.

"Just in time," the detective said, giving them a chastising glance that Liz assumed had something to do with them not staying put in her father's apartment. "I was just telling everyone that the time of death seems pretty certain, but we still have to wait for the medical examiner's confirmation. I can answer a few questions, but for now, I'd like to keep it simple and get back to my job. Fenton has assured me that everyone in this room had been together well before the murder-robbery took place."

Liz couldn't help herself. "Of course we were together. And of course we didn't murder or rob anyone. Why would you think someone from the Indialantic would be involved, anyway?"

"I'm not allowed to discuss what we have or haven't found. But I can say we are following every lead in looking for a suspect."

Kate raised her hand like she was in English class. "Did David Worth see the person? How badly was he hurt?"

Agent Pearson put her hand on the door leading into the hotel. "He was taken to Indian River Medical. I'm going to head there now." She turned toward Fenton and said, "I will need to have fingerprints taken of anyone who was in the Worths' suite."

"Of course," he answered.

"What about Captain Netherton and Iris?" Aunt Amelia asked. "They aren't missing or hurt, are they?" She put her hand to her heart.

"No. They're accounted for. In fact, after they're finished being interviewed, I'd like to send them here so we can search the entire upstairs. The Worths' suite will be off-limits for a while. No one is allowed in or out."

"Of course," Fenton said for the second time.

Agent Pearson walked out and into the hallway. She turned and said, "Give us another an hour or so, then you can return to your rooms. I'll see everyone in the morning. Get some sleep."

Yeah, right, Liz thought. How could Aunt Amelia sleep on the same floor where a woman had just been murdered? After Agent Pearson left, she said, "Auntie and Betty, you can sleep in the beach house with me."

Aunt Amelia said, "Thank you, darling. That would be a relief. Naturally, I'll have to bring Barnacle Bob and Venus."

"Naturally." Liz wondered how the bald-headed parrot and bald-bodied cat would get along.

"I appreciate the offer," said Betty, "but I plan to sleep in my own bed. I'm not that worried someone will come after me for my jewels."

Liz looked at her. "Are you sure?"

There was a knocking from the outside door to the office. Ryan, who had remained mute during the exchange with Agent Pearson, got up to answer it. Liz overheard Ryan introducing himself to Iris. To Captain Netherton, she heard him say, "Good to see you again, Captain. Sorry it's not under better circumstances." Then Iris entered her father's living room/dining room and took the seat vacated by Pops. Ryan and Captain Netherton remained in her father's office. She heard the low buzz of conversation, but couldn't make out any of it.

Liz poured coffee into a cup for the housekeeper. Iris's face was a pasty white, and her right leg jiggled nervously. Liz wanted to ask her what had happened, but thought better of it. She asked, "Milk? Sugar?"

"No. Nothing," Iris said in her raspy smoker's voice. "I could go for a shot of tequila if you have any?"

Fenton took a few long-legged strides to the small kitchen, opened an upper cabinet, and retrieved a bottle. "Will brandy do?"

"Yes, please."

Captain Netherton and Ryan entered the room. The captain said, "I could use a spot of brandy myself, old chap."

Aunt Amelia said, "Pierre, how about you? I'm sure you could stay here, in my nephew's apartment."

"I'll be fine, Amelia. Like Betty, I'd rather sleep in my own bed. I'm on the opposite end of the hotel from the Oceana Suite, and lately I sleep like the dead."

Iris gasped, but Pierre didn't notice, not realizing his faux pas.

"Iris, how about you? Do you want to go to your mother's or somewhere else? I can't ask you to stay at the hotel after what happened."

"Yes, that is a good idea," Iris replied. "I will pack a few things and be on my way."

Captain Netherton stood. "I'll escort you to your rooms. This is no time for a lady to be alone."

The housekeeper shrugged her shoulders and downed the brandy in one gulp.

After a long period of silence, Ryan finally said, "I think our hour's up. We can retire. Captain Netherton, you're free to bunk with me in the caretaker's cottage."

"Oh, thank you, my boy. I will stay in the hotel to protect Betty, although I doubt she would say she needs protection."

Betty glanced at the captain, opened her mouth, then closed it. Liz saw the tug-of-war between her feminist side and the romanticist in her.

There were many questions Liz wanted to ask Iris and the captain, but for Aunt Amelia's sake, she wouldn't bring them up now. Plus, her father had the inside track with Agent Charlotte Pearson. Liz would have to wait until tomorrow.

Before leaving the apartment to help Aunt Amelia collect Barnacle Bob and grab a few items to take to the beach house, she pulled Ryan aside and asked, "What were you talking to Captain Netherton about?"

He looked down at her, but remained silent.

"Look, buster, my great-aunt's life's work is tied up in the Indialantic."

"I thought she was an actress most of her life?"

"Semantics. She has put everything she has made for almost four decades into this hotel, and now the emporium. If you know anything about Regina's murder, then I want to know. I'd also love to hear what you've learned from Brevard County Fire and Rescue. I'll be agreeable to work with you on Dad's case if you're forthcoming with me on anything you can dig up on the murder."

"I'll have to think about it."

"I guess you like to work alone."

"Okay, okay. Meet me tomorrow morning at the caretaker's cottage, and I'll tell you what I know." He looked down at her hand still holding his wrist. "Now is it okay if I take my seventy-five-year-old grandfather home? Or do we have to make a deal on that one, too, Bossy Pants?"

Ugh. He was back—"*Here's Johnny...*" At least she knew what she was dealing with. The kinder, gentler Ryan had thrown her off balance. Never again.

Later that night, when Liz was in bed and Aunt Amelia and her animalia were secure in the guest room, something hit Liz like a proverbial brick. Where was Captain Netherton's cane? And what had happened to his limp?

A few hours later, she woke in the pitch dark with her heart pounding. After the night of the scar, Liz had spent weeks living through nightmares, waking up drenched in sweat, shivering, and cold. She prayed they wouldn't come back to haunt her after what had just happened. As she drifted back to sleep, she remembered why she'd woken. She'd dreamt that a ghostly Regina Harrington-Worth had entered Liz's bedroom, her arm outstretched, holding an emerald-and-pearl necklace dripping with blood, her head floating above her shoulders where her neck should have been.

Chapter 19

Liz sat on her deck, looking into a cup of black sludge topped with swirling coffee-ground flotsam. Aunt Amelia wasn't just a bad cook, she was a bad beverage maker, too. Her great-aunt had set up the automated coffeepot the night before and was still asleep in the guest room. Liz had checked on Aunt Amelia earlier and saw Venus snuggled in the crook of her great-aunt's legs. Even though she wore a nose strip, Aunt Amelia still snored. When Liz had carefully backed out of the room, she'd heard Barnacle Bob say from under his covered cage, "Snoring to beat the band. Snoring to the beat the band."

She loved early mornings on her deck overlooking the ocean. A congregation of white ibis pecked at the shoreline with their long, curved orange beaks, scavenging for sand crabs. If any of the other authors in her Manhattan writing group knew about Liz's ocean-front beach house with its glorious views, they'd never feel sorry for the fact that she'd barely written a word since coming home to live on the barrier island. As she stared out at the mesmerizing waves, her thoughts switched to Regina's murder.

"A gold doubloon for your thoughts?"

She turned and saw a handsome, distinguished man walking up the steps leading to the deck. "Dad!" He came toward her and gave her a kiss on the forehead. "I hope you were able to sleep?" he asked as he sat on the lounge chair next to her.

"A little." She didn't have to ask how he'd slept, because he had stubble on his chiseled jaw. Her father greeted each day with a clean-shaven face, smelling of citrus aftershave, but not today. The look made him even more handsome, but she was sorry it came at the price of a sleepless night.

They sat in silence for a few minutes sharing the peaceful view. Liz was the first to speak.

"I would go get you a cup of coffee, but Aunt Amelia made it."

He smiled. "That bad, huh?"

"Oh yeah."

She tipped her cup toward him and he laughed. He said, "I wanted to stop over to tell you that Charlotte will be coming by the hotel around eleven for the fingerprinting. Until any DNA results come in, we can't ask for samples. This is a small town, not like you see on television. All these tests cut into the budget."

"It would be a pretty dumb robber who didn't wear gloves."

"Agreed. I told Charlotte I'd try to round up everyone and we'll meet in the library."

"Who is 'everyone'?"

"Anyone who has been in the Oceana Suite. You, me, Iris, Captain Netherton, Aunt Amelia, Pierre, and Ryan. I have no clue on how to get ahold of Iris. Do you know where she went last night?"

"No. Sorry."

"David Worth is coming home from the hospital today. He asked if he could stay for a couple of days until he figures things out—not in the Oceana Suite, of course. I called Charlotte and she thinks it's a good idea. I hope your great-aunt agrees."

"Is something going on with you and the beautiful homicide detective, Father Dear?"

He smiled, but didn't answer.

Liz said, "I'm sure Aunt Amelia will want to rescue David Worth like she did Venus."

As if on cue, Aunt Amelia opened the French doors and stepped through them with Barnacle Bob on her right shoulder. She was the only one who could handle BB, and there wasn't any worry he would fly away. He knew where his bread was buttered, or more aptly, his kiwi was halved.

"Why don't you have a cup of coffee, Fenton?" Aunt Amelia asked. Then she turned to Liz. "Lizzy, you didn't offer your father coffee after the night he's had? Hell, the night we *all* had."

Barnacle Bob said, "Good to the last drop. Good to the last drop. Maxwell House."

Not Aunt Amelia's Maxwell House, Liz thought, as she glanced inside her mug.

Fenton said, "I'm good, Auntie. I must get back anyway. Everything's fine at the Indialantic. I just left Betty, Pierre, and Captain Netherton in the kitchen. The police should be leaving by noon. I'll let Liz fill you in on the rest." He got up and went over to Aunt Amelia. He clasped her hands in his and gazed into her matching sea-green eyes. Barnacle Bob moved his beak in Fenton's direction. He released his aunt's hands and took a step backward. "I don't want you to worry about anything. This is a simple case of a robbery gone bad. I doubt that anyone at the Indialantic is involved, but I think it might be better if you stay here with Liz for a day or two."

Barnacle Bob squawked, "Robbery gone bad. Robbery gone bad."

"Hush, BB!" Aunt Amelia said, and the bird obeyed. "I promise to stay here at night, but during the day I want to be at the hotel. I'm sure your lovely Charlotte will catch this monster very soon. Also, I need to put a sign on the door to the emporium that we will be closed for the time being."

"Sounds like a plan," Fenton said. "Okay by you, Liz?"

"Of course. Tonight, Auntie and I will turn the AC on high, put on our footie pj's, make popcorn, and watch some of her old shows on DVD."

Her father left, and she filled her great-aunt in on what he'd told her about meeting in the library at eleven.

After showering and dressing, Liz said good-bye to Aunt Amelia, who was sitting on a bar stool cuddling Venus in her arms like a newborn. As she walked across her deck, Liz heard her great-aunt crooning the melancholy song "Memory," from the musical *Cats*.

When Liz reached the caretaker's cottage, the door was open, so she stepped inside. She surveyed the open living room and kitchen floor plan. It had been ten years since she'd been in her former home. Nothing remained the same except the white kitchen cupboards, countertop, wood table, and old stove. There'd been no reason to update the kitchen when Liz and her father had lived there, because they'd taken most of their meals at the Indialantic. There were doilies on every chair back and tons of knickknacks, mostly consisting of china bird figurines. A large framed print of two cockatiels hung over an old television produced before the advent of the flat screen. After Aunt Amelia's friend's passing, her great-aunt must have felt too sad to have anything removed.

"Hello. I'm here," Liz called out, moving next to a lumpy-cushioned plaid couch. Under a side table, scarred with drink rings that a dozen crocheted coasters couldn't hide, was a basket. Inside the basket was a half-finished knitting project. Liz had an urge to rescue the lacy aqua something that Aunt Amelia's friend and costar from *Dark Shadows* had started. But first, she would have to learn to knit.

Ryan came out of the front bedroom, Liz's former bedroom. His thick dark hair was perfectly messy, and his navy Brooklyn Engine 205 FDNY logo T-shirt clung to his muscled torso like a second skin. Liz thought she saw a tattoo on his upper arm, but she looked away, not wanting him to think she was interested.

"You're late," he said brusquely.

"How can I be late? There was no set time. You said 'morning'. This is morning."

"Wow, you always go that extra mile to irritate, don't you, Bossy Pants?" Now who was being childish?

Ryan stepped into the kitchen, and Liz sat at the small, rectangular table in the tiny breakfast nook. There were marks in the wood from the impression her own pens and pencils had left after years of doing homework at the table. There was the faint indent of the cosine symbol, bringing back memories of her father sitting with her night after night as she tried to master trigonometry—her least favorite subject, unlike English.

"Want some?" Ryan held up a glass carafe of coffee, and she inhaled the rich scent of the dark roasted beans. "I make a mean cup of coffee, taught by the best."

She thought about refusing, but this game they were playing was getting old. She didn't have room in her world for a Ryan, or any other male. And if Pops had taught him how to make the coffee, then she wanted in. "Sure."

He put the pot back under the coffeemaker, left the kitchen, sat at the table, and began thumbing through a file folder bulging with papers. Without looking up, he said, "Well, princess, what are you waiting for? Pour yourself a cup of joe and let's get going."

Liz banged her fist on the table, her face prickly with heat. "You say, the 'P word' one more time, you'll be sorry. And that *is* a threat. You don't want to cross me. You obviously know what happened when someone else did." She didn't care. Let him believe what he wanted. She had nothing to prove to anyone. Ryan had hit the largest of her many raw nerves. Travis's nickname for Liz had been "Princess," and because of their age difference, it had always made her feel uncomfortable. "Princess" was more of an endearment a father might call his daughter, not his girlfriend.

The same night when she and Travis had celebrated a year of being together, they'd both fallen apart. Liz had first met the Pulitzer Prize–winning author while at the New York Public Library on Fifth Avenue, researching *Let the Wind Roar.* They met in the archives, both reaching for the same pencil to fill out a microfilm request. Travis was gathering information on WWII for the sequel to *The McAvoy Brothers*, and Liz was researching WWI for her novel.

Travis's book *The McAvoy Inheritance* would never be published, and Liz was to blame. Or so everyone thought.

Liz looked at Ryan's smug face. *Jerk!* She got up, stomped over to the kitchen, grabbed a mug from the cupboard, and poured herself some coffee. After returning the carafe to the coffeemaker with a thud, she opened the fridge, took out a carton of milk, smelled it, wrinkled her nose, and said, "Yuck," even though the milk was fine. When she put the milk back, she slammed the door extra hard, rattling the contents inside.

She hated drinking her coffee black, but it was well worth it when she saw Ryan glance inside his mug for curdled milk. Score one for the good guys. Liz changed her mind about not playing games—let the jousting commence.

When she sat back down at the table, they faced each other like a married couple in a divorce proceeding. Ryan insisted they discuss her father's case and what role each of them would play, before he would tell her what Captain Netherton had told him last night.

"Okay. I've fulfilled my side of the bargain," Liz said a few minutes later. "I promise to work with you on Dad's case, but I also know we might have to postpone it, especially after everything that happened last night." She got up, went back to the kitchen, and filled her cup with coffee, then without thinking, she took out the milk from the fridge and poured it into her cup.

From behind, she heard, "Touché."

She came back and sat at the table. "Okay. Spill it. Your turn. Start with what you learned from the first responders."

Ryan opened the folder in front of him and took out a legal-sized piece of paper with handwritten notes. He noticed Liz looking at the paper. "I take notes on everything. A sign of a good investigator."

What Ryan didn't know was that Liz was looking more at what was sticking out of the folder—a ripped-out page from a newspaper. The header read *The Daily Post*, with a date that coincided with the morning after her and Travis's night of terror. She would bet her life that the thick sheaf of papers in the folder had as much to do with her as they did with her father's case and Regina's murder.

Ryan said, "Captain Netherton made the nine-one-one call at seven forty. When the first responders got to the scene, a limo was waiting under the port cochere at the entrance to the hotel. The fire and rescue guy I talked to didn't go inside, but he did see David Worth when he was carried out on a stretcher by the ambulance crew. He'd been stabbed once in the back on his right side below his shoulder blade. David seemed pretty coherent and kept asking about his wife. Then one of the officers from the sheriff's department started asking him questions. My guy overheard David tell the officer that he'd gone down to get ice for his wife's knee to take with them in the limo for their night out. When he got back up to the suite, he saw that the shutters had been closed in the bedroom and the lights turned off. He walked into the dark room and discovered his wife lying on the bed at a twisted angle. As he bent toward her, someone, who must have been hiding behind the door, stabbed him in the back, then ran out."

Liz shivered. "Wow. That's a lot of info for a stranger to divulge."

"Bill used to live on Long Island. His company was one of many who were called to the Trade Center on nine-eleven. Just like the police force, there is a comradery between first responders and the fire department."

"What did Captain Netherton tell you?"

"He said he was in the dining room, which is below the Worths' suite. First, he heard scuffling. Then he called the housekeeper in and they both listened. When they heard Mr. Worth scream, they ran up to the suite. The door was open, and they found him crawling on the floor from the bedroom. Captain Netherton called nine-one-one. The housekeeper entered the bedroom, checked Mrs. Worth for a pulse, and didn't find one."

"Was Regina stabbed?"

"No, choked."

"What was she choked with?"

"The captain didn't know, he didn't go into the bedroom. Said he was too overcome when he saw the cat sitting on top of Regina's chest. He stayed with Mr. Worth in the sitting room."

"How tragic. My father got a call from Agent Pearson. She wants anyone who was in the Worths' suite to meet in the library at eleven so her officers can take prints for elimination purposes. I guess you fall into that pool, because you carried the woman up to the bed after her fall. And one other thing, I know it's still early, but my father wasn't able to track down Iris."

"Didn't she tell your aunt where she was going last night?"

"Great-aunt," Liz corrected. "No, and Aunt Amelia hired her without checking her references. She had a feeling in here"—Liz thumped at her chest—"that Iris was 'honorable'."

"She didn't put an address on her employment forms?"

"No. Because she would be living at the Indialantic." Liz didn't want to tell Ryan that if Iris didn't show up at eleven, she planned to check her rooms for any clue of where she'd gone.

Ryan got up and put his coffee mug in the sink. She assumed that meant their meeting was over. Liz stood, reached over, and pulled out the front page from the *Daily Post* with her and Travis Osterman's photo and the headline "Writer's Rampage." She walked up to him, crumpled the newspaper-clipping into a ball, then pushed it into his chest. "If you want to know what happened, even though it's none of your damn business, ask me sometime, Mr. Investigator." Then she strode out the door.

Chapter 20

Liz stepped inside her favorite room at the Indialantic, the library. The furniture in the library was similar to the lobby's: light wood, bamboo, three rattan cushioned sofas and armchairs, a humongous area rug, and a large desk. There was even a fireplace. Each wall was filled with floor-to-ceiling bookshelves, with volumes dating all the way back to the late 1700s.

After Liz's great-grandmother Maeve's parents passed away, Isle Tor in Cornwall was willed to Maeve's brother, Connor, but the books in the castle's library were left to Maeve. During the Indialantic's early years, Liz's great-grandfather William Holt commissioned a ship to bring every book from Isle Tor's library to America as an anniversary gift for his beautiful Maeve. The addition of a fireplace in the library was also a gift from William to Maeve. Florida's steamy climate didn't necessarily call for many roaring fires, but its presence in the library helped Great-Grandma Maeve feel less homesick for England.

The library had been Liz's oasis as a child. The hours and hours spent inside fostered Liz's desire to become a writer. Her love of reading had been passed down from both of her parents. Before her mother's death, Chloe Holt had been an assistant acquisitions director for the rare books and documents division at the New York Public Library. Liz remembered her mother and father taking her to the library on her fifth birthday for an insider's peek at the library's legendary children's collection. That day, Liz imagined that the mammoth lions at the top of the library's steps had been part of her birthday present. Years later, every time she rode down Fifth Avenue and passed her marble feline friends, *Patience* and *Fortitude*, she smiled with the memory.

The library was the only room in the hotel that was kept locked. As children, Liz and Kate were only allowed inside under her father's watchful tutelage. Kate's habit of talking to books like they were old friends, even chastising characters like Heathcliff and Edward Rochester for their bad behavior, had come from the hours spent with Liz in the library. As Liz got older, the library became a refuge from the growing pains of crossing that rickety bridge from adolescence to tweenhood. Many a time, after finishing a book, Liz would walk out of the library feeling like she was the story's main character, sometimes even speaking with an English or French accent. Everyone had their little idiosyncrasies, so when Kate talked to her books, it had never seemed strange to Liz.

Guests weren't allowed inside the library, and no matter what financial difficulties the Indialantic had gone through in recent years, not one book had ever been sold. Which made it a strange place for Liz's father to allow fingerprinting to be done.

Agent Pearson sat behind the huge bamboo glass-topped desk like she was at command headquarters at Quantico. An officer from the sheriff's department had pulled up a chair at the side of the desk, and he motioned Liz forward like she was a truant called into the principal's office.

After her fingerprints had been taken, Liz turned to Agent Pearson and asked if she could go up to the Worths' suite and collect Regina's cat collar and crate, along with any food or toys for the feline.

"I thought I made it clear to your father that no one is allowed in the Worths' suite until I say so," said Agent Pearson. "I'll send Officer Martinez when he's done."

"Oh, and there's one more thing. Did anyone tell you that someone threw a brick at the Worths' car yesterday? Supposedly there was a note attached."

"No," she said. "Do you know what happened to the note?"

"Pierre, our chef, told me that Iris Kimball might know. She saw David Worth come into the hotel with the rock sometime in the afternoon."

"I sure wish we knew where that woman was. If you see your father, please tell him I must cancel tonight and that I'll explain later."

"Will do. Dad said that you know David Worth plans on staying here for a few days, until he can get his affairs in order. You're okay with that?"

"Yes. But I told your father, Mr. Worth isn't allowed to go into their suite without a police escort."

"Understood. I'll also tell Aunt Amelia. Are you allowed to share how Regina was strangled?"

"No, I'm not allowed to tell you, and I hope your father knows better than to give out any information in an ongoing murder investigation."

"Um, yes. I'm sure he knows that."

Agent Pearson changed her tactics and attempted a smile before continuing, "I am aware of how disliked Mrs. Harrington-Worth was in this area because of the proposed demolition of her family's mansion. Do you know of anyone else who might have wished her harm?"

"I thought she was killed because of a robbery? I do know about the shoddy way she treated people, including her husband. And about all the rumors." Liz didn't like to talk ill of the dead, but if anyone could conjure up a dozen enemies, Regina would have been the one.

Agent Pearson looked up from the papers in front of her. It was the first time since Liz had walked into the library that she'd looked directly at her. "What rumors?"

"That she'd killed her father." Liz regretted what she said as soon as it came out of her mouth. Hadn't she been crucified in the press herself because of rumors and false innuendos?

"I know Mrs. Worth didn't like you. She accused you of stealing her necklace, right?"

"Um, yes. But her husband found it, remember?" Charlotte wasn't going where Liz thought she was, was she?

"Why were you in the Worths' suite? You're a writer, aren't you?"

So, the detective knew all about Liz's past. "I cleaned their suite to help my eighty-year-old great-aunt, because Iris, the housekeeper, was missing, per usual. I hope you're not suggesting I killed Regina for a necklace and earrings? I think if you look in my financial records, you'll see I don't lack for money."

"The jewels she was wearing were very rare and valuable. I'll be looking into everyone connected to the hotel and shops. Can you send in Ryan Stone?" Then she hesitated a few seconds before adding, "Please?"

Liz left the library and stepped into the corridor. Ryan was there alone, intently typing a text to someone on his phone. It was possible he had a girlfriend back in New York. Hell, maybe even a wife. Though he didn't wear a ring, and she thought Aunt Amelia or Pops would have mentioned that by now.

"Your turn, Snoopy Pants."

He laughed as he passed her. "That all you could come up with, Bossy Pants?"

At least he hadn't called her "princess."

Chapter 21

It was time for Liz to do some snoopy-pantsing of her own. She went to the housekeeper's closet and took the ring of room keys off the hook. On her way to the service elevator, she noticed that the dumbwaiter that stood next to the ice machine wasn't completely pulled shut. Liz had been warned as a child, first by her father, then Aunt Amelia, to stay away from the dumbwaiter and keep her games of hide-and-seek with Pierre confined to the lobby, dining room, or kitchen. She would tell her father about the dumbwaiter at the same time she told her father about his buddy Charlotte's aspersions regarding Liz and the missing necklace and earrings. She'd also tell her father that his date for the evening had been canceled.

As Liz took the service elevator up to the second floor, the key ring jangled in her hands. She was never one to slow down at an accident, and she felt relief when she passed the door to the Worths' suite and saw that it was closed, crime scene tape crisscrossing the door frame. She headed to the other end of the hallway and used the key to open Iris's suite.

Iris's rooms appeared the same as she'd seen them yesterday, untouched with personal effects. Liz went to the housekeeper's closet and found white long-sleeved collared shirts, pressed below-the-knee khaki shorts, khaki pants, a rain slicker, a windbreaker, one black dress, one pair of low black sandals, and four pairs of white sneakers with thick rippled soles. The woman's wardrobe would fit in an airplane's carry-on, befitting of her no-frills personality. Liz was about to give up on finding anything in the closet, when she spied a green beach towel in the back right corner. She pulled it out and opened it. Inside was a black scuba-diver suit, flippers, and a mask. Not unusual for anyone living on a barrier island. The towel was damp and smelled of the briny ocean. Next to the towel was a duffel bag. Liz looked inside. Captain Netherton's missing chart of the water depths surrounding the barrier island lay on top. She zipped up the duffel and backed out of the closet.

Liz rummaged through Iris's desk and dresser drawers and didn't find anything. Not one clue to where she'd gone. She'd saved under the bed for last. There was only one small shoe box there that she had to crawl halfway under the bed to retrieve. There weren't any dust bunnies or cobwebs. Liz had to give Iris credit, she was a meticulous housecleaner. She grabbed the box, then sat on the floor with her back to the bed and opened it. Inside were birthday cards addressed to Iris at a military APO address in California. Liz had been right that Iris had served in the military. Each envelope had the same Cocoa Beach return address. Liz opened the first five cards, all signed Love, Mom, with a hand-drawn heart. Liz returned the cards to their envelopes, but stuffed one of the envelopes in her pocket and put the box back under the bed just in time to hear, "What the hell are you doing in my rooms!"

Iris had returned.

"I was searching under your bed for Venus. You know, the bald cat."

"Why would it be in my rooms?"

Iris stepped into the room and looked around. Liz quickly passed her, went through the open doorway, and stepped out into the hall. "You're right, she's not here. I thought with all the commotion last night that she might have snuck in when you were packing to leave the hotel. Did you find a good place to stay?"

"Yes." Iris placed her suitcase on the bed.

"Nearby?"

The housekeeper didn't answer.

"I'd better check Betty's room. Oh, by the way, you missed the fingerprinting session in the library. Agent Pearson was looking for you."

Color seeped into Iris's pale face. "Well, I'm here now."

"You can check the library and see if she's still there. Agent Pearson also wanted me to ask you about the rock with the note tied around it that David Worth showed you yesterday afternoon. She wanted to know what the note said."

"I don't know. He mumbled something about it saying, 'You better leave things as they are or else'."

"Do you know what he did with the note?"

"He handed me the rock, which I threw in the bushes, then he tossed the note in the trash."

"In the lobby?"

"Yes."

"Thanks. I'll tell the homicide detective." Liz said the word "homicide," louder than the rest of the sentence, trying to gauge Iris's reaction. Iris remained stone-faced. Liz said, "I'm really sorry you're the one who found Regina Harrington-Worth dead. It must have been a shock. Especially when you saw that thing wrapped around her neck."

"It was a shock. The Ace bandage was wrapped so tightly, she didn't have a chance."

"Good thing Captain Netherton was with you."

"I guess."

"David Worth is coming home from the hospital today and staying here, although he can't stay in his old suite—for obvious reasons. I would check with Aunt Amelia and see which suite needs to be cleaned and aired out for him. I'll touch base with you later."

Liz turned and walked toward Betty's suite, thinking about the strange murder weapon. If, as Agent Pearson postulated, someone related to the Indialantic had murdered Regina and stabbed David, then Liz would keep Iris near the top of her suspect list. The woman was sketchy and always disappearing.

She made a mental note to try to corral Captain Netherton, recalling the absence of both his cane and limp last night and the fact that he'd called Regina by her first name. Though Liz had a hard time pegging the charming sea captain as a killer—after all, he was the distinguished Captain Daniel Gregg from television's *The Ghost and Mrs. Muir*.

Iris was another story.

Chapter 22

Before reaching Betty's suite, Liz saw Officer Hernandez, whom she'd seen earlier in the library, coming out of the Worths' suite. In his arms were a large pet carrier, a small pet carrier, and a leopard-print diaper bag bursting with cat paraphernalia.

Liz wondered if she would ever think of the Oceana Suite as anything other than where Regina had been murdered. When the police were done with the suite, Liz would call in Kate and the crew from Home Arts by the Sea to redecorate it.

She waved at the officer. "I'll take those."

They met halfway at the iron railing overlooking the lobby and made the transfer.

"Thanks. This will be one happy cat." Then, Liz thought, how happy could Venus be after her human had been murdered? Sadness enveloped Liz. She felt a little coldhearted that she hadn't taken a moment to mourn Regina's death. They weren't friends—far from it—but she'd never wished the woman dead.

Liz continued to Betty's and turned the knob to her door. It was locked. Usually, she left it open 24/7, which confirmed that Betty had been frightened last night. Who wouldn't be? She knocked, and Betty came to the door dressed in jean capris, a white button-down blouse that came below her knee, and a pair of red ballet flats—very Audrey Hepburn. Betty's hair was a silver-white that she wore in a French twist. Betty didn't dress like a grandma, even though she was one.

Betty took the small carrier out of Liz's left hand. "What do you have here? Carolyn Keene has enough toys for a dozen cats—the captain keeps buying them for her. Whenever he buys one for Killer, he makes sure

Caro isn't left out. Plus, Kitty Keene prefers more classic playthings and bedding. She's not into bling."

Liz laughed. "These are Venus's things. I asked Agent Pearson if I could have them. Venus is staying at the beach house for now. Although David Worth is coming back to the hotel sometime today." Liz stepped inside and dropped the carriers and the kitty diaper bag onto the floor.

"He's coming here? Why in the world would he do that?"

"Dad said he needs time to decide where to go and make arrangements, etc. You're right, I wouldn't want to stay where my wife was murdered and I'd been stabbed. Oh, Betty, it's starting to hit me. I think I've been in shock."

"I'll make some tea. You'll feel better in no time." Tea: the magic elixir of the Indialantic by the Sea Hotel.

Liz picked up the leopard-print cat bag and started rifling through it. "Damn. It's not here."

"What's not there?"

"When I cleaned the Worths' suite on Friday, Venus was wearing a pink collar, with what I swore were real diamonds. I wonder if the killer took it?"

"Have a seat," Betty said, as she moved toward the kitchenette.

Liz sat on the sofa. A few minutes later, Betty brought over a silver tray laden with a teapot and all the accoutrements, including a few of Pierre's orange scones. Liz filled Betty in on everything that had happened since she'd seen her the previous night.

"Are you sure Captain Netherton didn't have his cane, or a limp? Everything was so crazy last night, I didn't notice."

"I'm sure. I mean, I'm pretty sure." She looked into Betty's pale gray eyes. Maybe Liz had been mistaken?

"Well, we have three things to go on: One, Agent Pearson thinks someone related to the Indialantic is our culprit."

"Yeah. She suspects me."

"Nonsense. Two, we need to research the return address on those birthday cards from Iris's mother, and find out where she keeps disappearing to."

"And three," Liz said, "we need to go down to the lobby and fish out the note that was attached to the stone that someone threw at the Worths' car."

They both shot up and headed to the door. Betty peeked out to make sure the coast was clear, and Liz followed her to the center of the hallway, to the railing that overlooked the lobby. Betty peered over, waved Liz on, and they crept down the stairs.

There were two trash cans in the lobby, one by the doors leading outside and one behind the registration desk. A safe bet would be the trash can by the doors. Liz moved toward it. Betty zipped ahead and beat her there. Betty took off the top of the trash can and stuck her arm and head inside. "Voilà! I think I see it. But we need to preserve any fingerprints." Spoken in true Nancy Drew style.

Liz stepped behind the desk, grabbed a box of tissues and a manila envelope, and brought them over to Betty. Betty plucked out a tissue from the box, making sure her hand only touched one side, then reached into the can and grabbed a crumpled piece of paper, while Liz held open the envelope.

Betty dropped the paper inside, then said, "Let's go to the kitchen and get some gloves. We need to photograph the note before we turn it over to the police. Do you have your phone?"

Liz answered. "It's in the butler's pantry, in my handbag."

"Good."

They walked through the dining room and into the empty kitchen. Betty laid the envelope on the wood farm table. Liz went to the pantry and retrieved her phone and a pair of gloves from the box Pierre used when preparing meals using hot peppers.

Back at the table, Liz put on the gloves and reached in the envelope. She laid the note on a clean section of paper toweling, then carefully smoothed it out. In handwritten blue ink, it read: Abandon your plans or else. This is your last warning.

"Quick, take a picture."

Betty picked up Liz's phone and took a burst shot of the note. The camera on the phone *click, click, click*ed away.

She put the note back in the envelope and said to Betty, "I'm not giving it to Agent Pearson. You can."

"Not giving what, Ms. Holt?"

Oops.

Agent Pearson walked in, holding a teacup and saucer.

Betty said, "We were about to give you the note that had been tied to the rock thrown at the Worths' windshield. I fished it out of the trash and made sure not to leave any prints. You might want to check outside the lobby door for the rock."

"Thanks for saving that task for the professionals. You need to keep out of my investigation." She directed her stare at Liz, not Betty.

Betty grabbed Liz's elbow. "Come on, dear, let's go find your auntie. I'm sure the nice detective will thank us later." Betty handed the envelope over to Agent Pearson, who stood with her mouth open. Liz admitted, Betty made a pretty impressive figure for an eighty-three-year-old. She wouldn't want to be on Betty's bad side, and luckily she never had been in the past.

They left the detective in the kitchen, then went through the doorway leading to the hallway with the service elevator. As they passed the ice machine, Liz told Betty how the night before, there had been water on the floor near the ice machine. "I don't know if it means anything? But it might prove what David said about getting ice for his wife's knee."

As they entered the elevator, Betty said, "We need to write everything down and pretend this is the outline for your next book. I know how much you love to research. I'm going to give you a few projects that will get the ball rolling. Like your Agent Pearson, I have a feeling that whoever killed Regina might be right under our noses."

"She's not *my* agent Pearson, she's Dad's."

Betty gave her a knowing look. Was it that obvious that Liz was concerned about how the detective's relationship with her father might alter their father-daughter bond?

Liz said, "But we were all together last night when the murder took place…"

"Exactly. But who wasn't with us?"

"Iris Kimball, Captain Netherton, Minna Presley, Francie Jenkins, Brittany Poole, and Edward and Nick Goren. However, it might just be a random incident."

"Indeed, it might," Betty said. "But it can't hurt to find out a little more. You've already got a good lead on Iris. Follow it through, and I'll do what I can on my iPad."

Liz and Betty performed the secret handshake they'd used since Liz was eight, which included complicated hand movements and real spit. For a moment, Liz was back in time, then the adult Liz surfaced and she realized this wasn't a game. She planned to protect those she loved, and if that meant putting her own self in danger, she would do it.

Chapter 23

"Road trip! Yay!" cried Kate. "I never get to catch all the good garage sales on Sundays. I'm always at the shop." She took a bite of her English muffin pizza and said, "Delish, Aunt Amelia!"

Liz begged to differ, but said, "Yum," anyway. Her great-aunt had been let loose in Liz's kitchen. Aunt Amelia had ignored all the gourmet lunch choices in the fridge, including Pops's homemade pâtè de champagne— country-style pâtè. Not that Liz didn't live on English muffin pizza when she was in college, but even then, she'd sprinkled Italian seasoning on her tomato paste and used fresh mozzarella cheese. Her great-aunt's heavy-handed choice of curry powder and blue cheese didn't scream "pizza"; it screamed Pepto-Bismol.

Aunt Amelia clapped her hands. "Road trip! Let's hit the trail. I call shotgun!"

Now Kate had done it. Per Betty's assignment, Liz planned to head to Cocoa Beach with Kate and check out Iris's mother's return address on the envelope she'd stolen from under Iris's bed. The envelope was safely tucked inside her handbag. But Liz didn't want Aunt Amelia to know she was looking into Regina Harrington-Worth's murder, or questioning her great-aunt's choice of a housekeeper.

Liz said to Aunt Amelia, "I thought you had to wait for David Worth to come back from the hospital?"

"Oh, didn't I tell you? They're keeping him for one more night, which is a good thing, because the Windward Shores Suite hasn't been used in decades, and Iris has a full day ahead of her."

A half hour later, everyone was loaded into Kate's aqua-colored van, which was probably built in the same decade when Aunt Amelia had starred in *Dark Shadows*. Kate loved it because it had lots of room in the back for her bike, surfboard, books, and the precious junk she rescued to go into her shop. When Kate dragged Liz to estate sales or antique shops, the hippie van perfectly fit the bill. Liz was always the designated map navigator, because Kate was one of those people who had no sense of direction. In Kate's case, she seemed to enjoy getting lost. Everything was an adventure.

After Kate's big announcement about their plans, Liz had texted her to keep quiet about their covert assignment involving Iris, saying their cover story would be that they were going to a potential client of Kate's who was looking for a rare book. Aunt Amelia had been given a new cell phone for Christmas from her nephew, but she never used it except to call Liz, Fenton, or Betty. Unlike Betty, she didn't grasp the "smart" part of a smartphone. Betty had tried to teach her a million times, to no avail. When things settled down, Liz had a great idea to motivate Aunt Amelia to use the Internet on her phone. She would download the YouTube app and let her search for clips from her past roles in TV Land.

They took the scenic route via A1A to the northern tip of the barrier island, turned left at Patrick Air Force Base, and headed west. Silhouetted against a startling blue ocean sky was the barrier island's black-and-white Cape Canaveral Lighthouse, its working light having been a beacon to sailors for a hundred and fifty years. Once over the Indian River Lagoon, they turned right onto Highway 1.

Halfway to Cocoa Beach, Kate stopped at their first garage sale. Liz realized they needed a book as a decoy for their covert mission. While Kate was filling the back of her van with boxes of UFOs, unidentified found objects, and Aunt Amelia was looking through a stack of old movie-star magazines, Liz spied a vintage Dick and Jane children's book that she quickly paid for. She stuffed the book in the front waistband of her long, gauzy cotton skirt and untucked her blouse to cover it. At the thought of the word "gauze," Liz was reminded of the Ace bandage used to strangle Regina, a strange weapon to use when you were already carrying a knife. As Liz pondered these dark thoughts, a single cloud in the bright blue sky smothered the sun.

Two yard sales later, they entered historic Cocoa Village. Quaint Main Street was lined with palm trees and awninged storefronts. There were all of the typical shops found in most small Florida towns built in the late 1800s, including a quilt and fabric shop that Liz knew Francie frequented. Could Francie really be considered a murder suspect? Liz couldn't picture Francie strangling Regina and then stealing the necklace and earrings as subterfuge to stop the demolition of Castlemara. Francie had been upset at the plans for tearing down the mansion, but upset enough to kill?

As they passed I Dream of Jeannie Lane, Aunt Amelia said, "I can picture astronaut Tony Nelson walking down Main Street looking for his mischievous genie. Did I ever tell you about when I was—"

Kate interrupted. "Yes. Great episode of *I Dream of Jeannie*. When onlookers think Tony pushed Jeannie overboard, but really she'd blinked her way back to her bottle in Cocoa Beach."

"I played Young Woman Number One. All I said was, 'Look!' and then pointed."

Kate added, "And you did it perfectly, in your bubble gum–pink lipstick and platinum-blond hair."

"A wig, of course. I think I still have it somewhere."

Liz laughed. "It's probably in my trunk of dress-up clothes in the hotel's luggage room."

At the end of Main Street, Kate turned left. The map server on Kate's phone directed them to the return address on the envelope Liz had pilfered from Iris's bedroom. They turned onto a small shaded street on the water side of town. The phone broadcasted, "You have arrived," as Kate pulled into a gravel drive.

Liz said, "Don't forget the reason you're here." She handed Kate the Dick and Jane book titled *Guess Who*, the irony of which wasn't lost on Liz.

Kate looked down at the book. "Wow! This is a classic. Worth at least sixty bucks."

"Kate, you act like you've never seen it before?" Aunt Amelia said.

"You know Kate and her books, Auntie," Liz said. "She hates to give them up."

Aunt Amelia took the book from Kate's hand and said, "I remember Fenton reading Dick and Jane books in elementary school, but the ones he read had the word 'New' next to the title. I hope the woman buys it. I feel bad we had to close the emporium shops today and you're losing out on sales. If she doesn't buy it from you, I will."

"Don't worry, Aunt Amelia," Kate said. "If she doesn't purchase it, I'll find the perfect home—it's what I live for. Plus, if the shops weren't closed, I wouldn't have gotten those two boxes of treasure I rescued at that first yard sale, or the sailboat weather vane from the second sale."

The musty odor from Kate's treasure boxes filled the back of the van. A few minutes earlier they'd set off a series of sneezes from Liz that almost caused the van's windows to explode. Kate's prized sailboat weather vane was missing its east-west indicator—not much help during one of the barrier island's frequent gales.

Aunt Amelia handed over the book. Kate left the engine running, got out, and scurried up the chipped and potholed walkway toward the small brick house. The yard was overgrown with the typical, spiky Florida grass that caused you to yelp if you walked barefoot on it. That was one thing Liz missed about Manhattan. Central Park in the summer, lying on a blanket with a book or your boyfr—She let the image fade.

Liz watched as Kate peered into the front picture window. The blinds were closed, but there were gaps where numerous slats were missing. Kate rang the doorbell. After a few minutes, she banged on the door. Then she looked back at the van and shrugged her shoulders.

"Kate might need help," Liz said. "Stay here, I'll be right back."

Aunt Amelia didn't hear her—she was too busy reading an article from one of the vintage magazines she'd bought at the second garage sale entitled, *Tattletales from Television.*

When Liz caught up with Kate, she said, "I'll go check the back. You look in the windows to see whether there's furniture and maybe grab some mail from the mailbox. On second thought, you'd better not. Stealing mail is a felony." She knew better—she'd just dared Kate.

"It's only a crime if you steal mail, not take a picture of it and place it back." She opened the mailbox and clicked her tongue. "Doesn't matter. There's only a coupon flyer for Space Coast Pizza addressed to 'Current Resident'."

"Darn," Liz said. "I have to report back to Detective Betty. Failure is not an option."

"Excuse me, young ladies, can I help you?" A man came toward them from the house next door, brandishing a hand rake. His yard looked like the Garden of Eden compared to the unkempt property on which they were now standing.

They walked toward him.

"We're looking for Greta Kimball or her daughter, Iris," Liz said. "Will they be home soon?"

He chivalrously took off his Atlanta Braves baseball cap and looked them over. "You're not selling anything, are you? We don't allow door-to-door salesmen or saleswomen around here."

"We aren't selling anything," Kate said. "We've lost touch with the Kimballs. We're down here on vacay and wanted to look them up for old times' sake."

Liz quickly waved the envelope in front of him. "We got a Christmas card last year and we wanted to stop by and catch up." She strategically placed her hand over Iris's name.

The man ran the fingers of his free hand through his thick mane of white hair, making furrows ready to seed.

"I love your sausages," Kate said.

Liz whipped her head around to face Kate, then she followed Kate's gaze, which was aimed at the man's front yard. Sure enough, there was a tree sprouting two-foot-long sausages.

He said, "Ain't she a beaut! *Kigelia Africana.* Saw one in the Africa section at Walt Disney World's Animal Kingdom and discovered that our local nursery sells them. Two years later, I have sausages up the kazoo. The sausages are the fruit. Have you ever seen the flowers up close?"

"No," Kate said. "I'd love to see them. Come on, Liz, let's go check out his sausage…" Liz held her breath. After a two-second pause, Kate finished her sentence, "…tree."

They walked into the yard and saw, among the sausages, bell-shaped magenta flowers that, instead of hanging vertically, hung horizontally. After Liz and Kate oohed and aahed, the man smiled, and the gates opened to any misgivings he had about sharing the whereabouts of whom he called "poor Greta Kimball."

After getting everything they needed and more from Pete Foster, former semipro golfer and wicked shrimp-boil maker, they got back in the van. Aunt Amelia was engrossed in another vintage movie-star magazine. Liz leaned forward from the back seat and saw a full-page head shot of the actress Anne Francis, with a caption, "Private Detective—Honey West."

Kate looked over at the open pages. "I have a pulp fiction copy of the first Honey West book, *This Girl for Hire,* by G.G. Fickling. Honey West was one of the first female private eyes in fiction. G.G. Fickling was a pseudonym for a husband-wife writing team. The wife was a fashion editor for *Look* magazine and *Women's Wear Daily,* and the husband a former U.S. Marine. Aunt Amelia, I'll give you my copy of the book, if you want it?"

"Oh, sweetie, I appreciate it, but I'm more of a visual person, always have been. I love watching faces and gestures—a window to the soul, I always say."

Liz couldn't help but ask, "What kind of soul did Regina Harrington-Worth have?"

"We aren't our outward appearances, Liz. You know that better than most. For all we know, Mrs. Worth could have been a scared and lonely child, hiding behind a façade of anger and entitlement."

Liz didn't think so, but she let her great-aunt believe what she wished. "Then I wonder what the soul of the person who killed her looked like?"

They all remained quiet after Liz's comment.

Chapter 24

When they were about twenty miles from the Indialantic, Liz called out, "Wait. Kate, stop the car! I need to visit someone at the Sundowner. An old friend from school works there, and I promised to give her my new contact number."

Kate pulled the van into the parking lot.

"Don't tell me someone you know works in this joke of a 'retirement home'," Aunt Amelia said. "Millicent was here until I rescued her and made her move into the caretaker's cottage. I supposed it could have changed from when she was a resident, but from the looks of the outside, I doubt it. I'll never forget the horrible smell when I first came to visit her. At the end of my days, I'd rather walk out into the ocean than stay at a place like that."

"Auntie, Dad and I would never put you anywhere but right by our side."

"Some people don't have a choice, if it's all that their retirement benefits will pay for. Tell your friend, I can give her the name of a wonderful place to work, right on our island."

"Will do," Liz said. "Be right back."

Liz got out of the van, avoiding the potholes on the blacktop as she made her way up the driveway. She walked into the dingy lobby and was immediately hit with an awful odor. It was so bad she put her nose to her sleeve to inhale the scent of fabric softener on her blouse. In a small TV room to her right, four elderly people sat in wheelchairs. Each wheelchair was positioned to match the four directions of a compass. North, South, East, and West were slumped over, chins on chest, not cognizant of the television or anything else going on around them. Liz thought it was a sad state of affairs to be reduced to living in these conditions after a life of vibrancy and autonomy.

Security was pretty lax at the Sundowner. Liz wasn't asked for ID or whether or not she was a family member. They probably wondered who would want to steal one of the residents anyway? But Liz knew someone who would love to—Aunt Amelia.

The sleepy-eyed woman at the registration desk told Liz that, indeed, Greta Kimball was a guest at the Sundowner. Then she pointed at the person in the wheelchair Liz had designated as North. Liz walked up to Iris's mother. When Liz put her hand on Greta's soft, wrinkled hand, her head shot up and her eyes opened wide. Greta didn't have the filmy, highly medicated gaze Liz would have thought; instead her hazel eyes were sharp and alert. Her long white hair looked unwashed. Her face had few wrinkles; with a good haircut she would be an attractive woman.

"Yes? Can I help you?" Greta said. "If you are trying to get me to take a sedative, I told you I refuse. If you have a pill for the pain in my hip, I will also tell you nay. If you need to talk to my daughter, Iris, I will give you her number. She's my designated advocate. So there!"

"Oh, I am sorry. I have the wrong patient."

Greta Kimball replied, "We are not *patients*, we are *residents*. As soon as my daughter gets enough money for my operation, I'm out of this dump."

"Again. I apologize."

"Let me give you some advice. Lean down."

Liz crouched next to her.

"Whatever resident you are here to see, get them out as soon as possible. This place stinks. The food is the best of it, if that tells you anything."

"Thanks for the advice," Liz said as she stood up. "I hope your daughter comes through for you real soon."

Greta smiled and gave Liz a thumbs-up, hope shining bright in her eyes.

Liz hurried out of the Sundowner.

When she got back in the van, Aunt Amelia asked, "How was it?"

"Just as you said."

"Did you tell your friend what I said about finding another place to work?"

Liz didn't want to lie, so she said, "My friend wasn't there."

"Good. Maybe she found a better place of employment."

Traffic was light on the way back to Melbourne Beach, people hunkering down for the forecasted storm scheduled to hit after midnight. Kate dropped Aunt Amelia at the Indialantic and Liz at the beach house. Liz made a quick dinner of sautéed shrimp in mango chutney and a green salad, then went to her office and turned on her laptop. It was only the second time since she'd been home that she'd turned it on. The first was to type out the synopsis her publisher had requested for her supposed next novel. Once she'd pushed the button and sent the synopsis off into cyberspace, she'd never thought of it again. She started a new document with the simple headline of Notes, filling the page with everything she'd learned from Ryan yesterday and ending with what she'd discovered today. Liz printed it out, stuck it in her pocket, and took off for the hotel, wanting to fill Betty in on the day's events.

A few minutes later, Liz was sitting on Betty's sofa, holding a cup of chamomile tea.

"We can't rule out Iris completely," Betty said. "She does need money for her mother's operation. However, I would put her at the end of the list because, as she has been telling Amelia, she does have an ailing mother. I did a little research on my own, let my fingers do the walking. Iris was honorably discharged from the navy ten years ago. She'd been a navy diving specialist, which explains the wet suit."

"And the water depth chart Iris took from Captain Netherton's room. It still points to her as being a thief, though."

"Perhaps. But not a murderer. Time for assignment number two. Namely, David Worth."

"How could David be his wife's killer? Are you saying he stabbed himself?"

"Crimes of passion by family members are one of the top reasons for homicides. And many people have been known to stab or shoot themselves as a way of creating an alibi. You will have to wait to hear from the police—they'll be able to tell whether it was self-inflicted."

"Let's hope Agent Pearson shares things with Dad. I don't think she and I will be getting any girl-bonding mani-pedis in the near future."

"If that's the case, you might want to bring Ryan Stone into the loop. He most likely has ties to the NYPD and their databases."

"Ick."

"Is that a good 'ick,' or a bad 'ick'?" Betty asked.

Liz wasn't sure.

Chapter 25

Monday dawned dark and brooding, reminiscent of Ryan's face the previous evening when Liz had spotted him coming out of the caretaker's cottage. He either didn't see Liz, Aunt Amelia, and Killer, or he pretended not to. He walked with his head down, toward the emporium's parking lot.

Liz had awakened at 6 a.m. from a restless night with Killer snoring next to her on the "man side" of her bed. The ever-gallant Captain Netherton had loaned the Great Dane to Liz and Aunt Amelia for the purpose of protection. The idea of Killer as a guard dog was humorous; he rarely barked and the only way he could stop someone from breaking into the beach house would be to lick them to death.

One of the reasons for Liz's restless night had to do with the eerie *Twilight Zone* episode Aunt Amelia had picked for them to watch, "Jess-Belle." Her great-aunt chose it because it starred Anne Francis in a part completely opposite her glamourous Honey West role. In the episode, a poor mountain girl had a local witch put a curse on the rich girl who was dating the man whom Jess-Belle was obsessed with. Things didn't turn out well, which was not unusual in the *Twilight Zone*.

As they were watching, Aunt Amelia had remarked that Anne Francis's and Tina Louise's moles made them look so distinctive. "Liz Taylor had one, too, but it was farther back on her jawline. Moles, or 'beauty marks,' were all the rage back then, kind of like puffy lips are today. Maybe I'll add one for my next performance at the Melbourne Civic Theatre. I'm going to try for the part of Cat in *Cat on a Hot Tin Roof*." Aunt Amelia never got the ingénue parts anymore, but that didn't stop her from trying. Whatever part she won, she always made it distinctively her own, and usually to much applause from the audience. Aunt Amelia had fallen asleep five minutes into "Jess-Belle." If she'd had a cameo in the episode, she would have stayed awake until the credits rolled. When Liz was young, she never got scared from any part her great-aunt played, no matter how gory. She knew it was all make-believe. Now, as an adult, she took stock in the adage: True life is stranger than fiction.

At eight, Aunt Amelia left to have breakfast at the Indialantic; then she was going to the emporium to open the main doors, praying there would still be customers after the news of Regina's death.

Liz sat in a chair next to the French doors, looking out at layers of gray: sand, ocean, and sky. Every morning, except in foul weather like today, Liz followed the same routine. She would take her mug of coffee, sit on the bottom step leading to the beach, and thank the universe for another day of living in paradise, then plan the day's activities while staring out at the fathomless sea. Today's weather would be considered most foul: The surf was high, along with the tide. Tornado and gale warnings had been issued for Brevard County. Luckily, no hurricanes were on the horizon this time of year, but the rain came from all directions, bringing with it grains of sand that sounded against the panes of glass like pellets shot from a BB gun. The wind chimes hanging outside the kitchen window clanged against each other in an earsplitting cacophony.

She took a last gulp of coffee and viewed a lone figure walking the beach. She stood and reached for the binoculars she used for spotting rare seabirds, a perk to having America's first wildlife sanctuary, the Pelican Island National Wildlife Refuge, nearby. When Liz looked through the lens, though, she didn't see a rare bird, just a drenched Ryan Stone. For a split second, he lifted his head. He wore the same pained expression she'd witnessed the previous night—as if he'd lost his best friend. *Please don't let it be Pops*, she thought.

It was strange that he would pick this stretch of shoreline for a melancholy stroll in a storm. Liz had one of Aunt Amelia's urges to rescue him. She put on her rain slicker and waited until he was near the steps leading up to the beach house, then went out into the deluge.

She called down, "Ahoy there!"

Ryan didn't hear her over the howling of the wind. She grabbed the wood railing and went down three steps. When he finally glanced in her direction, she pantomimed for him to come up to the house.

He trudged up the steps and followed Liz onto the deck. Liz removed her raincoat and left it on the chaise. Ryan left his sandals outside the door as she ushered him inside.

"I'll go get you a towel," Liz said. "Wait here."

When she returned, she handed him a large bath towel.

"Thanks." He stood there, dripping like a wet seal.

"Take off your shirt and shorts. I'll throw them in the dryer. Despite what you've read about me, I won't take advantage of you."

Ryan remained still, not even offering a comeback. He took off his shirt, wrapped the towel around his waist, then discreetly slipped off his NYU-emblemed shorts.

Her gaze lingered on his muscled upper right arm. What she thought was a tattoo from when she'd seen him at the caretaker's cottage, turned out to be a purplish raised welt in the shape of a continent.

He noticed her looking and said in an irritated tone, "I know, it looks like Africa or Australia. And before you ask, it's not from a fire. Only a birthmark."

"Have a seat," Liz said. "I'll be right back."

She couldn't believe she'd done to him what others had done to her when focusing on her scar too long. It was just that his appearance was so perfect. Not that the birthmark was ugly, just unusual.

Liz threw Ryan's wet clothing in the dryer and returned to the great room. She said, "Is everything okay with Pops?"

He glanced up at her, a lock of wet hair falling across his right eye. "Granddad's fine."

"Then what's the reason for the glum posture? It's not about me, is it?"

"Not everything is about you, Elizabeth Holt." Then he quickly added, "I'm sorry." He stood and shuffled to the door.

"What about your clothes?"

"I have others."

As he reached for the doorknob, she put her hand on his. "It might help to talk. Even though you are a big jerk, we are still partners on Dad's case." His mouth made a slight upturn. "Sit. I'll get some coffee and actually bring it to you."

He laughed. "Make sure to check the expiration date on the milk."

When she brought back the mug of coffee, he was looking through a book of Florida wildlife on her coffee table trunk. The inscription inside was to an eighteen-year-old Liz from Kate's brother, Skylar, wishing her a lifetime of happiness in New York.

Ryan closed the book and took the coffee. Liz sat on the chair across from the sofa.

The wind and rain picked up, and all the windows were covered in an opaque film.

After a few sips, he put down the mug. "You make a mean cup of coffee, Ms. Holt. Not as good as mine, of course."

The joking Ryan was back. Liz had learned from therapy that it was good to talk things out, but once you did, to leave them in the past where they belonged. She said, "Okay, spill. What's up?"

"One of the guys in my company is on life support."

"Oh my God, from a fire?"

"No. That's the kicker. A car accident. We all know the risks when it comes to fighting a fire, but we forget about the danger of going to the grocery store for some Pampers."

"Is there a chance he might pull through?"

"Yes. There's a chance."

"Then hold on to that."

Liz thought about Betty's advice to bring Ryan into the loop about their inquiries into Regina's murder. It might be a good distraction.

She filled Ryan in about everything she and Betty had learned. After she told him about Captain Netherton's disappearing, then reappearing limp, she asked if he had anyone back home who could look into the captain's background.

"I can do that. I know some people, and I have access to certain databases I use when investigating an arson." Ryan seemed on board, even welcoming the extra assignment. "I think you and Betty should be careful, though. This isn't a game. This is murder. I'm not one hundred percent sure that someone here was involved in the murder, but it can't hurt to consider everyone who wasn't with us as a suspect. I'll do what I can. Do you have surveillance cameras at all the hotel exits?"

"No. Only outside the revolving door of the lobby. The dumbwaiter in the hall next to my father's apartment was slightly open the night of the murder. It would be the perfect way to exit the second floor with no one seeing you, then go out my father's office to the back of the hotel. The limo driver was out front and the other emergency exit doors would set off an alarm. The kitchen and Dad's office are the only doors that weren't set on the alarm. Whoever killed Regina could have exited through my father's apartment, knowing he was still at the emporium with the rest of us, then out through the office to the outside. And if that's the case, I would say that Regina's killer was someone who knew the hotel. There's also the unlocked door in the kitchen, but I would think that whoever killed Regina wouldn't take the chance of running into someone in the hotel's kitchen."

"Did you tell Agent Pearson about this?"

"No, but I mentioned it to my father. I'm sure he'll pass it on." She told him about the note Betty had pulled out of the trash that had been tied around the rock thrown at the Worths' Bentley. "We took a photo of the note before giving it to the detective. Betty is trying to match the handwriting to someone at the Indialantic." Then Liz filled Ryan in on the detective's aspersions against Liz.

"That's ridiculous. Why would you do such a thing? Plus, you have an alibi."

Liz liked the new, on-her-side Ryan much better than the Ryan she'd been dealing with, but she wouldn't let her guard down quite yet. Plus, he owed her a *big* apology for his past behavior. If he was any kind of investigator, he should search for the facts of what had really happened the night of the scar. Liz wasn't going to tell him; it would only be a case of "he said, she said."

Ryan took a sip of coffee. "One of the things I find strange is why David Worth would want to come back to the hotel after what happened. He definitely needs to be looked into. Do you know how long he'd been married to Mrs. Worth?"

"No, but Minna and Francie told me that following Regina's death, Castlemara would go to the Barrier Island Historical Society and the jewelry from her father's treasure dives to treasure museums. She wasn't allowed to sell a piece—only to wear them."

"A lot to figure out, that's for sure. I'd better get over to Deli-casies. I told Granddad to stay home because of the storm. I have to try to re-create a few of his salad recipes."

"I can come by and do a taste test for you."

"Sounds good. Kate said you're a gourmet cook. I think you'll find that I'm not too bad myself."

Liz smiled. "I was taught by the best. Pierre Montague."

"And I was taught by my grandparents, and my first chief at the fire station."

"We'll have a cook-off then. Best man or woman wins."

"You're on. I think it should take place here. The kitchen at the caretaker's cottage is lacking."

They both stood.

Liz's mind switched back to Regina's murder. "Wait, before you go, I want to give you something."

She left him and stepped into the hallway, then inside her office and printed out another copy of the notes she'd taken about the murder. When she walked back into the room, he was standing at the door, towel and all.

"Don't you want your clothes?"

"I'll get them later. I'm sure they're still wet. Or they will be again, once I step outside."

"Here are the notes I've taken so far," she said, then handed them over. He looked perplexed on where to stow them.

Liz laughed. "Let me get you a Ziploc bag."

She walked to the kitchen, got a bag, and brought it back.

Ryan folded the pages in half, put them inside the plastic bag, then sealed it. "Did I inspire you to write everything down?"

"No. Research is my forte. I had to do a lot of it for my novel."

"*Let the Wind Roar*," he said as he opened the French doors and reached down to pick up his sandals. "I just read it. Good book." Then he walked out, into the storm.

Chapter 26

After Ryan left, Liz phoned Betty and told her that he was on the case. Betty had placed a call to the makeup and hairstyle artists who had come to the Indialantic to get Regina ready for the Treasure Coast Ball, but hadn't learned anything helpful to their investigation. Liz had forgotten about them. She also told Liz that she'd compared the photo of the note tied to the rock against Iris's handwriting on the shopping list in the kitchen, and she didn't think they were written by the same person. At the end of the conversation, Betty asked if she could get copies of the canceled rent checks for the emporium shops. Another great idea. Liz had access to the Indialantic's online banking account.

Because of the weather, Liz decided to take Betty's baby-blue Caddy over to the emporium. She hadn't needed a car in Manhattan, and barely needed one now, but in this monsoon of a morning, walking and golf-carting were definitely out of the question. Driving the half mile to the emporium reminded Liz of being out to sea in her father's vintage forty-foot Chris-Craft motorboat, *Serendipity*, moored at the Indialantic's dock. Earlier, Liz had received a text from her father that said he would be out on a case until late afternoon. She'd texted back, *Good luck. Don't text and drive!*

Liz parked in the emporium's lot, noticing that the only cars there were Kate's hippie van and Minna's BMW. She decided against an umbrella; in this wind she might end up like Mary Poppins, floating into the air. She got out of the car and ran toward the emporium doors. Rogue palm fronds flew at her from every direction, scratching at her bare legs. She wrestled with one of the doors and finally tugged it open, then flew inside with the next big gust of wind and rain.

Kate was standing in the entryway, watering a potted palm. She helped Liz push the massive door closed. "Look what the cat dragged in," Kate said. "The cat!"

Liz looked down and Bronte rubbed against her ankle.

"You have a friend for life. When are you taking her home?"

"I thought she belonged to the emporium! Your only chance to have the kitten you've always wanted?"

"Well, if you took her to the beach house, I could visit. I'm afraid Brittany will do away with her, or at least leave a door open purposely so she gets out. That meanie found a single strand of Bronte's hair on her black pants and went ballistic."

"I thought you said Bronte hides all the time."

"She does. She loves lying on top of the books in my bookcases. If it wasn't for the white tip at the end of her tail, I don't think I'd ever find her. She never comes out when there are customers. However, who knows what she does at night when no one's around."

Liz took off her rain slicker and laid it on the bench under the window, then picked up Bronte. The kitten looked up and Liz almost melted onto the plank wood floor. "Stop being so adorable, Kitty." Liz could barely take care of herself, let alone a pet. "I'll think about it." She put Bronte down and the kitten scurried away, but not before turning back and giving Liz a green-eyed, soulful look.

The lights flickered and Liz held her breath until she remembered that, like the hotel, the emporium had an emergency generator installed by Aunt Amelia to protect Deli-casies by the Sea's perishable food.

Kate put the watering can on the floor and sat on the bench. "Come. Sit a spell. I want to know what happened when you talked to Iris's mother. We couldn't chat because of Aunt Amelia."

"Sorry, last night was crazy and so was this morning." Liz filled her in on Greta Kimball and told her about Ryan's morning visit.

Kate said, "There haven't been any customers. Only one person came in, the lucky winner of one of the raffles at Home Arts by the Sea. She was very inquisitive about Regina Harrington-Worth's murder. Francie didn't come in today. Minna said she's not feeling well. She's been in bed since Saturday night."

"Do you know what's wrong?"

"A stomach bug, Minna thinks."

The lights were on in Brittany's shop, but she wasn't inside. She had a new sign posted by the entrance: By Chance or Appointment.

Kate noticed Liz looking at the sign. "I know. Isn't it obnoxious? It doesn't look good if one shop is closed for business when the other three are open."

"I'm going to tattle to Aunt Amelia, although my sunny great-aunt has a hard time when it comes to business confrontations, especially with Brittany Poole."

All of a sudden, they heard Nick Goren's booming voice coming from the direction of Gold Coast by the Sea.

"Let's investigate," Kate said to Liz.

They tiptoed toward the voices, passing Minna in Home Arts and waving. The lights were on in Deli-casies by the Sea, but no one was up front. Liz assumed Ryan was back in the kitchen making salads.

Kate ushered Liz into her shop and they both crouched down by the half wall and listened.

"What right do you have to give your girlfriend of two minutes a piece of my estate jewelry? I want it back," Edward said in a very calm, but loud voice.

"You have tons of stuff. You won't miss one little bracelet," Nick said. "Come on, Brittany, let's get out of here. Once again, my father treats me like a second-class citizen. I quit. Find some other minion to work for you."

"I'll take the cost of that bracelet out of your wages."

"You have a showcase of jewelry. You're just jealous you don't have a love life."

Edward raised the decibel level. "I'm not giving you one thin red dime if you walk out. Your mother must be turning over in her grave."

They heard Brittany say, "Come on, pooh bear. You can stay with me until this all blows over."

"It won't," Nick said. "The damage has been done."

As they marched past Books & Browsery by the Sea, Liz poked her head up to get a look at the bracelet. It wasn't anything spectacular, and it didn't look like something belonging in a sunken treasure chest. As they walked away, she was almost positive that they were the two people she'd seen on the beach: the hulking, no-neck Nick and the diminutive Brittany.

When they heard the front door slam, Liz and Kate stood up.

"Should we go check on Edward?" Kate asked.

"Uh, no. Not a good idea. Let him cool off."

"What do you think of the idea that Nick and Brittany killed Regina for the necklace and earrings?"

"I certainly wouldn't take them off the list, that's for sure. Let's go over to Deli-casies. I'm curious about Ryan's cooking ability."

"Hey, missy. Do I feel a little wavering in your feelings for the guy?"

"No. He's still a jerk. But maybe not as big of a jerk as I thought before."

She grabbed Liz's hand and gave her a very serious, unlike-Kate look. "Don't you think if people knew everything that went down with you in New York, they might be more compassionate?"

"I don't want compassion. I can't change what the papers or Travis say about me. I still haven't told Aunt Amelia everything. She doesn't judge me."

"Okay. All I'm saying is, if you want any kind of a future relationship, then you have to give the guy a chance by telling him what really happened."

"He's from New York. I'm not going back there, so there's no chance for a relationship with him, anyway."

When they walked into Deli-casies, Ryan was at the coffee bar staring down at a piece of paper. Kate sat on his right, Liz on his left.

"Are you going to close up?" Kate asked. "There's only been one customer all day."

"No, I'll stick it out," Ryan said. "I was just looking over a recipe of my granddad's for conch salad. Where do you even buy conch?"

Liz took the recipe out of his hands. "It looks yummy. Conch usually comes from Key West, known as the 'Conch Republic'."

Ryan said, "Sorry, but I can't imagine eating conch. The rubbery insides of a giant seashell that you hold to your ear to hear ocean waves? But I guess at that point they've vacated their shells. What's the name for a group of conch? A school of conch?"

"A concert of conch," Liz said, laughing.

"Or like a murder of crows, a murder of conch," Kate added.

Ryan turned to Liz. "Speaking of murder, your great-aunt called. She asked me to come to dinner. Apparently, David Worth has just arrived and insists on eating dinner in the dining room. She wants me there as backup in case he faints or needs help because of his wound. Not that I'm a paramedic, but I've had some training."

Liz said, "I was going to eat at home, but I think I've changed my mind. I'll make something, and give Pierre the night off."

"Good, as long as it's not seashell innards," Ryan said.

Liz smiled. "Someday, I'll make you try some of my conch ceviche."

"Ugh," he said. "Raw conch!"

"I bet you've eaten the worm at the bottom of a bottle of tequila before," Kate said.

Ryan answered, "Yeah, in college, but that was on a fraternity dare."

Liz handed him back the recipe. "'Ceviche' means that the raw seafood is placed in a bowl and marinated in lime juice. The acid in the lime cooks it, so it's not actually raw."

The rain on the terra-cotta roof was relentless; the wind so fierce, it sounded like a Black Hawk from Patrick Air Force Base was trying to land on the emporium. Ryan got off the stool and said, "I better get back in the kitchen to put things away. There's no sense in making anything in this weather. If someone does come in, they can have their choice of anything except Granddad's salads. Kate, did you tell your friend about our other visitor, Agent Pearson?"

"She was looking for Francie," Kate said.

Liz was relieved the detective wasn't looking for her. "Ryan, before you go, I wanted to ask if you've ever talked to Edward or Nick at Gold Coast by the Sea? They might be more apt to share something with another guy."

"I've only been here since Thursday, but I'll try to strike up a bro-convo with them." He flexed his upper arms in an attempt to look manly. It worked. Then he looked down at Liz's feet. "Hey, you've got an admirer."

She thought for a minute he meant himself, then she heard a soft mewing. "Bronte!" Liz hopped off the bar stool and scooped her up. "What are you doing here? I thought you were shy? You want some conch? I'm sure Ryan has some to spare."

Ryan laughed.

Kate sneezed and tickled the kitten under her white chin. "That's it, Liz! You're adopting Bronte. Come by tomorrow to pick her up."

"Yes, ma'am." Liz held Bronte close to her chest and the kitten closed her eyes.

"Good. I'll catch you guys later. I have some new-old Hemingways to unpack and the perfect vintage safari helmet to place on top of them."

Liz glanced at Bronte. "Do you want to take her with you?"

"No, she'll find her way back to the stacks," Kate said, as she practically skipped out of Deli-casies. Liz felt lucky to have such a perennially upbeat best friend.

Ryan made sure Kate was out of sight before he said, "You know tiny kittens grow into big cats. They're not as cute then."

"You're not an animal lover?" Liz knew there was something off about him. Now she'd found it.

"I'm more of a dog person," he said, as he scratched behind Bronte's ear. The kitten didn't even wake up. "Cats are too standoffish. With a dog, you know where they're coming from, always happy to see you and ready for a good time."

For a dog lover, it sure looked like he'd fallen under Bronte's spell. His description of a dog reminded Liz of Kate. She had missed her friend when she lived in Manhattan, even though Kate came to visit every few months. Kate, who was the friendliest of people, hadn't liked Travis from the get-go. How had Liz been so blinded by Travis's fame, then her own?

Liz left Deli-casies and joined Minna at one of the burnished-aluminum tables in Home Arts by the Sea. Minna had her feet up and was reading the magazine *Vero Beach Living*.

"No customers?" Liz asked.

"Nope."

"I heard about Francie. I hope she'll be okay?"

"Oh, she'll be fine. I think she's just traumatized from Regina Harrington-Worth's murder. Francie thinks someone put a voodoo curse on the treasure from the *San Carlos* and Regina Harrington-Worth was collateral damage. She'll rally."

"We'll all rally when we catch the person who did it."

"Amen."

"How late did you and Francie stay on Saturday?"

"Francie left around six. I left around six thirty. Francie set us up with another of her blind dates that she found on a Melbourne-members-only dating site."

Liz felt relieved they both had an alibi.

Minna continued, "I told Francie I wouldn't go unless she checked the guys out before I got in the car and drove over there. I always take my own wheels when Francie sets me up on one of her blind dates. I've been burned too many times. I said I wouldn't succumb to one more of her attempts at online dating—she had one last shot at redemption."

"How did it go?"

"After I went home and changed, then got in the car at seven to go to the Sebastian Beach Inn, Francie texted me the date was off. She'd gotten there ahead of me and looked in the window of the restaurant to see two dorks sitting at the bar drinking Shirley Temples topped with paper umbrellas. She knew it would be a waste of an evening, so she took off."

"Saved by an umbrella," Liz said. "What did you do?"

"I went to François Farrant's opening, *Bruised Shells*, at the Sun Gallery in Vero Beach. And guess what? I met a guy!"

Liz clapped her hands.

"Francie says even though I met someone, I still owe her one more blind date. I think she needs the moral support. You and Kate could join us on the next one. An eightsome. We can invite Pops's grandson. At least that way we could play musical chairs and let any attraction come what may. Speaking of attractions, what are your thoughts on Ryan? He seems a bit moody, but gorgeous. He might be too young for me or Francie, but he's perfect for one of you. So, what do you think? You up for a quadruple double date?"

"Yes. Let me look at my calendar." Liz took out her phone from her front pocket and tapped the screen. "Oh good, I see an opening. The twelfth of...never."

Minna laughed. "Well, you can't say I didn't try. Misery loves company."

Liz got up and said, "I'd better get going."

Kate entered Home Arts, her formerly white T-shirt black with soot. "Guess what, Minna? We finally found a kitten to adopt Liz."

"Don't you mean that the other way around?" Minna asked.

"Not in this case," Kate said.

Chapter 27

Liz drove to the hotel and parked in the rear. Her father's car was missing, so she decided to take advantage of his absence and use his laptop for a little sleuthing. Before getting out of the car, Liz texted Betty that Minna had an alibi; Francie, not so much. Then Liz asked Betty to tell Pierre that she would be making dinner tonight and that David Worth and Ryan would be in attendance.

A lightning bolt stabbed the ground next to the gazebo, and thunder rattled the car windows. Liz bolted out of the car and fought her way to the door, worried she might get zapped, or have one of the many palm trees swaying near the ground, fall on her. For the first time in Liz's memory, her father's door was locked. She ran back to the car, got her keys from her handbag, and sprinted back. She opened the door and stepped inside, leaving her raincoat and shoes on the inside area rug, then she sat at the desk and fired up the laptop.

After typing in her mother's maiden name and birthdate, Liz clicked on the icon for Treasure Coast Security. She spent the next hour reviewing the footage from the camera outside the emporium, along with the camera outside the main entrance to the lobby on the evening of Regina's murder. If Agent Pearson was any kind of homicide detective, then Liz was sure she already had the Indialantic's camera footage from the security company. But Liz wanted to see for herself the comings and goings on that fateful day.

Liz was disappointed. The footage from the front of the emporium didn't show anything unusual. As Minna had said, Francie had left around six-ish and Minna at six thirty. Brittany and Nick left together at around six twenty. Edward must have been gone already, leaving Nick to close their shop, as was their usual routine; father and son must have called a truce.

At six forty-five, Josie had loaded the plants from inside the emporium into her flower truck, then drove away. Once Liz saw the footage of Agent Pearson walking into the emporium, she switched over to the footage from outside the hotel. Around six, she saw the hair and makeup team leave, carrying large suitcases and a canvas director's chair like what was used on movie sets. An hour later, a white limo pulled up. She then fast-forwarded to seven forty, when the first fire truck arrived, followed by a Brevard County Sheriff's car. The footage was grainy and in black and white, but she could picture everything in vivid color, including the inky mass staining the area beneath the right shoulder blade of David Worth's white tuxedo shirt as he was carried out, lying on his side. After the ambulance pulled away, one of the officers could be seen talking to the limo driver, then the limo pulled away. Ryan looked calm and in charge as he walked up to one of the first responders. And handsome.

As Liz went to turn off the laptop, she hesitated. She rewound the hotel feed to the beginning of the day on Saturday to see if any of the people on their suspect list might have entered the hotel; they could possibly have hidden in one of its many rooms. She saw herself leaving in the morning; Aunt Amelia, shortly after; followed by David Worth. David returned a half hour later. Liz guessed that was just after she'd seen him in the emporium at Gold Coast looking for the "trinket" to give to Regina to get him "out of the doghouse." In the early afternoon, she watched footage of David leaving the hotel again. A few minutes later, an obviously perturbed David returned. He marched into the hotel, holding something in his hand, most likely the rock with the note. The time stamp on the video said three forty-five. Captain Netherton left around ten in the morning and returned to the hotel around five fifteen. No one else had left or entered the hotel the rest of the day from the front entrance. She knew Betty and Pierre always used the kitchen exit. That meant the only way the killer could have come inside was by way of her father's office, through his apartment, and into the hallway with the dumbwaiter. It was unlikely that the killer would have used the exterior kitchen door, since Iris and Captain Netherton were eating dinner in the dining room and would have been in and out of the kitchen. She postulated that the killer would have entered between five and seven thirty, because her father had said he'd left his office at five to go to the emporium, leaving the door, as always, unlocked. Unfortunately, the only footage from the hotel camera was the one she'd viewed at the lobby entrance.

Liz powered down the laptop, collected her things, and went back out the door. She would have liked to have had lunch with Pierre, Betty, and

Aunt Amelia, but first she wanted to go home and print out the canceled rent checks from the emporium so she could give them to Betty at dinner— the same dinner Liz planned to prepare to also knock Ryan's socks off. The first thing she did when she got home was change into her robe. On the short walk from the Caddy to her door, she'd gotten soaked. When she went into the laundry room, she spotted Ryan's neatly folded T-shirt and shorts. She'd forgotten to return them. Perhaps that was a good thing. Liz didn't want Kate inferring anything untoward about this morning. She held up Ryan's shirt and stuck her nose into the collar area, inhaling the lingering scent of his clean-smelling aftershave. "What's up with you and this Ryan guy, Elizabeth Holt?" she said out loud. She put Ryan's clothing in a bag and left them by the door. She would give them to him later when he came to the hotel for dinner.

At the thought of dinner, she shook her head. She still couldn't wrap her head around the fact that David Worth wanted to return to the hotel after being released from the hospital.

Liz made a late lunch of grapes, Pops's homemade country pâté, and rice crackers. She brought the plate into her office and opened her laptop, putting in her and her father's shared password, then logged in to the Indialantic's online banking website. She printed out the previous month's rent checks from the emporium, feeling lucky that Francie had signed Home Arts by the Sea's check, not Minna. Betty had checked Minna's alibi at the gallery, and the owner had said she'd been there at the time of the murder. Francie didn't have an alibi. If it did turn out that Francie threw the rock at the Worths' car, it didn't mean she'd murdered Regina or stabbed David. Nick Goren's was another signature she needed, because his father had signed the rent check for Gold Coast by the Sea. For Brittany's check, Liz had to go back two months. What a surprise, she thought sarcastically.

Liz jotted down a note as a reminder to tell Aunt Amelia that Brittany still owed rent for March and April. Brittany also needed to take down the ridiculous sign in her shop that said By Chance or Appointment.

Before going to the Indialantic to prepare dinner, Liz took a long, second shower and went through ten different outfits to wear before she settled on a simple sleeveless turquoise dress and gold flat sandals with straps that crisscrossed around her ankles. She added gold hoop earrings and a long vintage necklace with several gold charms that represented good luck and good health: an elephant with its trunk in the upright position, a wishbone, and a four-leaf clover. Kate had given her the necklace for her twenty-eighth birthday. It wasn't worth much compared to the necklace stolen from around Regina Harrington-Worth's neck, but to Liz it was priceless.

She was tempted to put some bronzer on her pale face, but she stuck to her usual routine of mascara, blush, and lip gloss. Her scar looked a thousand times better than it had after the first skin graft. Liz rarely held her own gaze in the mirror for more than a few seconds. When a child or someone walked by her and did a double take, she never got angry, but their actions always reminded her of that night. Days would go by when she wouldn't even think about the scar, forgetting it was there at all. Liz was never vain. When she'd modeled to help pay for her tuition at Columbia, she hadn't gotten caught up in the superficiality of it all. But when she'd won the PEN/Faulkner Award, that was another story. Her success went to her head, and when the dollars started rolling in, the reason she'd started writing in the first place—for the delight of her readers—got buried under the glitter and accolades. The night it all fell apart, Liz didn't really blame Travis; she was his enabler, like he'd been hers. Their life together wasn't real, just their fall from grace.

An hour later, Liz pulled the Caddy under the hotel's canopy. The sheriff's car she'd seen earlier that morning was parked in the same spot. Liz wondered why it was still there. Waiting for a return visit from Regina's killer, or was an arrest imminent? Aunt Amelia planned to sleep in her own bed tonight. Maybe Liz should talk her out of it? She parked the car a few feet from the revolving door to the lobby and got out. The storm hadn't let up, and per the weather report, it wouldn't until tomorrow.

Chapter 28

When Liz walked into the Indialantic's kitchen, her jaw literally dropped. Pierre was next to the center island with his toque askew, holding a scoop of flour, half of which had fallen onto the floor, making for a dangerous work space. Liz rushed over and took the scoop out of his hand. He looked disoriented, but his gaze cleared when he focused on Liz's face. "Surprise. I almost have dinner ready, although I seem to have misplaced the main protein." He went from counter to counter, searching behind canisters and bags of cornmeal. It seemed that everything that had filled the shelves in the butler's pantry had been brought into the kitchen.

She took Pierre's elbow and guided him toward the farm table. "Sit for a minute. I'll look for it." But Liz didn't have to look long, because she smelled it. "Pierre, was your 'protein' lobster?"

"Yes, Lizzy dear. Did you find it?"

Liz moved toward the double wall oven and opened the top oven door. Inside were the lobster tails she'd planned to use in the meal meant to impress Ryan. The spiny Florida lobster tails had been just one of the seafood components she had planned to use. She certainly hadn't meant to use all twenty-four on the tray in front of her. The lobster tails were charred on top, one second away from bursting in flames. A bottle of brandy sat on the counter next to the oven—Pierre must have intended on creating one of his famous flambés. She got an oven mitt and pulled out the tray.

Aunt Amelia charged into the kitchen, out of breath. "What's that smell?"

Pierre twirled the ends of his mustache, then said, "Surprise dinner!" He took off his toque and reached inside. His hand came out empty. "Have one more step to finish, just need to find the damn recipe. Where did I put it? Lizzy? Amelia? Do you see it?"

Aunt Amelia walked toward him. "Pierre, Betty told you that Liz—"

Liz gave her great-aunt the "shush" sign. Aunt Amelia understood that Pierre had forgotten what Betty had told him about Liz making tonight's dinner.

"Come, Pierre," Aunt Amelia said. "Let's get cleaned up. Liz will look for your recipe and finish it for you. You know how much she adores your...uh..."

"Lobster Louis," Liz said.

"Of course. Of course," he said, blinking a few times. "I think I might lie down a bit before our meal." Pierre got up and Aunt Amelia followed him to the left of the butler's pantry and into the hallway, toward the service elevator.

A tear coursed down Liz's cheek, causing a stinging sensation when it met her scar. No matter how much Pierre protested, Liz, her father, and Aunt Amelia would have to convince him to see a doctor.

Dinner was usually served at five thirty, six at the latest. Liz had only a short time to figure out what to make. The first thing she did was check the lobster. She removed one tail from its shell. The top was burnt, but when she turned it over the bottom was barely cooked. Pierre must have had the broiler on. Liz strode to the oven and sure enough, the Broil light was on.

There was only one thing to do; she had to cut off the charred tops, then cut the lobster tails into small chunks and make some kind of seafood risotto, cream sauce, or a chowder. She walked to the commercial refrigerator and opened the door. It seemed Pierre had already been inside. Carrot tops were missing their carrots, and unwashed leeks lay atop an unwrapped wheel of sheep's milk cheese with truffles that went for fifty dollars a pound. "Oh, Pierre, what a mess."

Barnacle Bob cooed from the pantry, "Oh, Pierre. Oh, Pierre. What a mess. Nothin' says lovin' like somethin' from the oven."

"BB, you're incorrigible."

Liz spent the next half hour cleaning the kitchen and refrigerator, while Barnacle Bob took a walk on the dark side, spouting every dirty word he'd ever heard.

Aunt Amelia stepped back into the kitchen. "I didn't hear BB use a curse word, did I?"

"No," Liz said. "He used all of them!"

"Pretty boy. Pretty boy," Barnacle Bob chanted.

Brownnoser, Liz thought.

Iris came into the room from the direction of the service elevator. She wore her usual scowl and didn't even glance in Liz's direction. She said to Aunt Amelia, "How many for dinner?"

Aunt Amelia said, "Let's see. There's me, Betty, Pierre, Captain Netherton, Liz, Fenton, Ryan, and David Worth."

At the name "David Worth," Liz saw the housekeeper's jaw clench.

"And if you don't mind, dear," Aunt Amelia said, not noticing Iris's darkening mood, "I'd like you to serve. Pierre seems under the weather."

Iris opened her mouth to protest, but apparently thought twice and closed it. Liz was glad. She wouldn't allow Aunt Amelia to be bullied. Finally, the housekeeper walked into the dining room like she was marching to orders.

Aunt Amelia came close to Liz and whispered in her ear, "What are we going to serve, darling? Should I run down to the Crab Shack and pick something up?"

"Not in this weather, Auntie. I'll come up with something, but don't expect too much. You're not trying to impress David Worth, are you?"

"No. We don't need anything fancy. He told me he was Florida-born, grew up in Orlando, of modest means. I spoke to him earlier, and he volunteered the information that when he met Regina Harrington he'd made a lot of money after selling his computer graphics company. Then the poor guy actually fell asleep in the middle of our conversation. He must be on heavy pain medication or tranquilizers. I realized then where I'd seen him before. It was at the grand opening weekend of the emporium shops. Oh, you should have seen it, Lizzy. It was one of the happiest times of my life."

"I'm sorry I missed it, Auntie. But I did catch it on the video Kate texted me when I was in New York. The closing on my loft took much longer than expected, or I would have been here in a heartbeat. You looked absolutely gorgeous, and the shops were packed."

"David was there. I know it. I told you, I don't forget a face. I remember spotting Shelley Winters at Schwab's on Sunset Boulevard even though she wore sunglasses and a head scarf. I'd just come from playing in a skit for the TV series, *Bob Hope Presents the Chrysler Theatre,* where Shelley had made a guest appearance. It was something about her chin..."

"Did you happen to notice Regina at the grand opening?"

"No. I'm sure someone would have pointed her out if she'd been there."

"Didn't you just tell me David said he'd never been to the Indialantic before?"

"He did. Although that was in front of his wife."

"Maybe he didn't want Regina knowing he shopped in such a 'lowbrow establishment'. I saw him the morning of the Spring Fling, buying something for Regina in Gold Coast."

"Nothing about the emporium is 'lowbrow,' Elizabeth Holt."

"I know that and you know that. But you must admit, we aren't Worth Avenue. How's he taking his wife's murder?"

"He seems numb—and sad," Aunt Amelia said. "Just plain sad."

Liz glanced at her watch. "I'd better decide what to make for dinner. Something that involves lots of lobster meat, obviously."

Aunt Amelia laughed. "Reminds me of an episode of *The Patty Duke Show*, when Patty wanted to impress a boy. She was a terrible cook, so Cathy said she'd do it, but then Cathy got called away. My part was cut, but it was so much fun to watch the twins work; I mean, to watch Miss Duke work. I have faith in you, my dear—you're more of a Cathy than a Patty when it comes to your cooking ability. But like Patty, were you planning on impressing a certain boy with your gastronomic delights? A certain boy with the first initial 'R'?"

"He's not a boy." *He's definitely a man*, Liz thought. "I wish I had as much faith in myself as you do about preparing this meal. I feel so bad about Pierre. I thought he was doing so much better these last few days. He even seemed to take what happened to the Worths in stride."

Aunt Amelia was an eternal optimist. "He will be as right as rain after his nap."

"Are we able to go into the Oceana Suite yet? I think it needs a makeover. And the sooner the better."

"Great idea. I'll put you and Kate in charge, and I don't plan on going inside until you're finished. I'd better go supervise Iris. She doesn't seem herself."

Liz begged to differ. "I see a patrol car is still parked outside."

"I promised your father I'd let him handle anything having to do with the police. I'm sure that lovely Agent Pearson will keep him updated."

Lovely? Liz felt something uncomfortable twist in her gut at the thought of Agent Charlotte Pearson and her father together. Was it jealousy? It had been twenty-three years since her mother's death; she didn't expect her father to stay alone forever. But there was something about Agent Pearson that bothered her. She was all business. Liz didn't see any warmth or compassion, but maybe that was because of their last encounter and the fact that the detective had to wear two hats: charming companion to her father at night and by-the-book homicide detective during the day.

After Aunt Amelia left the kitchen, Liz went to check the pantry and the fridge to see whether she had the proper ingredients to make a cohesive one-dish dinner. She'd given up hope that this would be the meal to impress Ryan, and so she looked forward to his invitation for their cook-off—the "best-laid plans" and all that.

First, she opened the fridge and found fresh corn on the cob; eggs; enough heavy cream to bathe in, because it was Pierre's favorite old-school French addition, butter; thick-slab bacon; and a large container of Pierre's homemade fish stock. In the pantry she located flour, shallots, fingerling potatoes, fresh garlic, paprika, dry sherry, salt and pepper, and dried thyme. She'd have preferred fresh, but the weather didn't call for her risking her life for fresh herbs.

Barnacle Bob, who had been snoozing, snapped to attention. "Ki-wi, ki-wi, ki-wi. Where in tarnation is my damn ki-wi!"

Iris was shirking her duties if BB had been three days without his favorite kiwi.

"Calm down, BB. I'll go ask Iris if she has any kiwi."

"Battle-ax Iris. Battle-ax Iris."

"Don't let Aunt Amelia hear you say that."

He turned around in his cage and did his version of dropping his pants by bending forward and raising his tail feathers.

"You're a dirty bird, Barnacle Bob."

As she walked out of the pantry with her tray of supplies, she noticed the parrot didn't repeat her words.

She set the tray down on the center island of the kitchen and went into the dining room to ask Iris if she'd fed Barnacle Bob. Iris wasn't there and the tables were only partially set.

Where was she always disappearing to?

Chapter 29

At six thirty, everyone in the dining room had a meal set in front of them. After Iris had served the dinner, Aunt Amelia had sent the housekeeper into the kitchen to clean up. Liz stood in the open doorway between the kitchen and dining room, surveying the tables, searching for reactions to the food. Pierre's dishes were usually flawless. Liz knew her meal wasn't flawless; she just hoped it was passable. She caught Ryan's eye. He lifted his wineglass in the air as a symbol of appreciation, then continued to work on what Liz had deemed Lobster Bisque Potpie.

David Worth and Ryan shared a table. Liz would have loved to join them, but she chose to sit with her father, letting Ryan have the chance to learn what he could from David. David seemed in pretty good shape for what he'd gone through—a little pale, but he was talking animatedly to Ryan, even gesturing with his hands. How could he not feel strange, sitting directly below where he'd just been stabbed and where his wife had been choked to death? Before dinner, Liz had handed Betty the copies of the canceled rent checks from the emporium. Liz hoped they found a match between the note and the handwriting, so that at least one mystery could be solved.

Aunt Amelia, Betty, Pierre, and Captain Netherton sat together at a different table. The storm outside was still raging, and the sky was as dark as midnight. There were lit tapers on all three tables, giving the grand old room a shadowy vibe. Liz was thankful for Captain Netherton. He was spinning one of his tall tales about a Coast Guard rescue he'd been a part of during one of Florida's worst hurricanes.

Everyone seemed happy. "Well? How is it?" she asked her father.

Earlier, he'd walked into the kitchen when Liz was in warrior-chef mode. She'd explained about the incident with Pierre and the lobsters. They'd both agreed that Pierre needed to see a doctor, no matter how "right as rain" Aunt Amelia thought he was.

Her father touched a napkin to his bottom lip and said, "It's delicious, hearty, filling, yet at the same time delicate. And the lobster is perfect."

"Well, thank you, kind sir. How did your day go?"

"Better than expected. A good day in court."

"That's great. When you have a few minutes, I have a lot to talk to you about, mostly things relating to Regina Harrington-Worth's death."

"Elizabeth, I hope you're being careful?"

"Of course. I have Betty, Kate, and Ryan all watching my back."

Liz heard her father's cell phone buzz. He held up his finger and said, "Hold that thought," then answered the call.

Liz got up, walked to the sideboard, picked up a pitcher of lemon-flavored water and took it over to David and Ryan's table. "Water, gentlemen?"

"I would love some," David said. "It's time for my next pill." He put his hand in his left pocket, then his right, and came up empty. He said, "Damn. I must have left my medication upstairs. I'll be right back." He put both hands on the table to push himself up, grimacing in pain.

Ryan said, "Mr. Worth."

"David."

"David, please sit down. I'll run up and get them. It's no problem."

"Thank you. Here's my room key. But don't you want to finish your dinner while it's hot?" He looked at Ryan's plate and laughed. "Looks like that isn't a problem. Did you inhale it?"

Ryan stood. "Just about. One of the best meals I've ever had."

"It is pretty tasty," David agreed, then he took a long swig of his wine.

After Ryan left, Liz asked David, "Can I get you anything else?"

"I'll be fine as soon as the meds hit." He looked up at Liz's face, his gaze lingering on her scar before he looked away.

Maybe he was thinking about his own wound? "Okay, well, let me or Iris know if you need anything else." She started to walk away, then turned back. "Mr. Worth, you don't know where Venus's collar is, do you?"

"No. I'm sorry. I haven't seen it. Did you ask Amelia? She still has Venus with her. I can't bear to look at the cat. She was Regina's child—she never had any of her own."

Liz touched his hand. "I am so sorry for your loss. Don't worry about Venus. Aunt Amelia is the Dr. Doolittle of the Indialantic. She will take care of Mrs. Worth's pet like Venus was her own."

"Thank you. You've all been so kind. I only plan on staying for a few more days, just until they release Regina's"—he took another gulp of wine. Liz had left a full bottle on the table and it was empty—"body for the memorial."

"Well, if we can help with any arrangements, please let us know."

"I will," he said. He looked out at the dark window leading to the courtyard and Liz walked away. She thought about opening another bottle of wine, but she knew firsthand he shouldn't mix pain medication with alcohol.

Liz went and sat with her father. She hadn't touched her food, but she'd done so much taste-testing she thought if she had just one more bite she might lose it—literally. Who would have thought anyone could get tired of lobster?

"Was the phone call about your new case?" she asked her father.

"No, it was Charlotte—Agent Pearson. She's a few minutes away and wants to talk to Mr. Worth about something. I told her to come into the dining room. She hasn't eaten. Can we offer her one of your marvelous lobster potpies?"

Liz looked down at her untouched dish. If she provided the detective with a homemade meal, maybe it would help to get her to open up about the investigation. She was still smarting from Agent Pearson's question about Liz having a connection to Regina's missing jewels. "This is the last one, but I'll take it back into the kitchen and heat it up a bit."

"What about you?" he asked.

"Don't worry. I've tasted so much lobster in the last few hours, I'll probably grow claws and a tail."

"Did I ever tell you that you're the best, dear daughter?"

"All the time," she replied. "But keep those compliments coming, dear ol' dad."

Liz went into the kitchen. Iris was gone, but the kitchen was spotless. In the pantry, Barnacle Bob's cage was missing. She hoped he wasn't in the same room as Venus; the two follicly challenged pets might tangle. BB was an expert at opening his own cage, and Venus—well, Venus was a cat.

She covered the potpie with a damp paper towel, then put it in the microwave on 50 percent power. Liz was breaking the cardinal rule of serving fine cuisine—to never use a microwave. But at this point, she really didn't have a choice. She would stick the potpie under the broiler for a few minutes after she took it out of the microwave. It wouldn't be as tasty as if it was straight out of the oven, but it would be darn close.

A few minutes later, Liz peeked into the dining room. Agent Pearson had arrived, and she was sitting in Liz's seat. Liz pushed the childish notion away that she'd been replaced by the stunning detective, and she pulled out the white-fluted pie dish from the oven.

She brought the lobster potpie and a hastily made salad into the dining room and placed them in front of Detective Pearson. Liz had served a more complex salad earlier, with freshly made goat cheese that Pops had gotten from a local farm, but as the saying went, "beggars can't be choosy." Looking at the elegant way the detective dressed, she doubted Agent Pearson would ever be considered a "beggar."

"Be careful," Liz instructed, "the serving dish is very hot."

"It looks delicious. Your father was just raving about it." Agent Pearson looked around at the other people in the room, and her rare smile turned upside down as she morphed back into a hard-to-read homicide detective looking for a murder suspect.

"Would you like some rosé?" Liz asked.

Agent Pearson put a napkin to her perfect lips. "No, thank you. I'm on duty."

"Water with lemon?"

"That would be great."

Liz hoped she was earning brownie points by waiting on the detective. She had a vision of everyone sitting in her father's office, discussing the murder, with Liz giving the police the one clue they needed to solve the case and catch the killer. She went to the sideboard and retrieved the pitcher of water, then came back to the table and poured some into the detective's glass. "Anything else?"

Before Agent Pearson could answer, her father said, "Pull up a chair, Liz. You've been on your feet for hours."

Agent Pearson didn't second the invitation, but Liz walked over to Ryan and David's table to steal a chair. Of course, there were closer tables with empty chairs, but she'd timed it perfectly. Just as she reached David Worth's table, Ryan returned, holding a prescription bottle. Liz was thrilled at the thought he'd taken so long to retrieve it. That meant he must have been doing some snooping in David's suite. Snoopy Pants to the rescue.

Ryan handed David the prescription bottle and said, "The bottle had fallen behind the nightstand. Took a while to find it."

David didn't seem to hear his words. He grabbed the bottle, poured several pills into his hand, then downed them with half a glass of wine.

Was he numbing his shoulder pain, or numbing the loss of his wife?

Liz took the chair back to her father's table. As soon as she sat, the conversation between her father and Agent Pearson quelled. Betty's table had also quieted, probably due to Betty shushing everybody so she could hear what Agent Pearson was saying to her father.

Agent Pearson must have liked the lobster, because it didn't take her long to finish it. Fenton recounted a story about a recent case he'd won involving a surfboard that a great white shark had chomped on. The bite mark coincided with the largest jaw measurement for any shark ever recorded and was sold to Ripley's Believe It or Not. The problem was, the owner of the surfboard was going through a divorce and his better half wanted a share of the proceeds from the sale. Her father had represented the wife and won the case. They all laughed when he described the surfboard in question, propped up on a table in the front of the courtroom.

"I have to ask," Liz said, "was the husband injured in the attack on his surfboard?"

"No, luckily he had wiped out. When the board shot out of the wave, the great white caught it in its mouth."

Iris came in and cleared away everyone's dishes.

Aunt Amelia called over to Liz, "Shall I bring in coffee and dessert, Liz?"

Luckily, before Pierre had tried to "surprise" Liz with the main dish, he'd already made dessert, Julia Child's Cherry Clafouti. Pierre had added a little lemon zest to the recipe and sprinkled sugar on top before baking the eggy dessert akin to Yorkshire pudding. "No, Auntie, Iris and I will bring it in. Stay put."

Liz stood and put her napkin on the table. As she turned for the kitchen, she heard David Worth's raised voice. "I will not keep quiet any longer. I refuse to sit in a room with that Casanova, Captain Clyde, acting like he didn't make a play for my dearly departed wife. I even have proof! I found a bottle of Chanel perfume with a note in my wife's Birkin." David tried to stand, but he wobbled and plopped back onto his seat. There was a second bottle of wine on the table, and it was half empty. David was high or drunk—or both.

Ryan said, "Steady, old boy. Let me help you to your suite."

"I don't want to go to my suite. What right did he have to give her Coco Mademoiselle!"

Both Betty and Aunt Amelia said in unison, "Coco Mademoiselle!" Then they each turned to Captain Netherton, who had a cat-that-ate-the-canary look on his face.

Uh-oh. It looked like Captain Netherton had been buying the same perfume for all his ladies.

"My beautiful wife was not a 'mademoiselle'! She was happily married to me!"

Agent Pearson stood, then went over to David.

David had lost all his bluster and his chin was on his chest, his eyes glassy from the wine and drugs. She said, "Ryan, please escort Mr. Worth to his suite." Then she turned and said, "Mr. Netherton, could you please meet me in the lobby?"

The captain stood and performed a little bow. "Of course. My pleasure."

Chapter 30

After dinner, Betty and Ryan met Liz at the door to the library. Liz put the antique key in the keyhole, opened the door, and ushered them in. Then she locked the door behind them.

Betty walked to the desk and rifled through her handbag for the printed photo of the note tied to the rock. She took it out, then dove back in for the copies of the rent checks Liz had given her before dinner. Liz could see why she was having a hard time finding anything in her handbag, which was more of an overnight satchel. She extracted an iPad, crochet hooks, tape measures, three granny squares and a neon orange skein of yarn, just to name a few of the items. Betty belonged on the TV game show *Let's Make a Deal*. Aunt Amelia had already been on the show in the late sixties, when she lived in Burbank. When Monty Hall had come up the aisle and asked Aunt Amelia if she had a tube of toothpaste in her handbag, Aunt Amelia almost fainted. She not only had toothpaste, but also a toothbrush, dental floss, and a pair of false buckteeth she'd used for one of her parts in the sitcom *The Beverly Hillbillies*.

Aunt Amelia's "pocketbook" held so many surprises that when Liz was a child, she would close her eyes, reach in, and call out an item. If she guessed it right, her great-aunt would allow her a single stick of Wrigley's Spearmint gum. She'd explained to Liz that when she was a young girl, during WWII, Wrigley's Spearmint gum wasn't available at her local candy store because the company sent their entire inventory overseas to the GIs fighting for America's freedom. To this day, when Liz was near Aunt Amelia and her handbag was open, the scent of Wrigley's Spearmint gum took her back to her own childhood.

Betty pulled out the copies of canceled rent checks and compared them against the writing on the note. Bingo! Francie Jenkins was the winner.

Liz wasn't surprised. They'd solved that puzzle, but it only opened the door to more questions. Could Francie also be the one who had murdered Regina and stabbed David? It seemed a big leap. "If Francie doesn't come in to the emporium tomorrow, I'll go to her cottage and talk to her. I don't think we should tell Agent Pearson anything about this until afterward."

"It might be too late," Ryan said. "Remember, I told you earlier that Agent Pearson was at the emporium looking for Francie."

Betty put the photocopies back in her bag. "Liz, I'd suggest that you get up early to go see Francie."

"I will. Now, why don't we have a seat and talk about what Ryan uncovered in David Worth's suite."

He grinned. "How do you know I found anything?"

"'Cause you're a snoopy pants," Liz said.

"Spoken like a true bossy pants."

Liz and Betty sat on one of the sofas and Ryan pulled an armchair up next to them. He retrieved his phone from his pocket and said, "What if I told you I'd discovered a copy of Regina and David Worth's prenup—and a copy of Regina's will?"

"I'd say, 'No, you didn't!'" Liz exclaimed.

"Did," he said. "However, just from all the photos I took with my phone, it doesn't look like he stands to inherit anything from her death."

He tapped his screen, then handed Betty his phone.

"May I e-mail or text these to my iPad? I need a bigger screen to view them."

"Of course," he replied.

Liz added, "I'd love a copy, too."

"Sure," Ryan said.

Betty stopped for a minute and looked over at Ryan. "Stellar work, Mr. Stone. You even took a photo of his prescription bottle, which gives us his doctor's name, where maybe we can find more about…"

"His wound and whether it was self-inflicted," Ryan finished.

"But if it was self-inflicted," Liz asked, "what would his motive be if he doesn't stand to inherit anything?"

"At this point, if it wasn't self-inflicted, it would just be a confirmation that he's not in the upper echelon of our suspect list," Betty replied.

"Speaking of a suspect list," Liz said. "What do you think of David's accusation against Captain Netherton?" Betty pretended to be busy e-mailing, but pink flushed her cheeks. "Come on, Betty, confession time. Did you happen to also receive a bottle of Chanel's Coco Mademoiselle from our captain?"

She looked up. "Yes. And I checked online. It wasn't cheap. If he's handing Chanel perfume out to all his women, he must be getting a whopping pension from the Coast Guard and lots of tip money from skippering *Queen of the Seas*."

"That doesn't make him a murderer, though," Ryan said.

"How about a thief?" Liz asked. "My father told me the necklace and earrings that were stolen were almost priceless."

"But very hard to fence," Ryan said. "If someone melted the gold and took out the emeralds, they'd only get a small percentage of their actual insured value."

"Minna and Francie told me Regina wasn't left anything in her father's will from the loot he'd recovered in his treasure hunts. She was only allowed to wear the jewelry, and upon her death everything would go to museums. The same with the property at Castlemara."

When Betty was done e-mailing Liz the photos of the will, the prenup, and the pill bottle, Liz stood. "I'd better get back to the kitchen and make sure everything is shipshape. And I want to check on Pierre."

Betty gave Liz a knowing glance, and Liz explained to Ryan about Pierre's recent memory loss and befuddled behavior.

"My nana had Alzheimer's and she did well on medication," Ryan said. "So there's always hope."

Liz and Ryan locked gazes, both thinking about the firefighter from Ryan's company who'd been in the car accident. There was always hope.

"I'll check on Pierre when I go upstairs," Betty said. "Liz, you should get some rest. You have an early day tomorrow."

"Thanks. Let's reconvene after I talk to Francie and we look over the photos Ryan took."

"I feel like one of the Hardy Boys. Do we need a name for our new mystery club?" Ryan grinned.

Liz laughed and turned to Betty. "Can I tell him?"

"Yes, but if he discloses my secret to anyone, it will be under penalty of death."

Liz told Ryan about Betty's ghostwriting career.

"My mom read Nancy Drew and my dad read the Hardy Boys," Ryan said. "I think Dad still has them somewhere. I read them all, too. They were blue-spined hardcovers."

Darn, Liz thought. Another plus to put under Ryan's Nice column, almost offsetting the Naughty.

Later, when Liz entered the lobby to make sure the hotel was secure, she found Captain Netherton sitting on a wicker chaise, sucking on the stem of his unlit pipe. It was the first time the debonair captain had looked his seventy years.

He gave Liz a weak smile that didn't engage the laugh lines near his blue-green eyes.

"Are you okay, Captain?"

"Yes, my dear. I always rally, even when I'm up against the perfect storm."

"Did you and Agent Pearson get everything straightened out?"

"Of course. I explained to her that I was just repaying Mrs. Harrington-Worth for the exorbitant tip she gave me when she chartered the *Queen of the Seas*."

"And Betty and Aunt Amelia?"

"Ah, the lovely ladies of the Indialantic by the Sea. Yes, I bought them the same perfume. Your great-aunt for all her generosity in letting me stay here and giving me something to do to fill my retirement days. And the lovely mystery writer for being so accommodating to my big mutt, Killer. That David Worth is out of his gourd with grief, I suppose. And he seemed as drunk as can be, so I'll cut him a little slack."

Liz remembered how badly Regina had treated her husband and wondered if there was a side to him that no one ever saw. If he didn't marry her for her money, that must be the Regina he was grieving for.

"Your suite is next to the Worths'—I mean, where the Worths were staying…um, prior to the robbery. Did you ever overhear anything? Arguing, any visitors?" she asked.

"Not that I can think of. These are all the same questions the lovely detective keeps asking."

"How about Saturday? Anything strange?"

"Well, just as you, I was at the emporium, manning the raffle table. Now that I think about it, before going down to dinner I heard Regina raising her voice at her husband. She asked him if he was drunk, because he was slurring his words. I didn't hear anything after that, and I went downstairs to the dining room, where Iris served me dinner."

"What time was that?" Liz asked.

"Around seven."

"And what time did you hear the commotion later?"

He put down his pipe and yawned before answering. "It was around seven thirty."

"Were you with Iris the entire time?"

"I know you're trying to make sense of everything. I myself have started a logbook about that night. Must be my military training, but there is no way that Iris was out of my sight for more than a few minutes. Between you and me, we actually shared dinner together."

Liz would probably find a bottle of Coco Mademoiselle in Iris's bathroom. "One last question, when you found David and Regina, was David conscious?"

"David was in a semi-stupor. He crawled into the sitting room and kept repeating, 'Why does it hurt so much? Why does it hurt so much?'"

After leaving Captain Netherton, Liz went back to check the kitchen. Iris had cleaned up and everything was sparkling. She grabbed her handbag from the pantry and went out the kitchen door. After the door closed behind her, she grabbed the handle and tested it. Locked. Would things ever return to normal?

Once home, she printed the photos that Ryan had taken on his phone while he'd been in David Worth's suite. He would be an asset to the CIA. Regina's will was as Ryan had said it was when he'd perused it. David stood to gain nothing from her death. What Minna and Francie had told her must be true. Castlemara would be left to the Barrier Island Historical Society and all the treasure would go into museums after her death, which was the reason Regina hadn't been allowed to sell any of the jewelry from the *San Carlos*. Any true assets that Regina had upon her death would go to her feline, Venus. That last fact said a lot for what Regina had thought of her husband.

Liz then looked at David and Regina's prenup. It stated that David had assets of a million dollars, which included real estate and the Bentley. Regina's assets were almost nonexistent: She received a monthly stipend of forty thousand dollars from her father's estate, nothing to sneeze about, but not enough to rebuild on her father's property after Castlemara was demolished. Nothing related to her father's treasure haul was listed.

The Barrier Island Historical Society had a lot to gain from Regina's death, but not David. Liz had a feeling that the knife wound wasn't self-inflicted. If it had been, Agent Pearson would already have him in a locked cell. Another motive for Regina's murder might simply be robbery. Pawn the pieces off, or find a collector from another country to buy them.

Later that night, when Liz got in bed, she picked up *Evil Under the Sun*. She was near the end of the book. Even though she'd already read it in her teens, she still felt the excitement at the fast approaching "aha" moment, when the loose ends would be neatly tied up with Agatha Christie's usual flair.

If only Regina Harrington-Worth's murder could be solved as easily.

Chapter 31

Tuesday morning, Liz pulled up a few doors down from Francie and Minna's cottage. She waited until Minna's BMW pulled out of the driveway. Betty's Blue Bomber was easy to spot, and Liz was happy Minna didn't glance Liz's way as she drove north toward the emporium. Earlier, Liz had talked to Minna on the phone, and she'd said Francie had planned on staying home for another day of rest.

Liz got out of the Caddy. Before leaving the beach house, she'd toyed with the idea of putting the ancient convertible top down. Betty said the automatic switch to lower the top was broken, but she was sure it would work manually. Liz hadn't wanted to take a chance, in case one of the island's sudden storms broke. Yesterday's storm had passed, but as usual in the tropics, another one looked to be approaching. She walked to the passenger's door, opened it, and retrieved two items from a box on the seat—one was a carafe of Pierre's French roast, the other a Bienenstich cake, or bee sting cake, made from brioche dough and filled with lemon custard, then topped with a crunchy honey-almond glaze. The aroma reminded Liz of early mornings in Paris when she'd walk by a boulangerie's open doorway and get drawn inside by the tempting scents wafting out onto the cobblestone streets. Her thoughts segued to Travis, who was fond of long weekends on the Seine. As she headed toward Minna and Francie's charming cottage, Liz realized that not all of her memories of Travis were bad.

Minna and Francie's cottage was painted pale yellow, with vintage aqua shutters worn by the sun and sea spray. It sat on the west side of the highway and had a small second-floor balcony with an ocean view. The cottage reminded her of those in Key West. When Liz was a teen, she and her father would take road trips down to the Keys. She smiled at the thought and climbed the steps to the cottage's front porch. One hand held the carafe, the other the cake plate, so she rang the doorbell with her elbow. Francie opened the door, blinking from the sunlight. Her skin was sallow, and she had blue-black bags under her eyes. Her hair stuck out in all directions, and her fifties-style housecoat had a huge yellow stain on it. On Francie's left foot, was a lavender bunny slipper, on her right, a pink piggy.

"Liz? Is everything okay? What's happened? Come in."

Liz stepped inside and set the carafe and cake on a table in the entranceway. "Everything's fine. I wanted to check on you and bring you something hot out of Pierre's oven."

Francie slunk over to the sofa in the living room and collapsed. On the walls were huge canvases of Minna's fabulous mixed-media art. The furniture in the room was vintage-modern with a Scandinavian flair. Liz took a seat on a leather and light wood recliner with matching ottoman. As she leaned back and put her feet up on the ottoman, she pictured herself in her therapist's office in Manhattan. Dr. Browning was another fan of midcentury modern décor.

Liz thought about how to delicately put what she wanted to say, but before she had a chance, Francie said, "I did it. I confessed to Agent Pearson. Oh, Liz, are they going to arrest me? Do I need to hire your father?" Francie began to sob. She grabbed the box of tissues beside her and blew her nose. She crumpled the tissue and tossed it on top of an already towering pile on the coffee table, then pulled out another from the box. Liz got up and went to the sofa, pushed aside a stack of sewing magazines, and sat down. She put her arm around Francie, thinking that these couldn't be the tears of a murderer. "Slow down, Francie. Deep breaths. Why don't you tell me everything, then we can decide whether you need a lawyer?"

Francie sniffled. "I did it. I threw a rock at the Worths' Bentley. I was so mad! I couldn't believe that witch was going to tear down such a beautiful mansion. My parents were friends with the Harringtons. My father and Percival Harrington II started the Barrier Island Historical Society together."

"Very understandable. I'm sure if you tell David Worth this, he won't press charges, just perhaps have you pay for the damages. What does Agent Pearson say?"

"She's not saying anything. Detective Pearson treats me like I'm a bug that's carrying a communicable disease. And she's right, too."

"Do you have an alibi for the time of the murder, around seven thirty Saturday night?"

"Yes. I was on a blind date at the Sebastian Beach Inn."

Liz removed her arm from Francie's shoulder. "Can you prove it?" Liz remembered Minna saying that the date had been canceled because the guys were a couple of geeks. "If you can, then there's no need for a lawyer." Could Liz be wrong about Francie? Just because she looked like TV's Gidget, with her large, trusting brown eyes and perky, cheerful persona, that shouldn't exclude her from being a suspect. Why was she lying about the date? If Francie was Regina's killer, there had to be more to the picture.

Liz said, "Why don't you take a quick shower, and I'll get the coffee and cake ready. Pierre's coffee and baked goods are the perfect balm for what ails you."

Francie looked down at the center of her chest and laughed. "Do you think I should incorporate this mustard stain into one of my new fabric designs?"

"Only if you add ketchup. Ketchup and mustard: the condiment choices of midcentury housewives everywhere. When I was small, on Pierre's day off, Aunt Amelia made me her version of spaghetti by adding ketchup and butter to the pasta."

"Yuck," Francie said with a smile. "Sounds like Chef Pierre was a good influence on your love of cooking, but Amelia, not so much. We're all are products of our formative years, aren't we?"

At the mention of her childhood, Francie then quieted, and her eyes lost their momentary sparkle.

"Okay, get!" Liz said. "Wait until you try Pierre's Bienenstich cake."

"His what?"

"Meet me in the kitchen and I'll translate."

Francie got up, then trudged down the hallway to her bedroom.

Liz collected the cake and coffee carafe and headed to the kitchen. Under a Felix the Cat wall clock whose tail ticked away the time, she placed the coffee and cake on the counter. She glanced around, feeling like she'd stepped into one of Aunt Amelia's episodes of *Leave It to Beaver* or *The Donna Reed Show*. Perfect, 1960s-television homemakers June Cleaver and Donna Reed had nothing on Francie. She removed a couple of jade-colored mugs and two matching cake plates from the clear glass-fronted cupboards, then found spoons, forks, and a cake server and placed them on the white enamel table with a black-and-white checkerboard border. As she put the coffee carafe and cake in the center of the table, her mind reeled from the lie Francie had told of her purported alibi for the night of the murder. Didn't she know Agent Pearson and the Brevard County Police Department could check her alibi and prove her wrong? She heard the door to the bathroom shut, and soon after, the sound of water running from the shower, then she crept down the hallway to Francie's bedroom. Her pulse quickened and her stomach did a little flip-flop when she walked inside. Sneaking around a new friend's bedroom didn't make for calm nerves. The room was neat and tidy, the bed made. It was covered in a chenille bedspread with matching shams. In the center of the bed was a sleeping feline. Francie's sixteen-year-old tortoiseshell cat, named Turtle, for obvious reasons, was so content he didn't even open his eyes. Liz was happy the cat wouldn't witness her violation of Francie's privacy.

Liz hurried and checked the dresser and nightstand drawers. She quickly glanced in Francie's closet, finding only her vintage-style dresses, jumpers, blouses, and shoes, Sweaters were at the top, enclosed in clear plastic bins and organized by color. If something incriminating was hidden inside one of the bins, Liz wouldn't have time to check. She then did a quick search under the bed. Turtle opened one eye, gave her a dirty look for disturbing his peace, then closed it. She couldn't find anything that might prove or disprove Francie's innocence.

As she moved toward the door, she observed a small trash can under the nightstand. Inside was a framed photo, the glass smashed into spiderweb fissures. She pulled it out and looked down at a framed photo of four people in front of Castlemara. They were surrounded by palm trees, and in the background was the glittering Atlantic. She recognized two of the people: Francie's mother, who had come into the emporium a couple of weeks ago, and Regina's father, Percival Harrington II. The other woman in the photo looked familiar; she had Regina's eyes, hair color, and sour expression, and heavy gold and precious-stone jewelry hung from her neck and ears. On her right hand was the same ring Liz had seen Regina wearing on the day she'd first met her. Liz assumed the unidentified woman in the photo must be Regina's mother, likely leaving the unidentified man to be Francie's father, who had passed away a few years ago. She grabbed her phone from her pocket and snapped a couple quick pics. She put the photo back in the trash can, then stepped from the room just as Francie exited the bathroom.

Francie gave Liz a quizzical look and Liz stumbled with her words. "I uh, left my, uh, phone in the car." She held it up for Francie to see. Unfortunately, she held up the side of the phone showing the photo she'd just taken. Quickly, she put the phone in her pocket, where it felt like it was burning a hole into her thigh.

"Come into the kitchen," Liz said. "Everything's ready."

"I'll be right there, but let me put on a pair of matching slippers. You're right. A shower made me feel much better, along with your confidence that David Worth won't prosecute me for throwing a rock at his car window."

She almost corrected Francie that it wasn't just the rock shattering the window, it was more the threat written on the note to someone who had been murdered just hours later. As they passed, Liz hoped she wouldn't notice her no-doubt flushed, guilt-ridden face.

Five minutes later, Francie came into the kitchen, just as Liz was adding an extra "spoonful of sugar to help the medicine go down" to her coffee. Mary Poppins had gotten that one right, and after a bite of bee sting cake, Liz might forget that sweet Francie was still a murder suspect.

"Thanks for coming over," Francie said. "You've really turned things around for me. I couldn't get up the nerve to set foot at the Indialantic after what I'd done. It was my bad luck I threw that rock the same day Regina was killed. Oops. That didn't sound right." She took a forkful of cake. "Oh my God. What is this delightful creation?"

"Bienenstich cake. *Bienenstich* is German for 'bee sting'."

"How did it get its name?" she asked, picking up the wedge Liz had served, then stuffing half in her mouth.

"Pierre says it's one of two things, either the creator of the cake was stung by a bee when he was working on the honey-and-almond topping. Or, when the dough for the brioche was put in the oven it swelled up like a bee sting often does."

"Which one do you think it is?"

"I would pick the second. I hate to think that the chef who created this recipe endured any pain, because it's such a luscious cake."

Francie nodded her head, and crumbs fell onto her plate.

When they'd finished, Francie got up and washed the cake plate and carafe and put them into a shopping bag. Liz knew it was a signal to leave, but she had one last question relating to the photo in the trash. "You said your parents were friends with the Harringtons. Did you ever hang out with Regina when you were young?"

"No one hung out with Regina. She was almost ten years older than me and attended private school. She was too good for the likes of us locals, even though her great-grandfather used to live in a shanty on the Indian River Lagoon. I might have been in the same room with Regina when I was younger, but she never once glanced my way, let alone talked to me."

"Do you have any idea who would have killed her?"

"I believe it was a robbery. Plain and simple."

Not so simple, Liz thought as she got up from the table. Francie handed her the shopping bag with the clean carafe and cake plate, then walked with Liz to the front door.

Francie said, "Maybe Regina got what she had coming to her because she murdered her father. I talked to one of the staff on Percival II's yacht about the day he was killed. He had a heart attack, but mysteriously the medicine that might have saved him was missing from his jacket pocket. He told me Regina was right next to her father, looking, or should I say pretending to look for his meds. I wouldn't doubt it if she swiped them so she could inherit his riches. I guess the joke was on her, because she didn't receive anything." She put her hand to her mouth. "I'm sorry, that sounded crass."

Liz didn't have a response for that one. All she could think about was why Francie had been questioning Percival II's death with his yacht staff. "Well, I'm glad you're better. I hope to see you at the emporium tomorrow."

She pushed against the screen door and stepped onto the porch. Coming toward them up the walkway was Agent Pearson. Liz brushed past and said, "Good to see you, Detective. I have to run." Then she booked it to the Blue Bomber, wishing she'd put the top down so she could hop over the driver's door and slide into the seat for a quicker getaway. Instead, she opened the door, got in, started the engine, and drove like a bat flying out of a *Dark Shadows* crypt.

Chapter 32

As Liz cruised north on A1A, her hair blowing in the breeze from the open windows, she was pleased with herself for getting Francie into the shower and a better frame of mind. However, she wasn't too proud of herself for snooping in Francie's bedroom. Liz needed to share with her father what she'd learned about Francie and have him ask Agent Pearson if she had an alibi for Saturday night. Minna had told Liz a completely different version of Francie's whereabouts at the time of the murder.

Instead of turning into the Indialantic, Liz kept driving north toward the Melbourne Beach Public Library, where her seventh-grade teacher, Mrs. Ingles, now the assistant director, might help Liz gather some info on Francie's family connection with the Harringtons, along with the history of the sunken treasure ship *San Carlos* that had netted Percival Harrington II the jewels that were to be eventually stolen from his daughter's neck and ears.

The ocean view out the car's windows was like no other. The temperature was in the upper seventies and the wind was mild. Liz turned on the radio. Betty's old DeVille didn't have a CD, cassette, or even an eight-track player. Usually, Liz alternated between a pop station and a country station. She liked all kinds of music, from opera to New Age, but since her ordeal with Travis, her new favorite was contemporary-country. She liked it for its simplistic message—enjoy the little things in life and don't put up with a good-for-nothin' man. As she pulled up to the library, a country singer crooned about a two-timing man and Liz thought about Captain Netherton. She parked and turned off the ignition, realizing that she'd never made a complete suspect list. Before talking to Mrs. Ingles, Liz would find a quiet corner in the library and use the note function on her phone to create one.

A short time later, she finished the list and e-mailed it to herself. Before she got ahead of things, she would first visit her father and bring him into the loop. Maybe she would learn more about the investigation because of his ties with his new gal pal, Charlotte. If he felt obliged to keep what he knew to himself, she would present her theories, then watch his face. Fenton Holt had an obvious tell when playing poker. Aunt Amelia and Liz called it the famous, one-sided Elvis lip-curl. After seeing her father, Liz planned to pick up her new bundle of joy. She hoped Bronte hadn't changed her mind.

Twenty minutes later, Liz was inside Mrs. Ingles's office sharing a cup of Earl Grey and a couple of Scottish shortbread biscuits from the open tin on her former English teacher's desk. It looked like the same tin Mrs. Ingles had had on her desk years ago. Whenever Liz saw a red-plaid cookie tin, she thought fondly of Mrs. Ingles.

"It's so great to see you again, Elizabeth. I heard you'd moved back to the island. We're lucky to have you. Hope you'll do a book signing for your next award winner?" Mrs. Ingles's hair might have grayed and thinned, and her face might be overrun with wrinkles from baking in the hot Florida sun, but her clear Isle of Skye–blue eyes remained as warm and bright as ever.

Liz laughed, "That would mean I'd have to write it first, Mrs. Ingles." Liz would never call her anything but Mrs. Ingles, and Mrs. Ingles would never call Liz anything but Elizabeth.

Mrs. Ingles searched Liz's face, concern showing in her gaze. "All in good time, I'm sure."

She'd always encouraged Liz to become a writer, and Liz would be forever grateful. "I wanted to ask you a few questions about the Harringtons. I'm sure you heard about Regina Harrington-Worth's death?"

"You mean murder, don't you?" She handed Liz another shortbread biscuit from the tin and Liz took it, even though she was still full from two slices of bee sting cake.

"I want to show you a photo. Maybe you can tell me who everyone is?" Even though Liz had pretty much guessed who was who, she knew Mrs. Ingles might add valuable insight into the past, seeing as she'd lived on the island all of her life. Liz handed her the phone.

Mrs. Ingles expertly put two fingers on the screen, then expanded the image. Librarians seemed pretty tech savvy nowadays. Liz was determined to add Aunt Amelia to that group.

"Celia Harrington, nicknamed Cece, is on the right, to her left is her husband, Percival II, then we have Mark Jenkins and his wife, Tina," she said, sticking her nose closer to the screen. "Mark and Percival started the historical society together. Cece was barely seen in Melbourne Beach. She was more into Vero Beach high society."

"Do you know who is still alive? Any juicy rumors or scuttlebutt about the people in the photo?"

"Tina Jenkins is the only one still alive. As for scuttlebutt…" She raised her right eyebrow. "There is one small rumor that my brother-in-law told me when he was working with Percival II on one of his treasure-salvaging expeditions."

Liz leaned forward, worried that Mrs. Ingles might see the saliva pooling in her mouth. "Yes?"

"Well, I guess it can't hurt now, because they're both dead. There were rumors that Mark and Cece were having an affair. I think if you look closely at the photo, you can see Mark looking directly at Cece, not his wife. Mark was much better-looking than Percival II."

Liz took back the phone, and sure enough, there seemed to be a definite connection between the two. It was like Francie's father and Regina's mother shared an intimate secret. "Speaking of treasure salvagers, can you point me in the right direction on any news or photos about Percival II's score on the *San Carlos*? I've been to the treasure museum, but the researcher in me wants to learn all I can about him and his finds."

"This past February, we held a retrospective of his life, including numerous photos that were displayed in the showcases at the entrance to the library. We also made everything available online." She pulled an empty pad of paper toward her and scribbled something on top. "Here's the IP address, where you'll be able to see everything. It was a great tribute." She handed Liz the piece of paper.

Liz stood, took the paper, then snatched another biscuit.

Mrs. Ingles smiled. "Take the whole tin. I have another. Oh, and I'll ask my brother-in-law if he has anything interesting relating to the *San Carlos*. Now you have me intrigued."

Liz walked over to Mrs. Ingles and gave her a hug.

She looked up at Liz. "You know, now that I think about it, something strange did happen on the first morning of Percival II's retrospective. Someone had opened one of the show cases—we didn't keep them locked back then—and stole a few photos. They weren't anything special, from what I could see. Just a couple of photos of Percival II's salvaging ship and his crew from the day they discovered the cargo section of the *San Carlos*."

"Are you a member of the Barrier Island Historical Society, Mrs. Ingles?"

"Yes. A lifetime member, my husband and I both."

Liz stepped toward the door and said, "It looks like I came to the right place. Thank you, teach. I promise not to be a stranger."

Mrs. Ingles closed the biscuit tin and handed it to Liz. "You know we're reading *Let the Wind Roar* in our book club on Tuesday nights. Stop in. Everyone would fall on the floor in a faint if you did."

"I might do that, just to see the fainting," Liz said, grinning, as she walked out of the office.

Fifteen minutes later, Liz was parked at the rear of the hotel. She strolled toward her father's office. Lining the walkway were waxy green bushes sprouting a profusion of delicate white jasmine. To her right, a huge roseate spoonbill with bright pink wings, like a flamingo's, foraged the lagoon's shoreline for aquatic treats. Liz took a deep gulp of the cleansing, scented air and knocked on the office door. She'd forgotten her keys and longed for the good old days when locking a door at the Indialantic by the Sea Hotel was considered a travesty.

Her father answered with a worried look on his face, which quickly changed when he saw Liz. He was clean shaven and smelled of citrus. His dark hair had a touch of gray and his unlined face made him look ten years younger than fifty-six. Aunt Amelia thought her nephew looked like a cross between Cary Grant, Rock Hudson, and Gregory Peck; Liz just thought he looked like "Dad."

Liz stepped inside. Light jazz played in the background. She glanced at his desk, covered in papers, and felt a stab of guilt for not coming by to help with the filing.

"I'm so happy you caught me," he said. "I was on my way to the kitchen to make a sandwich. "What can I get you?"

"I'll have whatever you're having. Do you mind if I use your computer to print out something I want to show you?"

"Sure, be my guest." He opened the door to his apartment and walked in, then closed the door behind him.

Liz sat in his chair at the desk and signed on to her e-mail account. She opened the suspect list she'd made at the library and added what she'd learned from Mrs. Ingles. She printed out a copy for her father and herself, e-mailed a copy to Betty and Ryan, then reread what she'd written.

David Worth ——Husband of murder victim. Got stabbed in shoulder, need to find out if it was self-inflicted, but doubtful because he wasn't arrested. Gets nothing from the will.

Iris Kimball—Needs money to help her mother. Captain Netherton was with her on night of the murder as an alibi. She went in and saw Regina first. Said Regina was choked with an Ace bandage. Had champagne bottle and two glasses in her room—Captain Netherton?

Captain Clyde B. Netherton—Had possible affair with Regina, Iris, and others. Bought Regina expensive perfume. Was with Iris at the time of the murder.

Francie Jenkins—Threw rock at the Worths' Bentley. Lied about where she was during the murder? Vice president of the Barrier Island Historical Society. Trying to stop the demolition of Castlemara. Her parents were friends of Regina's parents. Possible affair between Francie's father and Regina's mother.

Edward Goren—Former salvager and treasure hunter. Problems with his son, Nick. Alibi?

Brittany Poole—Known thief. Doesn't pay her bills. Materialistic. Dating Nick Goren.

Nick Goren—Son of Edward Goren. Doesn't get along with his father. Gave Brittany a piece of jewelry that was in the showcase in his father's shop, Gold Coast by the Sea.

Someone outside the Indialantic—Knew Regina would be wearing the jewels to Vero Beach Treasure Coast Ball. A simple robbery?

Her father opened the door from his apartment and said, "Lunch is on the table."

Liz shut down the laptop, pulled the papers from the printer, and went inside the apartment. On the table was a cream-cheese and green olive sandwich and a can of root beer. Her father's cooking ability was a notch above Aunt Amelia's. A wee notch.

She sat and said, "Thanks, Dad. I'm glad I got you alone. I wanted to go over some things concerning Regina Harrington-Worth's murder."

He raised his right eyebrow. "Why am I sure that I'm not going to like this?"

"Oh, you'll be happy, because it wasn't just me looking into things. Ryan and Betty are part of the team."

"'Team'?" He sat down across from her.

"We haven't really narrowed it down to a single suspect. That's why I want to bring you into the fold. And, of course, with your brilliant mind and close connection to Agent Pearson...I would value your input."

"I like the way you worded that, but I can't share anything having to do with the case that Charlotte has shared with me."

"Okay, then just look at this and tell me if there's anyone I should eliminate as a suspect?" She handed him the list.

"Eat your sandwich, young lady."

Liz took a large bite and mumbled, "I have more notes at home that I can e-mail you."

"Is Betty to blame for this?"

Liz smiled. "And you. Remember the case of Kate's missing surfboard? You told us exactly what to do. After we set up our sting operation, you were there to intimidate the culprits and get back the surfboard."

"There's a big difference between a stolen surfboard and a murder. Plus, I've only defended murder suspects, not prosecuted them."

They heard a knocking at the apartment's inner door leading into the hotel. Her father got up from the table and answered it. Aunt Amelia, Iris, and Agent Pearson stood in the hallway. Iris's usually stoic face was tearstained.

"What's going on?" he asked as they stepped inside.

Before Agent Pearson could answer, Aunt Amelia said, "Iris needs a lawyer. She's going to be arrested, and I assured her that you would take her case."

Liz got up from the table. "Arrested for what?"

Agent Pearson ignored Liz's question. "Fenton, are you going to take her case? I need to know. I have a deputy waiting outside."

Aunt Amelia came to him and took both of her nephew's hands in hers. "Everyone needs a good defense attorney, as you've told me yourself."

"I didn't kill anyone, if that's what you're thinking!" Iris shouted, breaking out of her stupor.

"Ms. Kimball, don't say another word. I'll meet you at the courthouse," Fenton said.

"Thank you, Mr. Holt," she said with tear-filled eyes.

At least he hadn't said the word "jail." The courthouse and jail were in the same building.

"And, Charlotte," he added. "I don't think you need to put her in handcuffs. Unless you're charging her with a capital offense?"

"Not as yet, I'm not. Okay. No handcuffs. We'll see you there."

Liz saw that one of the pages from her suspect list had fallen to the floor. Unfortunately, so did Agent Pearson.

Before Liz could grab it, Agent Pearson swooped in and snatched it up. "What do we have here?" she asked, adding a *tsk-tsk* sound.

"That is private," Fenton said.

She looked down at the paper. "I see Iris Kimball's name on here."

Iris shot them a dirty look.

Fenton snatched it from her hand. "Thank you, Charlotte. It's simply a list of all the people who were around at the time of the murder."

Agent Pearson didn't look at him in anger. Instead, the detective seemed to view him as a worthy opponent—the game now afoot. She glanced at Liz, then back at Fenton with a smile. "Well, I hope you aren't keeping anything from me?"

Liz broke into their moment. "Charlotte, we'll be willing to go over everything we have learned, if you'll let us in on a few things you've learned, as well." In all fairness, when Agent Pearson and Liz had first met, she'd been introduced by her first name.

Agent Pearson's lips turned slightly upward. "'Us'? Well, I see one thing on your list for suspect number one I can clear up right now—nothing was self-inflicted. But I'm not at liberty to share anything more. And the two of you"—she gave Fenton a chastising nod—"must report anything you know about this matter, or you could be charged with interfering in our investigation." She took a step closer to a now whimpering Iris. "Perhaps later, I might be willing to sit down with you and your father, but only if you're forthright with me beforehand."

Aunt Amelia moved to go with them, but Fenton held her back. Agent Pearson put her hand on Iris's elbow and guided her into the hallway. Liz heard the squeaking of the housekeeper's shoes as she scuffled away.

"Stay with Liz," Fenton said to Amelia. "I want to be there when they bring Iris in. Why do you think she's innocent, and what is she being charged with?"

Aunt Amelia sat on the sofa and fingered the iridescent beads around her neck. "They say she pawned one of Regina Harrington-Worth's missing earrings. They have her signature at the pawnshop and even have camera footage of her coming in with an earring and a cat collar with diamonds on it. Iris said the earring was lying on the carpet next to the collar when she went into Regina's bedroom and found her dead. Iris grabbed them both, knowing that whoever killed Regina would be blamed for the theft rather than her."

"Did she say any of this in front of Charlotte?" Fenton asked.

Aunt Amelia rubbed her hands in worry. "Yes. Was that a bad thing?"

"Not a good thing, that's for sure." He walked into his office and grabbed his briefcase from the floor next to his desk. He turned back before going out the door. "Auntie, did Iris say anything else to Agent Pearson I should know about?"

"Yes. She swore she didn't murder Mrs. Worth. She said she took the earring and collar to get enough money to help her mother get an operation. And I believe her."

As strange as it seemed, Liz tended to believe Iris, too.

Chapter 33

On the way to the emporium, Liz saw Captain Netherton pull out of the Indialantic's parking lot in his Ford Explorer, most likely heading to the police station where Agent Pearson had taken Iris. He was Iris's alibi for the night of the murder and vice versa. Liz thought of Greta Kimball waiting for her daughter to come through with the money so she could have her operation and leave the Sundowner Retirement Home. She understood Iris's in-the-moment temptation to grab the earring to help her destitute mother. However, Liz recalled when she'd pricked her finger on one the prongs on Venus's collar and noticed a missing stone. Had Iris been the one who had pried off a stone to verify whether it was a real diamond? Then a vision of the champagne bottle and the two flutes she'd seen in Iris's sitting room the day before the murder popped into her head. There was definitely someone else in Iris's life. As soon as her father came back from the courthouse, Liz planned to ask him to call the security company for a copy of the footage for the night before Regina's death, to see whether he could find Iris's champagne-sharing guest. The feed on his laptop was only good for seventy-two hours. Liz would also share everything she'd written in her notes involving Iris. She didn't know if the information would help or hurt Iris's case, but as Iris's attorney, he needed to know everything. As for David Worth, his wound wasn't self-inflicted, sliding him down near the bottom of the list.

After parking the Caddy, Liz walked to the emporium and stepped inside. Kate sat on the bench by the window, whispering into a book. The tips of Bronte's ears crowned from the basket next to her, and a huge shopping bag rested on the floor by Kate's feet. As Liz stepped closer, she heard Kate say to *How to Care for and Nurture Your New Kitten*, "You give good instructions to the newbie owner, but I noticed you didn't mention you must play with your kitten every day, so make sure Liz can read between your lines."

Brittany Poole stood next to a mannequin near the half wall to Sirens by the Sea, accessorizing a flowing, tropical-print sundress with a strand of chunky lime-green glass beads. After she draped the beads around the mannequin's neck, she glanced at Liz, then pointed to Kate. Brittany raised her right hand up to her ear, then extended her pointer finger and swirled it in the air in the universal "crazy" gesture. Clicking her tongue and shaking her head, Brittany turned and walked to the back of her shop. She stood behind the cash register and continued to watch them.

Liz agreed that Kate's conversing with books was a little on the idiosyncratic side, but Kate had once explained to her that every book written held a certain energy, an aura of connection to the heart and soul of the author who'd written it. As an author herself, why should Liz argue? Kate never cared about anyone else's opinion. Liz wished some of that confidence would rub off on her. She walked over to the basket, glanced inside, and saw *her* fluffy gray-and-white kitten nestled atop an apropos Hello Kitty flannel blanket.

"Yay. She didn't run away and hide in the Bronte section of your bookshelves. That must be a good sign."

"It's kismet. You're meant to be together," Kate said, then sneezed.

"Bless you!" Something about the ferocity of her sneeze suddenly flipped a switch in Liz's memory. "Hurry, let's get out to the car. Chop chop!" She took the basket holding Bronte.

Kate stood and put the book in the bag that held Bronte's things. "Boy, Liz, you're sure anxious for a new companion."

Liz prodded Kate toward the exit, noticing Brittany watching them with a strange look on her face. Liz hoped it had nothing to do with what Liz had just realized. When Brittany had made fun of Kate with her "crazy" gesture, there on her right hand was the same ring Regina Harrington-Worth had been wearing the night Liz had brought her husband's suitcases up to the Oceana Suite.

Once outside, Kate said, "Okay, okay. What's the rush?"

Liz kept her mouth shut about Regina's ring. She knew Kate too well. If she told her, Kate would charge back inside and read Brittany the riot act. "I'm just anxious to get Bronte settled." Then she told Kate about Iris Kimball's arrest.

"Wow," Kate said. "I never saw that one coming. I mean, she really is a sourpuss and all, and knowing about Iris's mother's situation, I guess it's a possibility she even murdered Regina."

"Aunt Amelia doesn't believe it. She's hired my father to be Iris's lawyer." Liz wanted to add, *Now that I've seen Brittany with Regina's ring, it will play to Iris's advantage.*

Kate opened the passenger door to the Caddy and put the bag of Bronte's things on the floor. Liz placed the basket on the seat and said to Bronte, "We'll be home in three minutes." She adjusted the seat belt diagonally across the basket in case she had to stop short for a crab, turtle, or armadillo crossing the road. She shut the door, then hurried to the driver's side and got in. Kate came over to the driver's window and yelled through the glass, "Text me if you hear anything. I have to get back inside. Ryan's stopping by to help me anchor my canoe to the wall."

If Liz attempted to manually roll down the Caddy's window, nine times out of ten, it would get stuck halfway. "Fun times," she shouted back.

"You know it!" Kate said, completely missing Liz's sarcasm.

When Liz returned home, she retrieved Bronte from the front seat. Cradling the basket in her arms, she walked up the steps onto the deck. She opened the French door and went inside. Glancing down at the tiny furball, she knew she'd done the right thing. Bronte hadn't mewed once on the way to the beach house. Liz said, "I won't let you down, little one. I promise."

She placed the basket near the sofa and went out to the car for the rest of the kitten's things. When she came inside, Bronte was perched on the cushioned window seat looking out at the ocean. Liz took a mental snapshot. Could there be a more tranquil, soothing picture than a kitten, a window seat, and the sea? Maybe Liz would become one of those spinsterlike Miss Marples, with a cat, a pair of knitting needles, and no man to complicate things. Liz had always toyed with the idea of penning a "cozy mystery," as her editor called them. She would use a pseudonym like Betty had, and there'd be little violence and gore, a sprinkling of humor, and a puzzle that was neatly solved, resulting in a happy ending—except for that of the murder victims, of course.

The fact that Brittany had been wearing Regina's ring meant she was somehow involved in the murder. But Liz's next thought segued to the fact that not even Brittany would be stupid enough to wear the emerald and chunky gold ring in plain sight—although her boyfriend, Nick, might have been stupid enough to have given it to her after *he* murdered Regina Harrington-Worth.

Liz made sure Bronte was settled, then she texted Ryan and Betty: *Meet me at the Indialantic's dock in ten minutes. New developments. Liz.* Ryan responded with *OK*, and Betty with a thumbs-up emoticon. Liz set out food, water, and a cat bed, then scattered a few catnip toys on the floor before leaving a sleeping Bronte on the window seat. She hated to leave her new housemate, but she had to share with Betty and Ryan about the ring she'd just seen on Brittany. Before leaving the beach house, she called her father and left a message on his voice mail, telling him about the ring on Brittany's finger, knowing he would pass the information on to Charlotte.

Exactly ten minutes later, Liz was sitting in her father's Chris-Craft, *Serendipity*. At one time, the Indialantic's dock would have been considered more of a pier. Almost a hundred years later, following a plethora of hurricanes and storms, it had been shortened and rebuilt with enough room to moor ten yacht-sized vessels. Today, besides the *Serendipity*, only *Queen of the Seas* and Edward Goren's skiff were in their slips. Overly kindhearted Aunt Amelia offered dock privileges to her hotel guests, as well as to her shopkeepers at the emporium.

It was perfect weather for a boat ride on the Indian River Lagoon. However, Liz planned to stay dockside, away from suspicious eyes and ears, namely Aunt Amelia's and Barnacle Bob's. She didn't want to go anywhere near the emporium and Brittany Poole. Her great-aunt had enough on her mind between Iris and Pierre. Liz and her father had convinced Aunt Amelia that Pierre needed to see a doctor. Liz's heart broke when she saw the resignation about Pierre's condition sink in and bury Aunt Amelia's sunny resolve and her penchant for looking at the positive side of life.

Betty walked up the dock carrying an umbrella. There wasn't a cloud in the sky. Betty called out, "You left this in my suite. Thought you might need it." She wore a pair of white capris and a navy-and-white horizontal boatneck top with a red bandana tied around her neck. On her feet were navy boat shoes. She carried a large white tote bag with an embroidered emblem of an anchor on the front that Liz knew was handmade and purchased from Home Arts by the Sea.

"Thanks, Betty. I rushed out without sun protection." Liz extended her hand and Betty hopped onto the deck with amazing agility. "You sure dressed for the occasion, but I wasn't planning on taking us out. There are new developments."

Betty sat on the stern's teak-cushioned bench. "Can't wait to hear them. You couldn't ask for a more perfect day. You sure you don't want to take a short cruise out to 'our' island?"

Betty was referring to a small uninhabited island south of the Sebastian Inlet. In the past, they would pack a picnic lunch, throw anchor, and wade toward shore. Then they would pretend to be stranded on the island, like in *Robinson Crusoe*, one of Liz's favorite childhood reads. The island had shrunk in size over the years from hurricanes and changing water surges.

She hoped it even still existed. Liz hadn't driven a boat since she'd been back, but she was familiar with every nuance of the *Serendipity*, even down to the correct amount and type of wax to use on the vintage teak deck.

"I'd love to. But I don't think we should leave port until we sort out all the latest developments."

Ryan strolled up to the dock wearing sky-blue shorts, a white t-shirt, Wayfarer sunglasses, and a blue Miami Marlins' baseball cap. He looked the antithesis of dark, enigmatic Brooklyn Ryan as he called out, "Hey, Skipper, what mysterious ports are we cruising to?"

"I haven't taken this baby out in ten years," Liz said, laughing. "Are you sure you want to take a chance?"

"Fear of danger is ten thousand times more terrifying than danger itself," he said as he climbed on board.

Liz almost fell into the lagoon. He'd just quoted Daniel Defoe from *Robinson Crusoe*. "We should stay near shore for the time being. I'm waiting for my father to come back from the courthouse. If we head out to sea, I might lose my cell phone signal."

Ryan stepped on board and took a seat next to Betty. He removed his sunglasses and hat, then gave Liz his full attention. "Okay, Captain, fire away."

Liz swiveled in the pilot's seat so she could face them. "There've been so many new developments in the last few hours that I thought I'd call in our little posse to help me see the big picture."

Betty reached in her tote and removed her iPad. "I have a few things to share also."

Ryan took out his phone. "As do I."

"Who goes first?" Liz asked.

"You go, Liz," said Betty. "Do you mind if I record you?"

"Not at all."

Ryan touched something on his phone. "Great idea."

Liz stood at the same time a huge powerboat sent a tsunami-sized wake in the Chris-Craft's direction. She teetered and tottered, then fell directly into Ryan's waiting arms. Liz laughed with embarrassment, even though she didn't mind the hand-to-hand contact or the smell of his neck before she reluctantly pushed up and righted herself. "Oops. Sorry, have to get my sea legs back. I've been a landlubber too long."

Ryan smiled. "If you can handle this boat all by yourself, then you're a better seaman than me. I've only been a passenger on fishing boats, and I have to admit I always get seasick for the first half hour. Then my stomach settles and I'm good to go for hours." He moved over and patted the cushioned bench next to him.

"Thanks, but I have to stay out of the sun." Liz returned to the pilot's seat under the canopy. "The first bombshell, and possibly the only one we'll need is…wait for it…I just saw Brittany Poole wearing the same ring Regina Harrington-Worth wore Thursday night."

Betty slapped her knee. "Holy smoke!"

"Are you sure?" Ryan asked.

"Beyond sure. You can't miss this thing. It's huge, with a humongous emerald. I know it doesn't necessarily make Brittany guilty of murder, but it could point the finger at her boyfriend, Nick."

"Speaking of Nick," Betty said, "I was talking to Captain Netherton, and he said that when he was swabbing the deck of *Queen of the Seas*, he saw Iris and Nick heading out on Nick's father's skiff, both dressed in diving suits."

"Interesting," Liz said. "That might explain the champagne bottle and two glasses I saw in Iris's suite the day before the murder and the fact that she's always disappearing. But with their age difference, it's hard to picture them in a relationship."

"Maybe it was a business arrangement, not romantic?" Ryan suggested. "They could be diving for treasure. By the way, I have a call in to the new owner of Edward's business in Miami. I also had a little chat with Edward, as you suggested, Liz. He claims he was at Squidly's during the time Regina was murdered and he has a charge receipt to prove it. Along with the bartender as an eyewitness."

"Squidly's is within walking distance of the Indialantic," Liz said. "He could have snuck out the back door, done the deed, then returned to the restaurant without anyone noticing. That place is packed from the moment they open their doors until closing time."

"Grandad said Squidly's makes an amazing Thursday night crab boil. I'll have to check it out and see if anyone can verify Edward's alibi. I also had a conversation with Brittany over a glass of wine. She claims that she and Nick spent the evening at her place, exhausted from the Spring Fling."

A glass of wine? "Ha," Liz said, a little too harshly. "What did she do? Break a fingernail ringing up sales?"

Betty looked at Liz. "It seems that all three of them have weak alibis."

"I left my father a voice mail about the ring Brittany was wearing. He's at the courthouse. Iris was arrested."

"Say what!" Betty held her iPad close to Liz's mouth.

"Agent Pearson arrested Iris for stealing one of Regina's earrings and trying to pawn it, along with Regina's cat's diamond collar."

Betty's eyes opened wide. "I didn't see that one coming. I had officially taken her off my list."

"Iris said she found the single earring and cat collar on the floor the night of the murder. But if she killed Regina, that would mean Captain Netherton was her accomplice."

"I don't think so," Ryan said. "I've looked into the captain's past, and he's squeaky-clean. Not even a parking ticket. He also volunteers with underprivileged high school kids on his days off, teaching them sailing. There have been no changes in his bank accounts, and he's received the United States Coast Guard Silver Lifesaving Medal." Ryan looked to Liz. "Captain Netherton was wounded on that same mission, and he has a metal rod in his left leg."

"So, maybe Iris and Nick are in it together?" Betty said.

"Hmmm. One more thing." Liz felt like a heel for having thought the captain was faking his limp. "I wanted to believe Francie is also innocent, but she lied about her alibi the night of the murder. Plus, her parents and Regina's hung out together and there are rumors that Regina's mother and Francie's father were having an affair. I also discovered something else strange. There was a retrospective recently held of Percival Harrington II at the library. Someone broke into the showcase and stole a few old photographs."

"Okay, let's recap. Our top suspects are Nick Goren, Edward Goren, Francie Jenkins, Iris Kimball, and David Worth," Ryan said, as he put on his sunglasses.

"You can take David off the list," Liz said. "Agent Pearson divulged that his wound was 'not' self-inflicted. That leaves Nick, Edward, Francie, and Iris. Brittany wouldn't kill Regina, then wear her stolen ring. Iris can only be an accessory to murder, because we believe Captain Netherton is innocent, and he swears Iris was with him the entire night. Hopefully, when my father returns, we'll get a clearer picture of everything and fill in a few more pieces of the puzzle."

After Liz battened down *Serendipity*'s hatches, the three went into the hotel and shared a pitcher of Pierre's lemon-limeade and a plate of coconut lime sugar cookies, Liz's childhood favorites, and waited for Fenton to arrive home.

Chapter 34

Upon waking Wednesday morning, Liz stretched, turned back the duvet, and reached for her phone. Peering through sleepy eyes, she saw it was 8 a.m. She placed the phone back on the nightstand and looked over next to her. Panic struck. Where was Bronte? Two white paws emerged from where she'd folded back the duvet. She peeled back the covers and exposed a gray-and-white-striped kitten.

"Bronte, I thought you'd abandoned me." Liz turned on her side and cozied up to the kitten, sticking her nose in the long, white fur on her belly, thinking Bronte must have some Persian ancestors in her pedigree. "It was quite a day yesterday. I hope today finds things back to normal." Bronte turned her head at Liz's voice, and she could already feel the calming effect of pet ownership. There had always been family pets at the Indialantic over the years. Liz luxuriated in the fact that Bronte was all hers. Maybe if she'd had a pet when she lived alone in Manhattan, she wouldn't have needed a man—as in Travis. She glanced out the floor-to-ceiling windows in front of her, which looked out to the sea. Dense fog eclipsed the view, and she relaxed back on her pillows. Blessedly, she had no pressing engagements for the day. She planned to stay inside and snuggle up with Miss Bronte.

Yesterday, when her father had returned to the Indialantic, Liz, Ryan, and Betty knocked on his office door and laid out everything they knew. Her father then called Agent Pearson and relayed a concise, detailed summary of what had been uncovered by the Three Detectiveteers.

After Fenton heard Liz's message about the ring, he'd accompanied Agent Pearson to the emporium just in time to catch Brittany and Nick as they were leaving. Brittany handed over the ring, a supposed gift from Nick. Agent Pearson and Fenton went directly to David Worth's suite, and he confirmed that the ring was, indeed, his wife's. Her father said David had seemed so upset that he worried he might have a stroke.

Her father had also passed on, per Agent Pearson, that Francie had an alibi for Saturday night. She was at the Sebastian Beach Inn sitting at the bar until midnight. Two men sitting next to her, and the bartender, collaborated Francie's claim. Apparently, Francie had lied to Minna, knowing the two men who'd showed up for their blind date weren't Minna's type. Francie decided to take a chance in case one of them was her soul mate. Plus, she wanted to drown her guilt about the fact that she'd vandalized the Worths' Bentley. They also learned that there was a drop of blood found in the dumbwaiter that matched David's blood type. Liz had been right in assuming the dumbwaiter had been used by the killer.

Liz scooped up Bronte and brought her to the kitchen. "Breakfast time, kitty."

As she filled Bronte's water and food bowl, she heard the tinkling of piano keys coming from the bedroom, indicating she'd received an e-mail or text on her phone. She placed the bowls on a cute plastic mat Kate had supplied and hurried to retrieve her phone. She tapped the phone's screen and opened an e-mail from Mrs. Ingles.

Liz, I came across this picture of the showcase taken the morning of Percival Harrington II's retrospective. The two bottom right photos are the ones that were stolen, I had one of our librarians enlarge them for you. I don't know if any of this will help with your investigation, but let me know if it does. XO, Mrs. Ingles.

She went to her office to look more closely at the photos on her laptop. So much for letting go and allowing the authorities to take over. There were still too many questions. An hour later, she was out the door, heading to the emporium. There was someone she needed to talk to.

Liz set out on foot for the emporium, afraid to drive even a golf cart in the miasma. She could barely make out the outline of the building in the dense fog. It wasn't raining, but by the time she walked inside, she was drenched from head to toe. There was still an hour and a half until opening and the shops were in darkness. Light filtered in from the single wall of windows, casting shadows onto the mannequins in Sirens by the Sea. As she hurried past the shop, she swore one of the mannequins moved, like in one of Aunt Amelia's black-and-white episodes of *The Outer Limits*. She rounded the corner at full speed, worried Brittany or Nick were hiding, ready to stab her with the knife that had wounded David Worth. A dim light glowed from Gold Coast by the Sea, and Liz moved toward it.

Edward sat at his small worktable, resembling a wax museum figure from one of her great-aunt's favorite 1950s movies, *House of Wax*, which ironically starred Vincent Price, Edward's look-alike, in the starring role as Professor Henry Jarrod.

Liz walked in and moved toward him. "Edward, can I talk to you?" A small desk lamp was the only light source in the shop. Still he didn't move. For a minute, Liz thought he might be dead, but as she edged closer, she saw a slight tremor in his left hand. "Edward, are you alright? Should I call a doctor?"

Slowly, his gaze moved up to Liz's face. "What do you want?"

"I wanted to ask you about your time on Percival Harrington II's salvager, *Ocean's Bounty,* and why you never told anyone you were part of the crew that brought up treasure from the shipwrecked *San Carlos.*"

Mrs. Ingles had sent Liz the two photographs missing from Percival II's retrospective. After Liz scanned them, she'd recognized someone familiar—a young Edward Goren. Edward was the only one of the crew on the *Ocean's Bounty* that didn't have a wide-mouthed grin on his face. In the photos, he wore the same scowl he had now, looking up at Liz.

"Why would I tell anyone that? It's not a crime. It was my first job. I was more of an indentured servant than a diver, not like the all-powerful Percival Harrington II, with his Midas touch. Prissy Percy never even went down to sift through the rubble on the sea floor—he sent us down, like coal miners into an unsafe mine, no high-tech equipment or safety gear, expecting us to pull up his loot, then hand it over, no questions asked. If it wasn't for the map I'd made of where the cargo hold of the *San Carlos* might be located, based on tide charts, past storms, and hurricanes, all Pretty Boy Percy would have found was a bunch of broken pottery."

"*You* found the treasure?"

"You're surprised? Percy waited at the surface, treading water in his brand-new wet suit, waiting for the treasure to be cranked up so he could grab the net for the perfect photo op. Instead of patting me on the back for finding a king's ransom, or should I say a queen's, because much of the jewelry had been a dowry for Queen Maria Luisa of Spain, he pushed me away. I'm sure you've seen the historic photo; it was plastered in every newspaper across the country." He opened the single drawer under his worktable, rifled through it, pulled out a sepia-colored page of newsprint, and handed it to her. He was right. It was the same yellowed front-page article Liz had seen framed on the walls of local treasure museums, restaurants, and gift shops—and at historical society events.

Edward continued his diatribe. "Afterward, when we laid everything out on deck to sort through, Percy threw me a few gold coins and said, 'Keep the change,' then laughed for the cameras. But I wasn't laughing."

"How did your son get ahold of Regina Harrington-Worth's ring from the *San Carlos*?"

"What the hell are you talking about?"

"You haven't heard?"

"Heard what?"

"Your son gave it to Brittany Poole. I know it's the same one, because I saw it on Regina's hand Thursday night."

White-knuckled, Edward gripped the table edge like he wanted to lift it up and toss it at her. But before he could, he received a phone call.

It was just as well, for Liz knew she was swimming in dangerous territory. She wasn't a daredevil like Kate, and she remembered the wise adage, "Never confront a killer without backup."

Edward stood, put his phone in his pocket, and turned off the lamp. He brushed past her and strode out of the shop without a word, leaving Liz in the dark—literally and metaphorically.

She felt her way out of the shop, the only light source in this part of the emporium from the Exit sign by the emergency door. She carefully stepped down the corridor, toward the faint light coming from the windows by the entrance. In front of Books & Browsery by the Sea, she received a phone call.

"There's news on the ring you saw on Brittany," Ryan said, skipping any form of greeting.

"What kind of news?"

"The ring is a fake. I just talked to Charlotte."

Charlotte? "But Regina's husband said it was hers...?"

"It's an excellent fake."

"What about the earring that Iris pawned? Was that a fake, too?"

"No, Charlotte said it was the real thing."

"This is crazy. Where do we go from here?" Liz told Ryan about the photos Mrs. Ingles had sent and her conversation only moments before with Edward Goren. "Did you ask Charlotte if they'd checked to see if there are any other copies of jewelry from the treasure of *San Carlos*?"

"Charlotte's doing that now. She's at the bank with your father. The same bank where Regina had a dozen safety-deposit boxes. Charlotte told me Regina's father had made it a stipulation in his will that a representative from the bank had to be on hand to sign off on what jewels were taken out of the boxes and what were put back in."

"Wow. Crazy. Let me know if you hear anything else? Can you fill her in on Edward? And also ask her to have my father call me."

"Of course. You be careful. I suggest you head back to your beach house and lock the doors."

"Yes, Mr. Bossy Pants."

Ryan laughed. "It's so foggy out there, it took me a half hour to get to my grandfather's. We're leaving now for Deli-casies. I'll call you when we get there, and you can come over for lunch. We'll wait together for any updates."

"Sounds good," Liz said, slightly surprised by the invitation.

Then he added, "Invite Betty, too." Her spirits took a slightly downward spiral.

After she hung up, she chided herself for being jealous over Ryan's possible attraction to forty-something Agent Charlotte Pearson. But the woman was gorgeous and competent, and well, gorgeous. Liz's thoughts segued to the fake ring—even David Worth had been fooled when Agent Pearson showed it to him. Who had made the fake? And why? She guessed, after Agent Pearson opened the safety-deposit boxes and had the jewels tested, they would know whether any other pieces from the *San Carlos* treasure had been duplicated. If that was the case, Liz wondered if Regina had been the one commissioning the fakes so she could sell the real thing without her father or the insurance company knowing. Then Liz circled back to Nick Goren, who'd given the ring to Brittany. Completing the wheel of confusion was Edward's confession that he'd been the one to find the original treasure, without getting any credit or compensation.

As Liz walked by Home Arts by the Sea, the main lights to the emporium switched on, and she heard voices, Nick's and Brittany's. Liz crouched down and went into Home Arts, then crawled under one of the worktables so she could eavesdrop.

"How dare you give me a fake piece of jewelry!" Brittany screeched. "I'll be the laughingstock of the island. What a bullshit story you gave me about finding the ring when you were with your father on one of his salvaging expeditions, saving it for when you met the love of your life."

"The part about the love of my life is true," Nick pleaded. "I embellished on the other part, but that doesn't mean I knew it was a copy."

"So where did you get it?"

"It was in a box that came in the mail, addressed to my father. I opened it because it came from the Cayman Islands, where he has a few not-so-secret-from-me bank accounts. I was positive the ring was something he'd found on one of his salvaging expeditions outside U.S. waters that he didn't want the ship's port-of-origin country knowing about. The laws of treasure salvaging are pretty strict. Three months went by and he never mentioned it, so I gave it to you. I told you not to wear it to the emporium, that it was too valuable, but you didn't listen."

"Obviously, it wasn't too valuable. Blah, blah, blah," Brittany said. "You can leave now. I have a shop to open. Oh, and if any of the other jewelry you've given me is fake, too, go to my condo and take them back—and be sure to leave your key or I'll change the locks."

"I'm not giving up," he said, his voice cracking. "Now that I have my diving certification, we can do what we planned. Start our own treasure-salvaging company."

"Ha. That won't be happening. Our plan depended on financial backing from your father. Do you think he's going to help you out now? Buh-bye, loser."

Nick didn't answer. A few seconds later, the double doors leading outside slammed with such force that the prisms hanging from the Baccarat chandelier crashed against each other, reminding Liz of her favorite scene in Broadway's *The Phantom of the Opera*. Liz waited under the table until she heard Brittany pass by, muttering a litany of curses that made Barnacle Bob seem like a choir-bird.

Finally, Liz stood. Pain shot up her spine from her lower back, and she let out a small groan that seemed to bounce off the tin-tiled ceiling. She held her breath, praying Brittany hadn't heard, then scurried out the main door, making sure to close it as quietly as possible. Then she stepped out into the dense fog.

Chapter 35

Brittany's car was the only one in the emporium's parking lot. Liz turned onto the path that ran behind the emporium. The Indian River Lagoon was to her right. The strong, pungent, fishy odor filled her nostrils. The summer before she'd left for college, thousands of dead fish lined the lagoon because of a record-breaking brown tide. That year, the hot summer weather and lack of rain had caused the algae to consume large quantities of oxygen, leaving little left for the fish and thus causing their death. Liz couldn't see, but she heard gulls emitting a high-pitched doomsday cry and the gentle lapping of the water against the boats moored at the Indialantic's dock. In the distance were the faint outlines of the *Serendipity*, *Queen of the Seas*, and Edward's skiff. She hurried along, engulfed by the suffocating mist.

Then she heard it. Not the wail of a seabird, but a wail nonetheless, followed by a faint "Help-p-p."

It took her a split second to stifle the thought that it might be a trap, someone out to get her, hiding in the mist. She crossed the road and crept toward the sound. Another "Help..." sounded, slightly louder. She stepped onto the dock, then stumbled, the toe of her sneaker catching in the gap between the planks of wood. The sound of footsteps echoed from behind, louder and louder, as they got closer and closer.

"Stop!" a male voice said.

She didn't. She moved faster toward the sound of the next garbled and whimpering call of distress. It was coming from Edward Goren's skiff. She held on to the piling and felt for the rope tethering the boat to its slip. She grabbed the rope and tugged, bringing the boat closer, then she made a blind leap onto the deck, landing on her knees.

The voice called out again, "I know you're there."

She swiped at the long bangs that blocked her vision, and saw the silhouette of a tall, muscular body. Then she heard that same body jump on deck. The boat rocked at the man's bulk.

"I told you to stop!" he said.

Liz stifled her own whimpering, as Nick Goren's huge hand grabbed her by the shoulder.

"What are you doing sneaking around my father's boat?" he demanded.

She ducked and stepped to the bow of the skiff, where the fog rolling off the water was thicker. "I um, I thought this was my father's boat. This damn fog is relentless."

"Brittany says I should stay away from you. You're a nosy bitch who likes to steal things."

Liz wanted to say, "*I like to steal things! Get real.*" Instead she said, "I'd better get going to meet my father on his boat. He's waiting there with Agent Pearson."

Suddenly the skiff moved to the right and they heard a guttural moan, like a bear trying to free its foot from a trap. Nick moved to the leeward side of the boat and called out, "Who's there?"

"Nick-k-k…"

"Father?"

Nick flipped up a bench, removed a lantern, then turned it on. At first, all they could see was the mist bouncing back at them. Then Liz saw a hand hanging on to a cleat on the edge of the boat. She peered over. Edward looked up at her from the inky water. She clasped his wrist in both of her hands and tugged. "Help me, Nick. He's heavy." She didn't have time to worry about whether Nick was Regina's killer. They had a life to save—his father's.

Nick pushed her aside. "I've got it." He leaned over and grabbed Edward's arm above the elbow and tugged. Thirty seconds later, Nick laid his semiconscious father onto the deck. A huge gash on Edward's forehead oozed red, and he mumbled, "David… David tried to kill me."

Nick put a hand on either side of his father's head. "David Worth? Why would he want to kill you?"

Except for the blood that trailed from his scalp into his left eye, the lantern made his face appear ghostly white. Through blue lips, he said, "He had me stab him. But I didn't kill her. I swear, I didn't."

"Stop. You don't have to tell us anything more right now," Nick said.

Edward closed his eyes and his head drooped to the side.

"I don't have my phone. Call nine-one-one, then run to the hotel to get help. I'll stay with my father," Nick said.

As Liz stepped off the boat, she heard Nick say, "I took diving lessons and I'm certified now. You can be proud of me now, Daddy. Hang in there. Help is on the way."

Chapter 36

Liz called 911, then ran toward the hotel, stumbling to her knees three times before she reached her father's office door. She banged her fist against the door like a madwoman, but no one answered. She sped to the outside kitchen door. It was locked, the kitchen empty.

When she finally made it to the revolving door at the hotel's entrance, she collapsed against the glass and was spit out into the lobby. She tripped on the Persian rug and landed on her knees, knees that were bleeding from her previous falls. Out of breath and wheezing, she pushed herself up to a standing position and saw Aunt Amelia sitting on the floor. Betty was crouched next to her, holding a glass of water to her great-aunt's trembling lips.

"Auntie! What's happened?" She rushed to her side. Her great-aunt's cheeks were flushed, and her scarlet hair had escaped its ponytail. Liz placed the palm of her hand on Aunt Amelia's forehead, just like her great-aunt had done to Liz when she was young and awakened from a nightmare. "Betty, what's going on?"

Betty set the glass on the bamboo table, and they helped Aunt Amelia onto a chair.

"Amelia saw David Worth in the lobby with his suitcases," Betty explained. "She tried to convince him to stay, but he flew past her, knocked her to the ground, then sped off in his Bentley."

"A rude young man," Aunt Amelia added.

Barnacle Bob squawked from his cage by the reception desk, "Rude young man."

"You said it, BB." Aunt Amelia attempted to stand, but sat back down.

"An ambulance should be here any minute," Liz said. "I'll have them take a look at you, Auntie."

Betty said, "I've already called Ryan. He should—"

Ryan flew through the revolving door and was at Aunt Amelia's side. "What's happened?"

Betty explained while Ryan checked Aunt Amelia's vitals. He said, "Your pulse rate is slightly elevated, but I think you'll be fine."

"Of course I'll be fine, Ryan. I'm a certified zumbaoligist. Could beat you in a relay race, I'm sure."

"I'm sure you could." he said, grinning. "What's a zumbaoligist?"

"An expert at Zumba."

"I'll explain later," Liz said hurriedly. "Ryan, can you step outside for a moment? I hear the ambulance."

"I don't think your great-aunt needs an ambulance."

Liz caught his gaze and nodded her head toward the front of the hotel.

"Okay, ladies, I'll be right back. I'll talk to the paramedics and tell them they aren't needed."

"Of course, they're not needed," Aunt Amelia said.

Liz and Ryan stepped into the same section of the revolving door. It was tight quarters, but after what Liz had just been through, the closeness was comforting.

Once outside, Ryan said, "Hey, you're bleeding."

"Just a couple of scrapes." She grabbed Ryan's elbow and led him onto the path on the south side of the hotel. "We have to hurry and meet the ambulance at the dock."

"I thought the ambulance was coming for Aunt Amelia?"

It was endearing to her that he'd added the word "aunt" to her title.

Liz continued to hold his arm as they walked through the fog, explaining what had gone down with Edward and Nick Goren.

When she'd finished, Ryan said, "Not even I would have guessed about Edward Goren stabbing David to give him an alibi for his wife's murder. When Betty called me about David Worth's behavior and his frantic exodus from the hotel, I called Charlotte. She sent a couple of cars to look for him, but I doubt, in this fog, they'll have any luck. I also told her about what Betty had texted us."

"What text? I didn't get a text." Liz took out her phone, brought it up to the tip of her nose, and read: *I called all the nearby hotels that allow pets, and none of them were booked for Thursday night, the night the Worths checked in. Their claim, that staying at the Indialantic Hotel was their only recourse, was a lie. I also talked to Josie from Josie's Flower Shop.*

She saw Edward Goren walking toward Squidly's around seven, when she went to pick up an outdoor potted tree she'd left behind, which means that his alibi might be legit, if the murder happened at 7:30, as Captain Netherton said. Let's meet later this afternoon. Betty.

Liz recalled that Regina had been the one who wanted to the leave the hotel. It was David who'd said he'd called around and found that all the hotels were booked.

"I can't believe David Worth is going to get away with killing his wife," Ryan said. "Hopefully, they'll catch him."

"What if Edward recants his story about stabbing David, giving David an alibi for Regina's murder? Edward was pretty delirious. What if he dies?"

Strobe lights flashed up ahead. When they reached the dock, an ambulance was already pulling away with its siren blaring—a good sign that Edward was still alive. Agent Pearson was standing next to Liz's father. Liz removed her arm from Ryan's and ran toward them.

"Dad! How badly is Edward hurt?"

Her father wrapped her in a bear hug and said, "It's pretty bad, but we won't know more until he gets checked out. He was unconscious when we got here."

Agent Pearson had a phone to her ear. She put the phone into her suit jacket pocket and said, "David Worth's Bentley just went off the Sebastian Inlet Bridge. There's no chance he could have survived. We are going to have the CSIs go over Mr. Goren's boat for evidence. Do you have any idea what went down here?"

Ryan said to Liz, "Why don't you go check on Aunt Amelia? I'll stay and explain everything to Charlotte and Fenton."

Liz felt relief, since she was so emotionally drained. The adrenaline rush she'd had earlier had sapped all her energy, and she was worried about her great-aunt. "Thank you."

She trekked slowly back to the hotel in the fog. When she entered the lobby, Barnacle Bob was in a frenzy, flapping his wings and squawking in parrot talk, not English. "What's wrong with him?" she asked.

"He's probably upset about the way that hooligan David Worth roughhoused Amelia," Betty said.

Liz moved toward Barnacle Bob, then lifted his brass stand and cage, then carried them over to Aunt Amelia.

Aunt Amelia said, "There's my pretty boy. Don't you lose a feather worrying about me."

"Rude young man," Barnacle Bob said.

"Yes, he was. But I am fine, my feathered friend."

Barnacle Bob calmed down. He whistled, then said, "Takes a licking and keeps on ticking."

Aunt Amelia let out a full-bodied laugh, her huge, dangling earrings slapping against her chin. "Don't you know it, old buddy."

"Where's Ryan?" Betty asked.

Liz looked at Aunt Amelia before she continued. Her great-aunt looked like she was back to her competent self, and so Liz told them what she'd witnessed at the dock.

Aunt Amelia said, "So Edward stabbed David Worth in order to give him an alibi?"

Betty said, "That explains something I just realized. The bottle of oxycodone that David Worth was supposedly using for the pain after he'd been stabbed, had actually been prescribed days before. The immediate pain from a stab wound would be much less if you were hopped up on megadoses of painkillers."

Wow. Liz should have picked up on that clue, but even "Mr. Investigator," Ryan Stone, had missed it. Pre-medicating also explained what Captain Netherton had told Liz about David's slurring and the behavior he had overheard coming from the Oceana Suite on the evening of Regina's murder.

"There's one more thing. David Worth's Bentley just went off the Sebastian Inlet Bridge. Agent Pearson said there is no chance he could have survived."

Aunt Amelia gasped. "Why do I get the feeling you two have been leaving me out of things? I'm not a fragile hothouse flower."

Liz took her great-aunt's hand. "We didn't want you to worry until we had more than just supposition."

"Then what you're saying is, David Worth killed his wife by strangling her with an Ace bandage? Why did he do it? For her money?"

"It wasn't for money, because he didn't get any," Betty said. "I think we will learn more when Edward confesses his role in the crime."

"I can't believe David Worth is dead," Aunt Amelia said.

Barnacle Bob repeated the old Timex watch jingle, "Takes a licking and keeps on ticking."

"Not this time, BB," Liz said.

Chapter 37

A month later, Liz was in the hotel's luggage room with her great-aunt.

After David's body had ironically washed up near Castlemara, Aunt Amelia arranged a double funeral for the Worths. Divers located the Bentley under the bridge. Nearby, on the ocean floor, they also recovered a suitcase filled with gold bars that Edward had given David in exchange for the jewels that, in his mind, he, not Percival Harrington II, had salvaged from the *San Carlos*. In a storage space leased by Edward, Agent Pearson found an entire glass display cabinet of priceless jewelry recovered from the *San Carlos*. There was even an easy chair in the center of the space, where Edward could relax and peruse his collection, finally one-upping "Percy."

Edward confessed that, months ago, he'd contacted David about buying a few pieces of Queen Maria Luisa's jewels from Regina before they were scheduled to go to the Sotheby's auction—the same auction that Minna said Regina's father had canceled because they weren't hers to sell. David and Edward then hatched a plan to make copies of the jewelry from photographs David took when Regina wasn't around. Edward sent the photos to the Cayman Islands, where he knew of a jeweler who made copies of famous eighteenth-century salvaged treasure for museums around the world. The only difference was that the pieces used in treasure museums were actually labeled as "reproductions." When Regina questioned the authenticity of a bracelet the pair had copied, David came up with the idea of a fake robbery. The morning of the Spring Fling, when David came into Gold Coast by the Sea, he wasn't really looking to buy something for Regina; he was complaining about the workmanship on a fake bracelet that Edward had commissioned. Edward swore he had no idea that David planned to kill Regina, saying he tried to leave when he walked in and saw

Regina's strangled body. David threatened to blame the whole murder on Edward if he didn't go through with the stabbing part of the plan. David had been recording their conversations and had followed Edward to his storage space. Edward paid David for the jewels with gold and cash. To Edward, it had never been about money. He wanted the treasure from the *San Carlos* because he felt he'd discovered it, not Percival II.

Liz had been right about the dumbwaiter being used. Edward said that David had waited until he saw Fenton leave for the emporium, then checked that the outside door to the office was open. Later, when David went down to the ice machine, supposedly to retrieve ice for his wife's knee, she was actually already dead. At that time, he let Edward in and brought him up to the Oceana Suite. After Edward stabbed David, he took the dumbwaiter back down and exited via Fenton's office, leaving behind a drop of David's blood from the knife he later threw in the lagoon. David faked the scuffle with his supposed knife-wielding assailant after he was sure Edward had safely exited the Indialantic via Fenton's office. The faked scuffle gave Edward an alibi, because he was safely on a bar stool at Squidly's at seven thirty. David got the idea of having Edward enter the hotel from Fenton's office on the same day Regina accused Liz of stealing her necklace. After Regina's fall, David watched Ryan carry his wife through Fenton's apartment and into the interior of the hotel.

Prior to the murder, David had been loading up on painkillers, so that when Edward stabbed him, the pain wouldn't be as intense—he was "premeditatedly medicated."

After Liz told Edward about the ring Brittany was wearing, he got a call from an irate David Worth, who'd just confirmed with Detective Pearson and Fenton that the ring was Regina's. David told Edward to meet him on the dock so they could come up with a plan. When Edward arrived, David whacked him on the head and dumped him in the water, planning on planting evidence that Edward was his wife's killer. Luckily, Liz and Nick showed up shortly afterward.

Liz also found proof of Edward and David's collusion. In the video Kate had texted to Liz while she was still in Manhattan of the Emporium by the Sea's grand opening, there was background footage of Edward handing something to David in a small box. No doubt, it was a forgery of a piece of jewelry from the *San Carlos*.

A week after David Worth's death, Agent Pearson's officers also found something interesting on Regina's father's yacht—a bottle of her father's heart medication. It was found in Regina's stateroom, under her mattress. The only fingerprints on the bottle were Regina's and her father's. No one would ever know whether Regina had kept the bottle from her father that day on the yacht, ultimately causing his death, but there were odds-on that she had.

"Here they are, Lizzy!" Aunt Amelia said excitedly, as she dug through her TV costume trunk. She pulled out an unopened package of what looked like small, white oval pillows and held them up in the air. "I stuffed two pairs of these babies in my brassiere for the episode of *The Wild Wild West* in which I played a saloon showgirl. I didn't have a speaking part, but I did get to stand next to President Grant's Secret Service agent extraordinaire, James West, I mean, Robert Conrad. I gazed into his ice-blue eyes, then gave him a wink and a great big smacker on his cheek. He was only an inch taller than me. Did you know he did all his own stunts?"

Liz would have sworn that over the past twenty-three years, she'd seen every part her great-aunt played. "No, I didn't. You never told me about that role—just the one in which you and Artemus Gordon had a three-episode flirtation."

"Ahh, Ross Martin. Boy, did we have more than a few laughs. I adored his sense of humor."

Liz opened the package, reached under her cropped T-shirt, and stuffed one of the pillows inside her bra. "My favorite part of the series is when the drawn pictures are filled in after each cliff-hanger scene, right before the commercial break." She stepped toward the full-length mirror hanging from the back of the door. "What do you think?"

Aunt Amelia said, "Bigger. Go bigger, I always say."

She looked at her great-aunt's colorful floor-length Japanese kimono embroidered with silk butterflies and cherry blossoms, and her brightly made-up face. Her long, wavy flame-red hair was held back by a large braid that was really a headband. If Aunt Amelia was going for demure, subservient geisha girl, something had gotten lost in the translation. But, as always, the total look was 100 percent Amelia Eden Holt.

Aunt Amelia handed Liz another package of falsies. "That should do it. Those Mary Quant hot pants look great on you. I can't believe I was once your size. Guess there's just more of me to love now."

"You're as beautiful today as you were the first time I saw you, Auntie."

"Now for the perfect wig," she said, wiping away a tear. "What color hair are you in the mood for?" She moved toward a stack of hat boxes and removed the lids. "I think chin-length brunette would be perfect. Although with what you've packed into the chest area, I don't think anyone on your covert mission will be looking anywhere else."

Liz put on the wig and looked in the mirror. She didn't recognize herself.

Aunt Amelia came at her with a large compact of makeup and a powder brush. "All you need is a little sparkle on your décolletage. Draw a little more attention. Too bad you can't borrow my white patent-leather go-go boots, but I think that might be a bit much. Nancy Sinatra gave them to me after I did a skit with her on *The Ed Sullivan Show*. I was in the background dancing the frug. But those wedge sandals will do nicely."

"The frug?" Liz asked.

"A very groovy dance, like the chicken dance," Aunt Amelia said.

Liz laughed and took another peek at herself in the mirror. "Let's go to the lobby and see if I can fool anyone."

Aunt Amelia said, "You go on ahead. It will look less conspicuous if I'm not tagging along."

Liz left the hotel via her father's office and went around to the front of the Indialantic. Betty and Captain Netherton were tossing a Frisbee to each other, laughing every time Killer leapt up and intercepted it. He was no "monkey in the middle." Liz smiled as she passed them. Betty winked as Captain Netherton frantically waved in her direction. Liz heard him ask, "Who's that? A new guest? She married?"

Would the captain ever learn not to let his libido lead the way?

Liz entered the revolving door, but she pushed too hard and almost broke her neck as she stumbled into the lobby, teetering on her five-inch wedges. Greta Kimball sat in a wheelchair *click*ing and *clack*ing away with a pair of knitting needles, the heel of a thick wool sock taking shape. Venus, the hairless cat, slept by her feet in her leopard cat bed. This was the fifth pair of socks Greta had made for her daughter, Iris. Like Betty and her granny squares, Greta liked to make multiples of her needlework projects.

Greta looked up and said, "Good morning." There was no sign she recognized Liz.

After Liz's father had gotten Iris off on a technicality for stealing the earring and cat collar, Iris had signed up for a tour of duty, training navy divers in Alaska. Instead of a romantic liaison, the champagne bottle and two glasses Liz had seen in Iris's room had really been from a celebration between Iris and Nick Goren, after Iris had helped him get his diving certification. The times when Iris had been missing around the hotel, she'd actually been moonlighting as a diving instructor, trying to save money for her mother's operation. Aunt Amelia had taken it upon herself to spring Greta from the Sundowner Retirement Home. Greta and the orphaned Venus immediately bonded, and Aunt Amelia allowed Greta to keep Venus with her in the Swaying Palms Suite. After Greta's operation, which Fenton would finance until she received the settlement he'd procured from her insurance company, Greta promised to take over her daughter's job as housekeeper and would live at the hotel rent-free. Liz had grown fond of Greta and had no problem helping out until after she was healed.

Pierre was on the other side of the lobby on a bamboo chaise reading *Peril at End House*, one of her favorite Christies because it took place in Cornwall, England, Liz's great-grandmother's birthplace. Cornwall had also been the setting for Liz's novel, *Let the Wind Roar*. Aunt Amelia had taken Pierre to a wonderful doctor, who'd checked all of their criteria. Dr. Helmer was both an MD and a homeopathic healer. There was no definitive diagnosis as of yet, but Liz prayed daily for a positive outcome.

Pierre looked up at Liz and took off his toque. "Hi, Lizzy. Here's your next book."

Drats, he recognized her.

Obviously, Barnacle Bob hadn't. He did one of his sailor's whistles and said, "Va-va-voom, Take it off. Take it all off."

Liz didn't know the midcentury jingle, but she got the gist of the bird's comment.

She took *After the Funeral* from Pierre's hand and put it in her handbag. Ryan was due to pick her up any minute.

Pierre said, "Does your father know how you're dressed, young lady?" She laughed. "Yes, he does. It was his idea."

Pierre raised a furry eyebrow, and his left hand twirled the end of his mustache. "Okay. Father knows best."

Hopefully, Liz thought. She heard the sound of a horn and saw Ryan's Jeep pull up under the canopy. She kissed Pierre and blew a kiss to Barnacle Bob. The parrot ruffled his feathers in delight. As she went out the revolving door, she heard a litany of catcalls—a gaggle of construction workers couldn't have done better.

Ryan got out of the Jeep. "You ready?"

"Ready as I'll ever be."

He walked to the passenger door and opened it. "After you. That is, if it's really you?" He brushed the brown bangs out of her eyes. "Yep. Same gorgeous cornflower-blue eyes."

Liz smiled, thanked him, and got inside.

As they pulled away, Ryan said, "You nervous?"

"A little. How about you? What if someone catches you?"

"I'm a trained assassin, didn't I tell you?"

Liz looked at his fit physique. He did look lethal.

"You distract," he said. "I'll infiltrate."

"Next time, you distract and I infiltrate. This is the twenty-first century."

"Yes, boss."

As they crossed the bridge over the Indian River Lagoon. Liz glanced out the window at the postcard-perfect day: Sailboats and cruisers passed beneath them, and fishermen lined the north side of the bridge, casting for a dinner of redfish or sea trout. Liz thought about Travis. They had tried to collaborate on a few writing projects, but both of their egos had gotten in the way and their projects were abandoned. Working with Ryan was easy, and she knew her father appreciated his help.

"Did you read in *Florida Today* about Edward's sentencing?" Liz asked.

"Yes. Your father told me. I think he should have gotten longer, but there was no proof he had anything to do with killing Regina. And dead men—as in, David Worth—tell no tales." Ryan looked over at her with a searching gaze.

"Eyes on the road, buddy."

He cleared his throat, then said, "Speaking of newspapers, have you seen today's *Daily Post*?"

"No. I'm allergic to that rag."

"Well, you might not be anymore, if you check page six. There's a copy on the back seat."

Liz reached behind her, then opened the paper to the headline, "Author's After-Rehab Apologetic Recant." Instead of vilifying Liz, Travis Osterman had told the true story of what had happened the night Liz got the scar. Staring back at her in black and white was everything she'd ever wanted in a confession—so why didn't she feel satisfied? When she reached the last line, it became clear: "Travis Osterman's new novel, *Glass and Blood*, will be out in August. The novel is a work of fiction, but insiders say it is not far from the truth about the Pulitzer Prize–winning Osterman and author Elizabeth Holt's days of wine and roses—and the night that culminated in violence and broken dreams."

Liz folded the newspaper and threw it back into the back seat.

Ryan took her hand. "I desperately owe you an apology for the way I treated you when we first met. But I want you to know that once I got to know you, I knew that what was being said about you wasn't true. *The McAvoy Brothers* was both my and most of the guys on at the FDNY's favorite male-bonding novel. I guess I was sticking to bro-code by believing every word that 'Pulitzer Prize–winning' Travis Osterman said about you was true." He squeezed her hand. "I promise to atone for myself. I'll do the dishes the next time we have a cook-off."

"The next three times, mister!"

"Deal."

They left the rest unsaid. Liz could understand the resonance readers felt with their authors. If Liz's favorite author had become embroiled in such a scandal, she would probably stick her head in the sand, too. No, that wasn't entirely true. Nothing would surprise her after what she'd gone through. She touched her cheek and felt a new sense of comfort as she traced the scar. She also realized that, if that night hadn't happened, she wouldn't be here now with her father, Aunt Amelia, Betty, Pierre, and Kate. Or Ryan.

Chapter 38

"We did it," Liz said, clinking her champagne glass against her father's and Ryan's.

"A job well done, team," Fenton said. "I had a hunch you two would work well together."

Liz took a sip of champagne. It was her first drink of alcohol since the night of the scar. When Liz had told her therapist that she'd sworn off drinking, her therapist had wisely said, "You weren't the one with the addiction to drugs and alcohol, Mr. Osterman was. It's okay not to drink for a while, if it makes you feel better. Just remember, the only time to drink is when you're feeling good with where you are in this world. Never drink when you're sad or depressed, because it will only lead to more of the same." *Wise therapist*, Liz thought.

Music filtered out from the speakers tucked under the eaves of the beach house. Kate and Pierre were nearby playing chess. Kate rarely let Pierre win, but Liz loved that it was Kate's idea to have a daily chess game with Pierre to keep his mind sharp. Every weekday after lunch, Pierre would walk to the emporium for a game with Kate at one of Deli-casies by the Sea's bistro tables. Liz had watched them yesterday when she'd brought over her conch ceviche for Ryan to try. He'd grudgingly admitted it was delicious, and Pops added it to his Friday seafood menu.

It was cooler than usual for Memorial Day. The ocean was calm, the temperature was in the low eighties, and there was a slight offshore breeze. Soon the weather would become so steamy, they wouldn't be able to catch their breath when stepping outdoors. Liz didn't mind, because she planned to be in the Indialantic's library, writing her next novel. She was five chapters in and might make her deadline after all. Not even Betty had seen her manuscript yet. Liz needed it to be hers alone for the time being.

Betty called out, "Liz, these Mexican chorizo and shrimp burgers are delicious. I've had two."

"Chorizo?" Kate asked. "Vegetarian chorizo, right, Liz?"

"Of course," Liz said, laughing. Kate was as much of a vegetarian as she was. "Don't thank me, Betty—thank Ryan." Liz looked at Ryan, with his Kiss the Cook apron that she'd loaned him. It certainly gave her ideas.

Ryan held up his glass to Betty. "Thanks, Betty. Not as good as the meal Liz made for Pierre's birthday, but I appreciate the compliment."

Liz smiled, because Ryan had actually been Liz's sous-chef for Pierre's eighty-first birthday dinner. Liz knew all of Pierre's favorite Julia Child recipes. Like a well-oiled machine, Liz and Ryan had turned out a meal of Pissaladiere, Moules Marinières, coquilles St-Jacques à la Provençale, and Soufflé aL'orange, which translated to savory onion tarts layered with anchovies and olives, mussels steeped in white wine and herbs, sea scallops in a creamy cheese sauce, and an orange soufflé.

She felt her spirits free-fall at the thought that Ryan would be leaving soon. Pops's second operation was scheduled for the following week. She excused herself and walked to the railing overlooking the beach. Aunt Amelia and Captain Netherton were both barefoot, running into the waves like children. Killer was behind them, digging a tunnel to Australia. His front legs were in a frenzy, spraying sand into the air. Maybe he, too, would find treasure and Aunt Amelia wouldn't have to worry about the Indialantic's bills.

Ryan came up behind her, lifted the brim of her straw hat, and said, "Your father just made me a proposition."

Liz turned to face him. "What kind of proposition?"

He pushed his sunglasses up onto his head. "He wants to hire me as his investigator. I'd work part-time for him and part-time for Grandad."

"You'd give up your job in New York to live here?"

"You don't think it's a good idea?" He took a step back.

She grabbed his arm. "Wait. I didn't say that. I just know what it's like to walk away from a career. Things are pretty slow and boring around here."

He looked at her hand on his arm. "I don't know about that. A murder, treasure, and…"

"And what?"

"You."

Her heart skipped a beat. "Welcome to barrier island living, partner!"

Acknowledgments

Thank you to my loving husband, Marc, for supporting my career, and for his wonderful editing on my new series. Thank you to my supercalifragilisticexpialidocious agent, Dawn Dowdle at Blue Ridge Literary Agency, for taking a chance, years ago, on a newbie author; your insight has been invaluable. Martin Biro, editor extraordinaire, it has been such a pleasure working with you and James at Kensington/Lyrical Underground. Your suggestions were spot-on, and I am looking forward to our future collaboration in the By the Sea mystery series. Thanks to my early readers, Mom, John, Lindsey Taylor, Ann Costigan, Michelle Mason Otremba, and Ellen Broder. And special thanks to gourmet home chef Lon Otremba for sharing his wonderful recipes.

Once again, I am in awe of all the support for the cozy mystery authors I've found on social media—from bloggers to readers, your passionate devotion to our COZY, warm community has been stellar and much appreciated.

Pops's Kalamata Hummus

1½ c. of canned chickpeas, drained and rinsed
¼ c. tahini
2 cloves garlic
¼ c. fresh lemon juice
1 tsp. cayenne pepper
2 Tbsp. olive oil
½ c. pitted Kalamata olives
1 small red pepper, seeded and sliced
1 tsp. ground cumin
1 tsp. curry powder
2 Tbsp. chopped fresh parsley (or snipped chives)
Combine chickpeas, tahini, garlic, lemon juice, cayenne, olive oil, olives, red pepper, cumin, curry powder, and parsley (or chives) in food processor and purée. Add enough cold water to achieve a spreadable mixture. Serves 4.

Pops's Baked Grouper Bites with Banana Salsa

Banana Salsa:
½ c. chopped green bell pepper
½ c. chopped red bell pepper
3 green onions, chopped
1 Tbsp. chopped cilantro
1 small jalapeño, seeded and chopped
2 Tbsp. light brown sugar
3 Tbsp. fresh lime juice
1 Tbsp. vegetable oil
¼ tsp. salt
¼ tsp. pepper
2 medium bananas, chopped
In a bowl, mix bell peppers, green onions, cilantro, jalapeño, brown sugar, lime juice, oil, salt, and pepper. Add bananas and mix gently. Chill covered for 3 hours.

Grouper:
1½ c. crushed potato chips

¼ c. grated Parmesan cheese
1 tsp. ground thyme
1½ lbs. grouper fillets, cut into strips
¼ c. milk

In a shallow dish, mix potato chips, cheese, and thyme. Dip the fish into the milk, then into the potato chip mixture, coating well.

Arrange in a single layer in a greased baking dish. Bake at 500 degrees for 8–10 minutes. Serve banana salsa on the side. Serves 4.

Pops's Coconut Rice

1 c. jasmine rice
1 c. unsweetened coconut milk, well shaken
2 tsp. grated fresh lime peel
1 Tbsp. fresh lime juice
1 tsp. kosher or sea salt
¼ tsp. freshly ground black pepper
1½ c. water

In a medium saucepan, combine all ingredients with 1½ cups water over high heat. Cover and bring to a boil. Reduce the heat to low and simmer for 20 minutes or until all of the liquid is absorbed. Serves 6.

Chef Pierre's Coconut Lime Sugar Cookies
(Liz's childhood favorites)

Preheat oven to 350 degrees.
Cookies:
2½ c. all-purpose flour
½ tsp. baking powder
½ tsp. salt
1½ c. granulated sugar
1¾ sticks unsalted butter (7 oz.), softened
2 large eggs
2–3 tsp. coconut extract
zest of 1 lime
Icing (optional):
1½ c. powdered sugar
2–3 Tbsp. lime juice

In a medium mixing bowl, combine flour, baking powder, and salt. Set aside. In a large mixing bowl, combine granulated sugar and butter; cream until light and fluffy, about 4–6 minutes. Add eggs, coconut extract, and lime zest. Slowly add flour mixture into larger bowl until thoroughly combined. Using 2 Tbsp. of dough at a time, roll into balls and place 2 inches apart on a baking sheet lined with parchment paper. Flatten each dough ball with the bottom of a glass into 2-inch circles. Bake at 350 degrees for 14 minutes, rotating pan halfway through. Cool on baking sheet 10 minutes, then place on wire rack. For icing, combine powdered sugar with 2 Tbsp. lime juice. Slowly add more lime juice until desired consistency is reached, then add lime zest and drizzle onto cookies. Makes approximately 24 cookies.

About the Author

Kathleen Bridge is the author of the By the Sea Mystery series and the Hamptons Home and Garden Mystery series, published by Berkley. She started her writing career working at *The Michigan State University News* in East Lansing, Michigan. A member of Sisters in Crime and Mystery Writers of America, she is also the author and photographer of an antiques reference guide, *Lithographed Paper Toys, Books, and Games*. She teaches creative writing in addition to working as an antiques and vintage dealer in Melbourne, Florida. Kathleen blissfully lives on a barrier island with her husband, dog, and cat. Readers can visit her on the web at www. kathleenbridge.com

Printed in the United States
by Baker & Taylor Publisher Services